Cast of C

Tommy Hambledon. A British spy, many years in Germany.

Alfred Reck. A wizened little man who is Tommy's longtime companion.

James Bellair. A junior intelligence agent whom Tommy takes under his wing.

Donald Macgregor. A foreman fitter from the Portsmouth Dockyard with a tale to tell. He never gets a chance to tell it.

The Albertinis. Father and son, proprietors of the popular Cafe d'Albertini.

Bettine Gascon. A flirtatious young governess and a policeman's daughter.

Stafford Wilkins. A teacher, one of Bettine's many conquests.

Rodney William Siddall. A handsome department store hairdresser.

Doris Baker. A stunning blonde, far more clever than she seems. She's been stepping out with Siddall.

Elsie Roberts. Nicknamed the Wax Doll, she has a sad secret.

Lewis Colville. The portly manager for a firm of naval wine merchants.

Molly and Eileen Trotter. Twin sisters who work at the Empire Theater, both sensible and observant young women.

Superintendent Gascon. Bettine's exasperated father.

Patrick Newton. An Irish garage keeper.

Dulcie Newton. His daughter, a conjuror's assistant.

Signore Maggiore. A conjuror.

Franz von Krug. Tommy's former manservant, now a refugee who has fled Germany and the Gestapo.

Mrs. Biggs. Tommy's charwoman, known to Reck as The Awful Woman.

Detective Superintendent Elliot. A very capable policeman who conducts his investigations strictly by the book.

Plus assorted police officers, witnesses, and innocent bystanders.

Books by Manning Coles

The Tommy Hambledon Spy Novels
Drink to Yesterday, 1940
A Toast to Tomorrow (English title: *Pray Silence*), 1940
They Tell No Tales, 1941
Without Lawful Authority, 1943
Green Hazard, 1945
The Fifth Man, 1946
Let the Tiger Die, 1947
With Intent to Deceive (English title: *A Brother for Hugh*), 1947
Among Those Absent, 1948
Diamonds to Amsterdam, 1949
Not Negotiable, 1949
Dangerous by Nature, 1950
Now or Never, 1951
Alias Uncle Hugo (Reprint: *Operation Manhunt*), 1952
Night Train to Paris, 1952
A Knife for the Juggler (Reprint: *The Vengeance Man*), 1953
All that Glitters (English title: *Not for Export*;
Reprint: *The Mystery of the Stolen Plans*), 1954
The Man in the Green Hat, 1955
Basle Express, 1956
Birdwatcher's Quarry (English title: *The Three Beans*), 1956
Death of an Ambassador, 1957
No Entry, 1958
Concrete Crime (English title: *Crime in Concrete*), 1960
Search for a Sultan, 1961
The House at Pluck's Gutter, 1963

Ghost Books
Brief Candles, 1954
Happy Returns (English title: *A Family Matter*), 1955
The Far Traveller (non-series),1956
Come and Go, 1958

Non-Series
This Fortress, 1942
Duty Free, 1959

Short Story Collection
Nothing to Declare, 1960

Young Adult
Great Caesar's Ghost (English title: *The Emperor's Bracelet*), 1943

They Tell No Tales

by Manning Coles

Rue Morgue Press
Boulder / Lyons

ISBN: 978-1-60187-026-1

Rue Morgue Press

87 Lone Tree Lane

Lyons CO 80540

Printed by Johnson Printing

Boulder, Colorado

PRINTED IN THE UNITED STATES OF AMERICA

About Manning Coles

Manning Coles was the pseudonym of two Hampshire neighbors who collaborated on a long series of entertaining spy novels featuring Thomas Elphinstone Hambledon, a modern-language instructor turned British secret agent. Hambledon was based on a teacher of Cyril Henry Coles (1895-1965). This same teacher encouraged the teenage Coles to study modern languages, German and French in particular, having recognized Coles' extraordinary ability to learn languages. When World War I broke out Coles lied about his age and enlisted. His native speaker ability in German prompted him to be pulled off the front lines and he soon became the youngest intelligence agent in British history and spent the rest of the war working behind enemy lines in Cologne.

The books came to be written thanks to a fortuitous meeting in 1938. After Adelaide Frances Oke Manning (1891-1959), rented a flat from Cyril's father in East Meon, Hampshire, she and Cyril became neighbors and friends. Educated at the High School for Girls in Tunbridge Wells, Kent, Adelaide, who was eight years Cyril's senior, worked in a munitions factory and later at the War Office during World War I. She already had published one novel, *Half Valdez*, about a search for buried Spanish treasure. *Drink to Yesterday,* loosely based on Cyril's own adventures, was an immediate hit and the authors were besieged to write a sequel, no mean feat given the ending to that novel. That sequel, *A Toast to Tomorrow*, and its prequel were heralded as the birth of the modern espionage novel with Anthony Boucher terming them "a single long and magnificent novel of drama and intrigue and humor." The Manning Coles collaboration ended when Adelaide died of throat cancer in 1959. During those twenty years the two worked together almost daily, although Cyril's continuing activities with the Foreign Intelligence Branch, now known as the Secret Intelligence Service or, more commonly, MI6, often required that he be out of the country, especially during World War II. Cyril wrote *Concrete Crime* on his own but the final two books in the series were the work of a ghostwriter, Cyril not wanting to go on with the series without Adelaide. While the earliest books had shown flashes of humor, it would not be until *Without Lawful Authority*, published in 1943 but set in 1938, that the collaborators first embraced the almost farcical humor that would come to be their hallmark. For more details on their collaboration and Cyril's activities in British intelligence see Tom & Enid Schantz' introduction to the Rue Morgue Press edition of *Drink to Yesterday*.

TO

A POLICE INSPECTOR

AND ONE OF

HIS

SORROWS

CHAPTER I

Salute the Day

HAMBLEDON WOKE up early, and switched on the light, blinking at the still unfamiliar room and listening to the unfamiliar country noises outside. A cart passed, iron-tired wheels grinding on the frozen road; a cow lowed near by, another answered, and there followed the sound of unshod hoofs accompanied by the clatter of the farmhand's nailed boots; further down the lane a dog barked as the cows went by. At the farm itself poultry were asking loudly for their breakfast, the cowman whistled "Good King Wenceslas," and the wind brought a loose trail of ivy slapping across the window. "England," said Hambledon to himself, "English country again. I think I'm going to like it," and he switched out the light and snuggled down under the bedclothes, for the morning was cold.

He felt no desire to go to sleep again, and lay thinking of the various things still to be done in the bungalow he and Reck had moved into two days earlier. A new washer on that dripping bath tap. The bolt was loose on the back door, it wanted a couple of screws. The kitchen was well fitted up though Reck wailed aloud at cooking over a coal fire instead of gas, a surprisingly good cook, Reck, considering all things. Of Reck's horror at finding it almost impossible to buy cooked meat in any variety even in Mark, the nearest town, of his struggles with the broad Hampshire dialect of their daily charwoman and of the charwoman's struggles with Reck's German accent. A rug would be nice in front of the fire in the lounge, one of those long-haired black bearskin ones, but that meant going to London probably, might get one in Portsmouth.

Portsmouth, they were going there that evening to meet young Bellair, who had got hold of a foreman fitter named Macgregor from the dockyard, with a story to tell. Might be interesting, that story; evidently Macgregor thought so since he considered Bellair not sufficiently important to hear it, and demanded a higher authority to whom to unfold his tale. So Hambledon had been sent down, not only, of course, to hear the Macgregor saga, but to look into the whole matter of these recent explosions on H.M. ships.

Bellair seemed a very decent fellow, one who had several good marks to his credit with the Department. Hambledon and Bellair had met for the first time at the Admiralty two days previously, Hambledon had looked the younger man up and down and decided that he might do.

The last day of the old year, New Year's Eve. At this time last year Hambledon was still in Berlin, though he knew the foundations of his life were cracking under him. Dear old Ludmilla had given a Sylvesterabend party full of worthy professors and their excellent wives, not an official reception but all Ludmilla's friends, dear good people, if a trifle dull until he had the brilliant idea of making a bowl of punch. They drank to 1938 then, no doubt some of them tonight were remembering the chief of police and his revered aunt, tonight they would drink to 1939 and hope for peace. Probably they would drink to his memory, bless their faithful hearts, saying what a nice funeral he had had and how movingly the Fuehrer had spoken of his murdered friend, whereas here he was if they only knew it, Tommy Hambledon still alive and kicking, and taking on another job. "I do take a lot of killing," he said sleepily, and shut his eyes again.

In his little room across the lounge Reck stirred, opened his eyes and immediately looked at the luminous dial of the clock. Barely seven, needn't get up for another twenty minutes, that Awful Woman never came before seven-thirty. Not that she would be so bad, presumably, if only one could understand what she said, though even Reck's bachelor ideas of cleaning and sweeping were outraged by Mrs. Biggs' methods. Speed, and speed alone, was her virtue. "I'm paid till twelve, and at twelve I goes," she said, and rushed round the bungalow like a female tornado till the clock struck noon, after which peace descended on the house of Hambledon.

He found it very strange to be living again in England after all these years, he had expected to dislike it intensely, to feel lonely, homesick for the familiar streets and speech of Germany, an outsider, an exile; but already after only four months the old spell was regaining strength. He quoted to himself—he had taken to reading Kipling again—

> "Beneath their feet in the grasses
> My"—something—"magic runs,
> They shall return as strangers,
> They shall remain as sons."

Of course, this downland country was not the England of his childhood; he was brought up in the flat Midlands where a gentle rise of fifty feet is called a hill, where men make wonderful hedges for the pleasure of the hunts, where the lift of the sky extends in an arc of a hundred and eighty degrees from horizon to horizon, and the great companies of cloud appear and gather, pass, and fade again into illimitable distance, their green shadows sliding across the green fields. That was what he had remembered when in a distant country he had thought of England; four months in London had not changed the picture and here in Hampshire the high downs constricted the sky. Still, there was already something homely and lovable about this place, or there would be when the sun shone again, for during the last two days and nights the east wind had never ceased to blow.

"Another ten minutes," said Reck and turned over, away from the clock-face. This job they had given to Hambledon should be child's play after what he had been doing for years, but one couldn't be sure. In Germany, people were unsuspicious because they were safe at home; here in England a German agent would fear everyone and trust no one, and men are dangerous when they are desperate. "Wonder what we're in for this time," thought Reck. "Start off all bright and easy and wind up in a burst of fireworks, I expect, as usual. If we bolt this time it'll have to be America, I suppose." He closed his eyes just for a moment and was awakened a quarter of an hour later by a furious banging at the back door.

"*Donner und blitzen,*" said Reck, "the Frau Biggs. Now she'll be cross all the morning."

Annie the chambermaid knocked at a bedroom door on the second floor of the King's Hotel in Southsea. At an inarticulate sound from within she entered, put down the tea by the bedside and pulled up the blind, letting in a colorless ray of winter sunshine.

"Ten to eight, Mr. Bellair, sir."

Bellair made a sound distantly resembling "Thank you," and dived further under the bedclothes; Annie left the room and saying, like Reck, "Another ten minutes," he lay still trying to remember a dream. Beyond the idea that it was something about a hippopotamus his effort was a failure and his mind turned to other things, mainly to the one subject which monopolized every waking hour, those explosions aboard H.M. ships. It was his job to find out who arranged them and how, so far the only step forward he had made was to get in touch with this fellow Macgregor and even he would not talk to Bellair. So Hambledon was coming down, primarily to see Macgregor, but actually to take over the whole enquiry, must be something pretty big if they sent down a fellow like that.

The explosions seemed to have only one point in common, that they always took place after the unhappy ship left Portsmouth Dockyard. The one odd piece of the puzzle was the swill-tub lorry which blew up just as it was passing out of the main gate. Most of the main gate went up with it and nearly a dozen men, including, of course, the lorry-driver who was literally never seen again. The "swill-tub lorry" was an ordinary three-ton motor-truck, hired from a firm of haulage contractors in Portsmouth by a farmer in the Fareham district. The lorry visited the dockyard daily to collect the contents of swill-tubs for the benefit of the farmer's pigs, of which he had several hundred, all hungry. After leaving the dockyard, it visited several Portsmouth and Southsea hotels for the same purpose and then went to Fareham to deliver the goods. It had done this regularly for upwards of two years without incident until Friday December the sixteenth, when with a flash and a roar which brought all Portsmouth into the streets, it blew up.

It was coming out, not going in. A saboteur might conceivably smuggle explosives into the dockyard in the lorry, but why on earth should he smuggle them out? Materials for making explosives, yes, perhaps, but the materials of explosives are seldom dangerous in themselves until they have been suitably blended. Besides, this was no desultory flare-up, but a very high explosive indeed, in a confined space, in a word, a bomb. Why bring a bomb out of the dockyard? And such a bomb! Fragments of debris had descended upon the United Services Recreation Ground.

Bellair sat up to drink his tea and thought of Hambledon. Who was Hambledon, anyway? Apparently he had a great reputation for dark doings in the Great War but no one seemed to have heard of him since. Hadn't he been presumed dead, lost overboard off a destroyer or something? There was a story extant that some woman had asked Hambledon where he'd been all these years, and Hambledon with a perfectly solemn face had answered that he'd taken refuge from the storms of life in a lamasery in Tibet, and there practiced contemplation. The enquiring lady had stared, and said, "Not really?" and one or two men had smiled. Evidently the story was untrue, but where had he been and why should he be treated with such deference? All the same, there was something unmistakably adequate about him in spite of advancing years, it might be interesting to work under him.

Bellair glanced at his watch which told him the time was a quarter past eight. He muttered something and sprang out of bed.

Lynbourne House stood in a small wood halfway up the slope of War Down, a steep lane passed the gate and entered the main street of Lynbourne village by the church. The window of Bettine's room looked down upon the village below, mostly upon ancient tiles and thick thatch, though at the top of Smithy Lane there was a line of bungalows, their bright roofs and roughcast walls conspicuous against the colorless wintry fields. At the back door of one of them a small angry woman was hammering with her umbrella to wake up the sleeping Reck.

Bettine's room had smooth walls painted a very faint shell-pink, a white door and window-frame, and gay chintz curtains at the window, cherry-patterned curtains which pleased Bettine, who loved cherry-red. It was, of course, a small room, as one does not give a governess one of the best bedrooms, but it had a huge built-in cupboard almost large enough to hold all Bettine's frocks, and a big dressing-table with a good mirror which had a light over it. There were several photographs on the mantelpiece and one more beside the reading-lamp on the bedside table.

Bettine was awakened as usual by the clatter in the kitchen below as the cook assaulted the stove with poker and tongs, at least, that was what it sounded like. Bettine switched on the bedside light and looked at her watch, just half-past seven, no need to get up for ten minutes. She looked without any particular enthusiasm at the photograph by the bedside, it showed a dark young man with a narrow line of mustache and that slightly stuffed expression only too common in portrait photography, across the corner was written "Bettine, from Stafford." It reminded her that today was New Year's Eve and tonight she was going to Portsmouth to meet Stafford, go to a show of some kind and have dinner afterwards. There would be something of a row if all this came out, as when the family were away she was not supposed to leave the children, but it would be so unkind not to go when Stafford had come all the way from Leicester to see her. Besides, it was such a good opportunity for an evening out, as the chauffeur had been given leave to take his wife down to her sister's in Portsmouth for the evening. Life was quite boring enough at Lynbourne House without throwing away opportunities.

Bettine lay back on the pillow and looked at the cupboard door. The navy blue suit tonight, it was smart enough for anywhere where they were likely to go, and nearly new. Stafford hadn't seen it before. But it meant wearing a hat, and Bettine hated hats, besides, she had an uncomfortable feeling that town clothes did not suit her nearly so well as country ones; there was the brown corduroy, much nicer, worn with a gay red and yellow scarf, and no hat on her brown hair. It was true Stafford had seen her in it before, but he always liked it, he might even think she had put it on to please him.

It was to be hoped he wouldn't be tiresome tonight about wanting to marry her, a man never seemed to understand that a girl might not want to get married and settle down, however fond she might be of him. "As it is, you see," said Bettine, getting her arguments ready in case they were wanted, "if I don't like the place or the people I'm with I can just leave and go somewhere else, it's so lovely to be free. Whereas, if we married, we might have to take a house in some horrid little street, with horrid neighbors looking over the garden fence, and it would be so boring with you out all day. I couldn't be happy polishing furniture all day long, besides, I don't want to marry anybody, not just yet. Heavens, it's a quarter to eight," said Bettine, scrambling out of bed, "I shall miss my bath."

Siddall's daily woman knocked on the door with his shaving-water, he rolled over and answered her without opening his eyes. He had, like Bellair, been dreaming, but unlike Bellair had awakened to remember that most of it was true. He dreamed that he was taking Doris out to dinner, she sat facing him across the table in one of those deceptively simple-looking dresses she wore so well, black, to show off her dazzling blonde hair and clear skin. It was true, he was taking her out tonight; there she would sit looking beautiful but stupid, saying "Oh, not reely?" and "Ever so nice," just like an English shopgirl, when in point of fact she wasn't a shopgirl, not even English, and anything but stupid. No, she was clever, too damned clever by half, she looked like a fluffy-headed fool, but precious little escaped Doris. Siddall told himself in a burst of frankness that she wasn't even beautiful, she was rather frightening, and he didn't know whether she was more frightening when she was being efficient or when she was being affectionate. "As soon be cuddled by a Bengal tiger, myself," said Siddall, and shivered. "If I hadn't such a good job with the Leviathan I'd pack and quit, besides, there are the other things. I'd like to lose some of them, including Doris, and I would, too, only—" he shivered again, for Siddall was that pathetic object, a pawn being played in place of a knight. "It's a bit hard," said Siddall, being sorry for himself, "when a man's worked up to a good position and is still young enough to enjoy himself, and he gets landed with all this. I'll ease off this somehow, I won't get dragged in further and further, I know how it'll all end, and anyway," he said, sitting up in bed and thumping the pillow, "if she calls me Siddie darling in public again I'll throw the gravy at her."

Doris Baker woke up when her maid came into the room with the early-morning tea and the letters, drew up the blinds, switched on the electric fire, and said "Shall I fill your bath, madam?"
"Not yet, thank you," said Doris, "I'll ring." She looked at the letters and found them all dull, lay back on her pillows, lit a cigarette, and reviewed the day ahead. New Year's Eve, tonight Siddall was taking her out. He was beginning to show signs of jibbing and that must be stopped, tiresome of him, one hated having to drive a man one cared about, it was unkind of him to make her do it. A new frock for tonight, have to run round the Southsea shops and see if they'd got anything fit to wear since there was no time to run up to Bradley's. How tiresome men were, making these plans at such short notice, they ought to know that women have things to see to. Black, or midnight blue for a change—not sequins, though, they fall off for inquisitive people to find. Siddall must be put into a good mood somehow, a little New Year's present, perhaps, cufflinks or something? Oh, she'd manage, besides,

he knew what would happen if he turned awkward, no need to worry. "I'll ring up and get him to do my hair," she said, "he loves doing that. He really is an artist in his line—in more than one line, really. I don't think it will be a dull evening," said Doris Baker.

Elsie Roberts did not wake till the shabby room was plainly visible even on a dark December morning, for the cretonne curtains at the window were thin and too narrow to meet in the middle unless they were pinned. She turned over in the bed which was too big for one alone and too ornate for the room, and remembered it was the last day of the old year, another year would begin tomorrow, just another year like all the others except that the boy would get bigger and stronger every day, in another year's time he would be as tall as she. It wasn't worth while getting up, if one stayed in bed and dozed off again one would save breakfast and there wasn't much in the house. It did cost a lot, keeping the boy at a school like that, but it was worth it even if one couldn't see him very often. New Year's Eve, she was married one New Year's Eve fifteen years earlier, funny to think of it now. "Suppose Ted comes back today," she thought, as she always thought on New Year's Eve, "shall I be glad to see him?" and decided as she always decided, that she didn't really want him. Aggravating man, Ted, always changing his mind right round to something just opposite to what he'd argued the month before, always losing his jobs because he lost interest in them and wanted to try something else. She had been glad when he joined the Navy because a man couldn't get out of that so easily and she thought they were settled at last, but were they? Not on your life! Two years they had of that, the two best years of her life, then, just after the boy was born, Ted went to China and deserted there of all places. Never been heard of since. Probably he was dead, China was a funny country by all accounts and Ted was always getting into trouble. No, she didn't want him back really. In another two or three years the boy would be earning and able to help her, if he went into the Navy he might do really well and make her a good allowance unless he married. Mrs. Roberts did not care for this idea, it made her feel lonely, so she pushed it away.

It might be as well to get up, after all, no use lying there making yourself miserable and a cup of tea would be nice, besides, there were stockings to wash and darn, she might wash her hair too, the soft flaxen hair which had given her the nickname of "The Wax Doll," it would dry while she was doing the mending. The room wanted tidying up, too, might as well start the New Year clean and neat, it might bring her luck. She threw back the bedclothes and got up.

There was a row of Charlet etchings on the wall opposite Colville's bed. He switched on the light to look at them, for they were a new acquisition. He liked to buy a picture sometimes, provided that it was a reasonably good bargain; he had not much knowledge of art or of values, but he had good taste and an eye for the uncommon. He always hung his latest purchase opposite his bed, by the time it had been there a month he knew whether it was a thing one could live with and should be moved to the lounge or the dining-room, or whether he should unload it again as opportunity offered and buy something else instead. These ferocious old French soldiers were distinctly decorative and seemed to improve on acquaintance, they would look rather well in the entrance hall if they were mounted in black passe-partout instead of those clumsy oak frames. The frames annoyed him, so he put out the light again and thought of other things. Another lucky day, let's hope, he had had some amazing luck lately.

He turned uneasily and laid a careful hand on his chest. Must remember to order some more olive oil capsules, 60 minims, all this port and sherry played the deuce with a man's digestion and if that went his nerves would go. It couldn't be helped, wine merchants always have to drink with their clients, and some of these naval officers have such incredibly hard heads. Must remember to tell Jackson to ring up H.M.S. *Araucaria* and ask the commander and first lieutenant to dinner at the King's the following night, probably the last chance of dining ashore that the poor blighters would get.

He heard the maid tap at his wife's room next door, and dived out of bed to reach the bathroom. "If she gets in there first," he said, hurling on a dressing-gown, "it'll be half-past eight before she's out again, goodness knows what she does all that time, I don't. But the result is easy to look at, so I'm lucky again."

There was complete peace in the room with the twin beds in it, apart from a faint snuffling sound from the further one because Eileen had a cold, and a faint snoring sound from the nearer one because the cat was asleep on Molly's eiderdown. The door opened and a voice said, "Molly! Eileen! Wake up, now, it's half-past eight!"

"Yes, mother," they said obediently, and the moment the door was shut dived down further under the bedclothes till only two handfuls of dark hair showed where the Trotter twins postponed the day.

"It's your turn to go early today," said Eileen eventually, in a voice muffled by blankets and catarrh.

"It is not, then, it's yours, I went yesterday."

"Oh, Molly, how could you? I know I went yesterday because I booked the box for that old fellow with side-whiskers for his niece from Scarborough or Whitby or somewhere."

"Or Blackpool," said Molly, getting up with a rush, "or Brighton or Buxton or Bristol or Bath, I never saw a man with so many nieces—the old goat!"

"Molly! They might be his nieces, you don't know."

"Oh well, I expect they're somebody's. Grrr, it's cold. Eileen, did you book those four third-row stalls for the second house tonight?"

"No, don't forget them, will you? There's mother calling again, do hurry up, I want to wash."

"You don't want to, you just feel you must. I say, Eileen, d'you remember the coffee with cognac on cold mornings before we went to school? Wish we had it now."

"That was in Wiesbaden, it costs too much in England—hi, those are my stockings you're pinching."

"Sorry. I say, did you see Mr. Bellair last night?"

"Only for a minute, did you?"

"Not for long. Eileen, did he ask you to go out with him tonight?"

"No, did he ask you?"

"No."

"Why?"

"Only thought he might, as it's New Year's Eve," said Molly.

"Shouldn't feel like going out if he did, with this cold on me."

"I expect you'd try and bear up," said Molly cheerfully. "Reggie will ask you, I expect."

"Oh, Reggie!"" said Eileen scornfully. "You can have Reggie, and anyway mother wants us to take her to the d'Albertini tonight."

"Tell you what," said Molly, between strokes of the hairbrush, "suppose Reggie takes mother out somewhere, then perhaps you and I could go to that dance for an hour."

" 'Do you believe in fairies?' " quoted her sarcastic sister. "When mother says—"

"Molly!" came the voice from the door again. "It's nine o'clock and past, and how you think you'll get a decent breakfast and to the Empire by ten-thirty the dear only knows, without ruining your digestion bolting your food—"

"Coming, mother! 'The telephone that rings,' " sang Molly, " 'and who's to answer? A fairground's painted swings, These foolish things—' "

" 'Remind me of you!' "

CHAPTER II

New Year's Eve

THE CAFÉ D'ALBERTINI was full of lights and laughter, the comfortable smell of food, warmth on a bitter night, and a crowd of people in the mood for celebration. Most of them were habitués with a mere sprinkling of strangers, even if they had never spoken to each other till that night they knew each other by sight, and on New Year's Eve there is little formality even among the English. By ten at night there was a real party in progress, all the more lighthearted for being unpremeditated, all the more enjoyable for the emotional solemnity which hangs across the threshold of every New Year. Women smiled at each other, an orchestra, consisting simply of a piano and two violins, was playing cheerful familiar airs, people laughed openly at an overheard jest from the next table, waitresses flew about, knives and forks clattered, and Albertini, son of the proprietor, walked up and down greeting everyone, overseeing everything, and ready for every emergency from an overturned wineglass to a too convivial guest.

At the far end of the room from the door a party of people rose from their seats, gathered up coats and handbags, and left, but the table was not long vacant for almost at once the door opened again and three men came in. Evidently Albertini knew the youngest, for he said, "Good evening, Mr. Bellair," and led the party through the length of the room to the table in the corner. Bellair was a man in his late twenties, his companions were plainly men of over fifty. One was a wizened little man with sunken eyes and deep lines in his face, but intelligent and alert as a terrier; the other a short spare man with the unmistakable air of one accustomed to considerable authority.

"This is a good place to know," said Bellair in a quiet voice, "sometimes people come here whom you might find it useful to meet."

The other two looked leisurely about the room, and the little man said, "I should think it likely. There seems to be a very assorted choice, doesn't there, Hambledon?" He spoke with a strong German accent.

"A diversity of creatures," said Hambledon. "Know many of 'em, Bellair?"

"Quite a lot, more or less," said Bellair, turning in his seat to survey the room behind him. "'Evening, Colville," he added to a civilian who was sit-

16

ting at the next table with two naval officers. They called him Mr. Colville and treated him with some deference, for he was manager for a firm of naval wine merchants and consequently a useful person to know.

"Good evening," said Colville to Bellair. "A cheerful scene."

"Very."

"Seems a popular place with the Navy," remarked Hambledon after the waitress had taken their orders. "There seem to be quite a lot of them here, and if I'm not mistaken the four young gentlemen at the middle table by the stairs are naval officers in mufti."

"Yes, it's a good place to meet them," said Bellair without emphasis. "One expects to see them everywhere in Portsmouth."

Hambledon nodded. "There's a wonderful head of hair down there by the door," he said. "The blonde enchantress."

Bellair did not turn this time, he looked in the mirror opposite him, behind Hambledon, which showed him the long room reflected. "Oh that, yes. That's Siddall's reigning beauty, the black-haired fellow next her. He's the head of the hairdressing department at the Leviathan Drapery Stores, and a swell at his job, I understand."

"Hence the marvelous coiffure, I suppose," said the third man. "Doubtless she gets it all dolled up at trade rates."

"Nice useful sort of boyfriend, eh, Reck?"

At the other corner table just across the gangway from theirs, sat a young man dressed in the usual tweed sports coat and wide gray flannel trousers, he was obviously not a naval man for he wore a small neat mustache. He had a rather conspicuous girl with him, and one of the naval officers at the center table caught her eye, lifted his glass, smiling, and bowed to her. She smiled back and her escort noticed it.

"D'you know those fellows, Bettine?"

"Oh no," she said. "They're just being friendly. I think it's such fun, don't you?" She had one of those voices which carry well and her words floated across the room. The young man scowled.

"I thought you were supposed to be out with me."

"Oh, Stafford darling, don't be so difficult! After all, it is New Year's Eve and I think he's got such a nice face."

"Minx," growled Reck in German.

"D'you generally smile at men you don't know?" asked the aggrieved Stafford.

"Not when I'm by myself, of course, but when I'm with you I'm quite safe, aren't I, sweetness? Oh, I do think you're being horrid to me, Stafford, on our one evening together, when I'm so happy I can't help smiling."

"Do I make you so happy?" he said, relenting, and she lowered her eyelids and smiled at him.

"Curiously mobile face that girl's got," said Bellair.

"Almost elastic," agreed Hambledon unkindly. "Remember those soft rubber faces you could push into any expression?"

Bellair looked slightly horrified, Hambledon noticed it and added, "But there, I'm probably unfair. I never did like brunettes."

"Minx," said Reck again.

The door opened abruptly and two men entered. They were wearing evening dress, and each held in his right hand a string with a balloon on it which bobbed about their heads. They walked with firm and rapid steps straight up the gangway without taking any notice of anybody, and ducked under the curtain at the end into the kitchen. The assembled company were so interested that they left off clattering cutlery and talking, and a hush ensued in which sounds of argument from the kitchen were plainly audible. There followed noises as of saucepan lids in motion and the two gentlemen emerged, one had lost his balloon and acquired a hardboiled egg instead which he carried carefully on the palm of his hand. They walked rapidly down the gangway again towards the door which was smartly opened for them by Albertini himself, and so passed out into the night.

The next time the curtain was thrown back by a waitress passing through, the lost balloon could be seen floating quietly about the kitchen ceiling, with the gray-haired old chef in his tall cap leaping like a salmon after the trailing string.

Two girls came in with a thin young man and had to stand by the door for a few minutes till there was a table to spare. The girls were obviously twins, very much alike and similarly dressed, one of them saw Bellair in the mirror and smiled at him, he turned to face them and lifted his glass in greeting.

"More girlfriends?" asked Reck.

"I rather like the look of those two," said Hambledon. "Who are they?"

"You're right, they may be useful. They work at the Empire, one's in the box office and the other sells chocolates off a tray. They know everybody much better than everybody realizes."

"Very useful," said Hambledon. "You know, tonight being what it is, I think we should have champagne. Do the resources of this house include a drinkable brand?"

"The revered proprietor worked at the Café Royal in his younger days," answered Bellair, and caught Albertini's eye. When the bottle was shown to Hambledon for approval, the girl Bettine opposite noticed it.

"Oh, Stafford, do let's have champagne!" The man looked a trifle dubious so she went on, "I'll pay for it, do let me."

"Why must it be champagne?"

"Because it's New Year's Eve, and because I like it, besides—" there was a loud pop as the cork came out of Hambledon's bottle, and in the little hush that usually follows that sound, Bettine's voice rang out clearly, "—I want the cork!"

Several people laughed, Bettine looked round with wide brown eyes to see what the joke was; apparently failing to discover it she turned to Stafford with an appealing feminine look as of one who would say, "These matters be too high for me."

"I wonder," said Bellair thoughtfully, "whether that girl is really so silly as she pretends to be."

"The beautiful blonde is leaving with her hairdresser," said Hambledon.

"She's very decorative, certainly," said Bellair, "and she's very friendly, but she's completely dumb in the American sense, and her only adverb is 'ever so.' You know, 'Ever so nice, it was.' In fact, we all think Siddall carts her round as an advertisement, he can't have any other use for her."

A woman came in alone and sat down by herself. She was considerably made up, with a very pink and white complexion and masses of golden hair which she wore rather like a medieval page-boy's. She gave an order to the waitress and sat quietly looking about her and listening to the music, she seemed perfectly contented although nobody went over to speak to her.

"Who's that?" asked Hambledon.

"They call her the Wax Doll," said Bellair. "She's a clever woman in her way."

"In what way?" asked Reck.

Hambledon looked at him and laughed, but Bellair answered, "I only meant she's very observant."

"That sort of woman generally is," said Hambledon, "but they usually talk too much."

"This one doesn't," said Bellair.

"I don't know who paid for the champagne opposite," said Hambledon in a low tone, "but I think our Stafford has had almost as much as is good for him."

The man was leaning towards the girl and saying, "But you are engaged to me, you know you are."

"Nonsense, darling."

"Even if you did lose the ring in the Isis, that's not to say the engagement's broken off."

"Nonsense, darling. Why, I've been engaged twice since then."

"Bettine! Who were you with when you lost the ring at Oxford?"

"With Edmund, he's very nice. He's so clever, too, he writes poetry."

"Does anyone read it?"

"And he sings beautifully, just like Richard Tauber."

"Curious," said Tommy Hambledon, "the effect on the female emotions of the male voice uplifted in song."

"I'll try it some day," said Reck.

"Here, where's your glass? You aren't drinking," said Bellair, suddenly noticing this.

"I never do," said Reck. "I'm a teetotaller."

"Even on New Year's Eve?"

"Oh, come on," said Hambledon, "champagne's practically a teetotal drink anyway. Get the party spirit, come on."

"Besides," said Bellair, "it's getting on for midnight, they'll be shutting up soon."

"Shutting up at twelve? Why?"

"Because tomorrow's Sunday."

"Oh, these English Sabbaths! D'you know, when I used to get homesick, 'Oh, to be in England,' all that sort of thing, I completely forgot the English Sabbath."

"I think I will have a drink," said Reck. "Even a teetotaller—"

"You're a shameless little flirt," said Stafford bitterly.

"Oh, Stafford darling, I'm ever so sorry. I just don't want to marry anybody just now."

"You're engaged to me."

"Nonsense, darling, that was all over long ago."

"It wasn't over at Christmas—only last week. You went about with me everywhere."

"You don't have to be engaged to a man," said Bettine, getting a little annoyed, "to go to a few dances with him. If your steps suit each other—"

"Yes, that's what you said about that fellow down in Kent, what was his name? Mick?"

"Well, that's all it was with him, and that's all it is with you, now. Of course I'm very fond of you, Stafford darling, and we'll always be friends, but I don't want to marry you. I know I'm changeable, you ask mother."

"You left Kent in rather a hurry, didn't you?" said Stafford unpleasantly. "I thought it was such a wonderful place."

"So it was, but I had to leave there, I couldn't marry Mick."

"What a wonderful life that young woman must lead," said Hambledon. "Platoons of men wanting to capture her."

"Wonder how much of it's true," growled the skeptical Reck. "She's a hussy, in my opinion."

"Our man is late," said Bellair, looking at his watch. "He said he'd be here at about eleven, it's past the half-hour."

"Oh, I expect he's just been celebrating and let the time get away with him," said Hambledon. "Your friend at the table behind you is fidgety about something, look at his ashtray. Besides, he can't keep his hands still."

Bellair turned leisurely in his chair to make a general survey of the room, including in his glance Colville's ashtray, half full of cigarettes just started and stubbed out again, and Colville's fingers below the table, pleating and repleating the edge of the cloth, though has face, seen in profile in another mirror across the room, looked perfectly normal and even animated. Beyond him, the Trotter twins with their escort were watching the people, Molly laughing as usual and Eileen looking disdainfully at a girl near the door who was making too much noise. The orchestra played a selection from "Maid of the Mountains," and the white-haired proprietor descended the central staircase from the Albertinis'rooms over the café to stroll among his clients, wish them the compliments of the season and confide to the few he knew best that he had seen so very many New Years, he did not expect to see another. They were too tactful to remind him that he had been saying this for years.

"Don't let's quarrel tonight, sweetness," said Bettine, sliding her long fingers between Stafford's short ones. "It's such a bad start for the New Year, and besides it's making me so unhappy. You don't want to make me miserable on our evening out, do you, angel?"

"Heaven knows I only want to make you happy all day long," said her infatuated escort, "but I do wish you'd—"

"Oh, that's all right then, precious, that's easy. You've only got to leave off being so difficult every time we meet, and we'll be so happy together, I'll dance for joy whenever I think of you. Look, angel, if you'll promise to behave nicely and not worry me, I'll promise you something."

"What's that?"

"I'll promise that if I don't marry anybody else I'll marry you. On my word of honor," said Bettine, leaning forward to look up into his face.

"Will you listen to that?" said Hambledon. "Then look at our Stafford's face. He ought to have his mother with him, he wants a nurse to hold his hand at crossings, he's no business to be allowed out without a keeper. She's jilted him once at least, she's been engaged twice since—so she says—evidently she made use of him to squire her about at Christmas, and now she has the brazen effrontery to suggest that he shall wait indefinitely while she has a thorough look round and if she can't find anyone better she'll marry him. Does he brain her with the champagne bottle? Does he throw the pepper at her? Does he spit accurately in her right eye? No. He goes all soft and gooey and holds her hand. Yet if you told him he was less like a man than an amorphous semitransparent jellyfish he wouldn't believe you. He wants clouting, and women like her ought to be drowned by the local sanitary inspector."

"Oh, I don't know," said Bellair. "If a man chooses to be such a fool as that you can hardly blame the girl for making use of him. Why not? She's pleased and he's happy and who cares, anyway? I wish this fellow would come."

"If he doesn't come soon," said Hambledon, "he'll be locked out, it's five minutes to midnight now. Something is about to happen, what is it? Everyone is standing up so I suppose we follow suit. They join hands, some parlor game—ah! Auld Lang Syne, of course. Everybody being matey, waitresses, proprietor, and all. Reck, you'll have to hold Bettine's hand to complete the chain."

"I won't," growled Reck. "I won't encourage her."

"Bellair, you'd better fill the gap, come on. Hands across the gangway. Your pardon, madam, my young friend wishes to hold your hand."

"What?" said Bettine. "Oh, Auld Lang Syne, I see. Stand up, Stafford darling. Oh, I do think this is fun, don't you?"

" 'For auld lang syne,' " sang Hambledon, " 'for auld—' why on earth do we have to flap our arms like this?—'cup of kindness yet, for auld lang syne.' What now? The King, of course."

The assembly, most of whom were service men, stood like statues till the orchestra played the final chord. Then the tension broke, chatter and laughter filled the room again.

"Happy New Year!"

"Quite a jolly evening."

"You stay here, I'll go and get the car."

"Same to you, and many of them!"

"Happy days, Stafford dear."

"I'll see if I can find a taxi, if not—"

"Enjoyed yourself, Molly?"

"Cheerio, folks, see you some more."

A woman called across the room, "Open the door, Mr. Albertini, and let in the New Year."

The door was flung open, admitting the cheerful noise of bells from the churches, laughter and shouting from the street and the sound of many voices singing in the Guildhall Square.

"It ought to be someone dark," said Eileen, "to be the firstfooter."

"Is that an Irish superstition?" said their escort. "Won't a fair man do?"

"Not only Irish, everybody knows that it's lucky to have a dark person—man or woman—come in first."

"No one seems to be in a hurry to come in and everybody's getting their hats and coats, what happens if nobody comes before the place shuts up?"

At that moment a man entered, took a step or two forward and paused as though looking for someone. Bellair saw him, and saying, "Good, here's Macgregor at last," rose to go and meet him.

"Oh, he is dark," cried Molly, "isn't that lucky!"

There came from outside a sound exactly as though someone had drawn a champagne cork in the street, and immediately there followed the roar of a high-powered car being driven off at speed. Macgregor, with a look of intense surprise on his face, suddenly gave at the knees, spun half round, and dropped to the floor.

"Look at that," said Hambledon, "that's what happens when you arrange to meet a Scot on New Year's Eve. He's been celebrating."

"We'd better collect him, I suppose," said Bellair, and the two made their way through the crowd while young Albertini shut the outer door again and bolted it, to prevent the entrance of any unauthorized revelers demanding refreshment. As for Reck, he stayed where he was, leaning one shoulder against the doorway to the kitchen and watching the people.

Tommy Hambledon looked down on the prostrate Macgregor, lying across the gangway with his head in the shadow under the first table. There was no one there, the people who had been sitting there had moved away to speak to friends.

"Completely and utterly corpsed," said Hambledon. "What an evening he must have had," but Bellair stooped over the man and said, "Good God!"

"What's the matter?"

"He is not drunk, he's dead, there's a bullet-hole in the back of the head. He's been shot."

CHAPTER III

New Year's Day

"LOCK THAT DOOR," said Hambledon to Albertini. "Oh, you have, good. Are there any more exits from this place? The door the other side? Lock that too, and telephone for the police. Tell them a man has been murdered."

"*Madre purissima*," gasped Albertini, and obeyed. It was fortunate that Macgregor had fallen in the space close to the door, there was no one immediately near them and no one realized what had happened. A few people stared with curiosity or averted their eyes in disgust because they thought the man was drunk, but they stayed where they were, waiting with the instinctive patience of the English for the nuisance to be removed so that they might pass by. Albertini came back and said, in a low tone, "The police are coming, they'll be here in a moment. They have only to come from the Guildhall, it's not more than a few yards."

"Shall I cover him up?" asked Bellair.

"No, don't," said Hambledon. "These people don't know he's dead, let the police tell them," and they stood there waiting.

One man came across to Albertini and said, "Could you open the other door, please? My wife and I want to get home."

"In just a moment, sir, in just a moment," said Albertini, and the man raised his eyebrows and went away.

The old proprietor came up to see what the trouble was, but his son seized him by the arm, pushed him into the tiny bar near by, and could be heard explaining what had happened in hushed but rapid Italian, till there came a knock at the door and Hambledon opened it to admit the police.

Detective-Inspector Grogan came in followed by two constables, took in the scene at a glance, and went down on one knee beside the body. Grogan turned the light of an electric torch on Macgregor's head; what he saw appeared to convince him for he rose to his feet and said, "Did anybody see it done?"

"No," said Hambledon. "He fell, but we thought he was drunk."

"Nor hear a shot fired? No? Well, has anyone left the place since this happened?"

"No, sir," said Albertini, "and the other door is locked."

"Good. Mullins, stay on this door and admit the superintendent, Dr. Buckland, Mr. Morgan and no one else. Has the body been moved?"

"I slipped my hand under his head," said Bellair, "I thought he was only drunk. I don't think I altered his position much."

"Apart from that, the body has not been touched?"

"No."

Grogan nodded, and Hambledon said, "I don't think any of these people know he's dead except Bellair, the proprietors here, and myself."

Grogan nodded again and said, "They'll have to know because I shall want statements from them, but I think he's died of a seizure—for the moment. If you"—to Albertini—"could produce a tablecloth or something we could cover him up. Mullins, see to it. Come with me, will you?" added Grogan to Hambledon and Bellair, and led the way into the main part of the restaurant. Here he paused and looked authoritatively about him, and the sight of his police uniform produced the hush he wanted.

"Ladies and gentlemen," he said, raising his voice, "I will not detain you a moment longer than I can help. But I am sorry to say that a man has died suddenly here, and I must have the names and addresses of everyone present in case their evidence is required at the inquest. If you will come across to me one by one we will get through it as quickly as we can. You, sir, first," he said to Bellair, and sat down at one of the tables with the constable beside him.

Bellair, who was already known to the police as a British intelligence agent, sat down at the same table, leaned across it, and said, "The dead man's name is Macgregor, he was a foreman fitter in the dockyard. He came here tonight by appointment to meet me and the two friends who are here with me on matters connected with the business which has brought me to Portsmouth."

"I see," said Grogan. "Will you tell me exactly what happened?"

Bellair told him that he saw Macgregor come into the restaurant, pause just inside the door, "probably looking for me," and immediately stagger, turn half round, and fall to the floor.

"Did you hear a shot?"

"No."

"Which way was he facing when he was shot?"

"He had his back to the open door and was facing up the room."

"Notice anything else?"

"No. Except that I heard a car—by Jove, I'd forgotten that. I heard a powerful car drive off suddenly at high speed, and the thought crossed my mind that it sounded exactly like my own."

"Yours is a Beverley, I think?"

"Beverley Barnes. I left it parked a few yards down the pavement to the right here, to avoid the bus stop."

"Wilson," said Grogan to his constable, "just look outside and see if it is still there." When the constable had gone, the Detective-Inspector said in a low tone, "Could he have been shot by anyone in the room, sir?"

"Not possibly, it was fairly quiet in here just at that moment. He was shot from outside, I'm sure of that."

"Which are your two friends, sir?"

"Hambledon, who spoke to you, and Reck, that man sitting at the far end of the room by the kitchen door."

The constable returned. "The car is gone, sir."

"The devil it has!"

"Number?" asked Grogan.

"PC 986."

"Get the Portsbridge police box and tell them to stop PC 986, black Beverley Barnes Saloon. Make a general call of it. They have probably got through by now unless they've been caught in a traffic block," added Grogan, as the constable dived for the telephone. "Are you in a hurry to get away, sir? Good, I should be glad if you'd stay while I go through the rest of these people. I'll have Mr. Hambledon first, he might have noticed something else."

Hambledon gave his name as Thomas Elphinstone Hambledon of East Bungalow, Lynbourne, but had nothing to add to Bellair's statement except that he had heard a pop outside which might have been somebody pulling the cork out of a champagne bottle, or might have been a silenced automatic. Grogan raised his eyebrows, but naturally did not ask a member of the British Intelligence Service how he knew what a silenced automatic sounded like. Alfred Reck, of the same address, had no information to give.

The rest of the customers provided nothing but their names and addresses, though Hambledon and Bellair, standing apart and watching their faces, extracted some amusement from their expressions.

"Never saw so many guilty faces in one place together in all my life," said Hambledon. "Dammit, every other one looks as though he'd got some horrid secret."

"Who hasn't?" said Reck.

"Even Molly and Eileen," said Bellair, "look thoroughly caught out. I bet they're not supposed to be here. Our Stafford and Bettine have got spots on their consciences, too."

"Most of the men with the more decorative ladies are trying to look as though they'd no idea how they got here," said Hambledon. "Observe that embarrassed bit of flotsam with the brunette."

"Did you ever see a painted corpse?" asked Reck.

"The Wax Doll? You're right, she looks ghastly. Perhaps she knew the man," said Bellair. "That finishes the clientele, now for the staff."

Albertini senior had seen and heard nothing, he was at the far side of the restaurant talking to friends at the time. His son said that he was just about to lock the door to prevent fresh customers from entering, when one of the lady customers—he did not know which—called to him to open the door for a moment to let the New Year in. He had laughed and complied; as he did so Macgregor walked in. Albertini was just in the act of shutting the door again when he heard Macgregor fall, he was not looking at him at the moment. Yes, he heard a pop in the street outside but thought it was either a champagne cork being pulled or one of those toys which imitate that sound— practical joke things. Yes, he also heard a car drive off, it sounded like Mr. Bellair's. In fact, he saw it pull up outside, and had thought it was Mr. Bellair's which some friends had driven to the door for him. He could not possibly tell how many people were in the car, it is difficult to see in through glass, but he did notice a lady in the passenger's seat beside the driver, she had the window down because he saw her hand holding the door. Her left hand, presumably. Yes, her left hand. No, he would not know the lady again, he only gathered the impression that she was dark-haired. It all passed in a moment, they would understand he had no reason then for taking any particular notice.

The waitresses had seen nothing, nor had the senior chef, who was not in the restaurant at all at that moment, but upstairs, changing to go home. The second chef was Chinese, and smiled politely on being questioned. His name was Ching and he lived in Portsmouth. When the last gentleman came in he was leaning on the half-door leading to the kitchen, looking down the room towards the door, thinking.

"Thinking?"

"About Canton," explained Ching. "In Canton are lots of clackers on New Year's Eve."

"Clackers?"

"Crackers," said the constable, who had talked to Chinese before. "Fireworks, like."

"No clackers here," said Ching, "till gentleman came in."

"No, I suppose not—hey? What's that you said?"

"No clackers till gentleman came in."

"Was there one then?"

"Yes, outside, somebody in car let off clacker."

"You saw that through the door?"

"Yes."

"Saw a flash from a car?"

"Yes. Big car went off quick, lots of noise."

"Here's something definite at last," said Grogan. "You're for the inquest, my lad. Make him understand what that means, Wilson. Here's the Super."

Detective-Superintendent Elliot came in, a square man in a dinner-jacket who still looked like the Lowland farmer that all his forebears were. He greeted Bellair, who introduced Hambledon and Reck.

"This is a life," said Elliot. "I take an evening off to go to a party for once, and this is the second time I've been hauled out of it tonight. Once for some trouble down in Portsea and now this, and even on the way here I was hung up by a fire at the top of Commercial Road, hoses all over the street and so on. Car ran into a paint-shop and caught fire, a hell of a blaze."

"Car?" said Bellair, with the uneasiness natural to an owner whose car has been stolen. "What sort of a car?"

"Big black saloon, can't tell you more than that. Couldn't see the number for smoke."

"I'll bet it's mine," muttered Bellair gloomily, but Hambledon asked, "Was there a lady in it?"

"No, sir. Only one man, they've got his body out. They think somebody else was killed when the car hit the shop-front, but they can't even be sure of that till they get the fire out. Now, what's all this?"

Grogan reported, and the superintendent turned to Albertini.

"Nothing must be moved till the doctor and the photographer have finished. When they're done we'll bring an ambulance and take the body away."

"Very good, sir," said Albertini in a resigned tone.

"Have all these people checked up as quickly as possible," said Elliot to Grogan, referring to the list of the customers' names and addresses. "If that Ching is right, he was shot from the car, possibly Mr. Bellair's car, I understand. I shall go round to the Guildhall now and see if there is any report from Portsbridge."

"If that's my bus blazing in the paint-shop," said Bellair, "there won't be."

"Eh? Oh, ah. Yes. Perhaps you'd like to come to the Guildhall too, in case it is."

On the way, Hambledon said, "I wonder whether anybody in the street saw somebody in a car fire an automatic pistol into the doorway of a perfectly respectable restaurant in the main street of a large town like Portsmouth. It almost seems as though someone ought to have done so, there are plenty of people about."

"You would scarcely credit," said the superintendent, "the wonderful things people don't see. Why, there was a bank messenger knocked down and robbed of fifteen thousand pounds in this very street some years ago, in the middle of the day with the pavements full of people, and how many of them saw it, do you think?"

"Precious few," said Bellair, "and those who did see it didn't do anything, I'll bet. I saw a smash-and-grab raid on a jeweler's in Bond Street once, from the top of a bus. Fellow smashed the window with a hammer, grabbed a tray of rings, and jumped into a car, and all the people on the pavement just stood and stared. There was one old retired colonel sort of fellow who stopped dead with one foot in the air, if only he'd put his stick between the thief's legs they'd have caught him."

"Show me the man," said Elliot sententiously, "who jumps towards a surprise when it occurs, and I'll show you a born policeman. The typical Englishman stands stock still."

"Is that why we're always caught napping by the outbreak of war?" asked Bellair.

"No, that's your pure and unsuspecting minds," said Elliot sardonically. "You never believe anybody could possibly be so wicked as to attack you—or so rash, I'm not sure which. I'm a Scot myself."

"What of the man who leaps the other way when startled?" asked the amused Hambledon.

"Probably Italiano," said Elliot. "Here we are, come up to my office."

There was some news about the fire at the top of Commercial Road. The paint-shop was that of Messrs. Shedd Bros., at the time the accident happened there was a sailor in the doorway opposite talking to a girl. The girl had screamed and run away, but the sailor had been persuaded to come to the Guildhall and make a statement then and there, as he was sailing for the China coast early next morning.

"Bring him up," said Elliot.

"Do they know yet whose car it was?" asked Bellair.

Elliot transferred, with a bushy eyebrow, the question to the inspector who was reporting.

"The number," said the inspector, consulting his notes, "was PC 986. The owner has not yet—"

"Look no further," groaned Bellair. "Damn the blighters, I hope they burn too."

"Ultimately they will," said the Presbyterian Elliot, soothingly, "ultimately they will. Was the car insured?"

"Yes, but that's no use," said Bellair, "I don't think there is another car like that in existence." He stared gloomily into space.

"Send up the sailor," repeated Elliot, who knew when consolation is vain.

The sailor, having given the usual personal particulars, said that he was standing in a shop doorway almost opposite Shedd's when he heard a big car coming fast from the direction of the Guildhall. His attention was attracted because it didn't sound like an ordinary car.

The bereaved owner merely uncrossed his legs, and crossed them over the other way; the sailor glanced at him with curiosity and continued his story.

When the car was about a hundred yards away it slowed down almost to a stop and a lady jumped from the passenger's door in front. The driver also got out, stood on the running-board for a moment, and leapt clear as the car gathered speed again with a roar. It came on, inclined towards the pavement and hit the curb. This evidently turned the front wheels, for the car cannoned off the pavement, shot across the road, crashed through the window of the paint-shop and immediately burst into flames.

"Oh," said Elliot. "You are sure the driver jumped out? There was another man in the car, you know."

"Yes, sir, but he was in the back seat. He was trying to hop over and grab the controls, but he hadn't time."

"You saw him standing up?"

"Yes, sir, saw him plain, there was a streetlight behind him."

"I see. Now the two who jumped out, did you see what happened to them?"

"The lady ran a few steps, like, as you would getting off a moving bus, and then stopped. The driver tripped or something and rolled over, picked himself up, and both bolted across the road and hopped into a taxi as was waiting the other side. Next time I looked they'd gone."

"Which way?"

"Towards Guild'all Square, sir, that's the way the taxi was heading. Not that I actually saw them go, 'cause that was when the fire broke out and I was looking at that."

"But you're sure it was a taxi?"

"Sure, sir. One of them yellow ones."

"Oh. Notice anything else?"

"No, sir. Can't think of nothing else, sir."

"About the lady who was with you, what's her name and address?"

"I dunno, sir," said the sailor with some embarrassment. "I'd only just met her, like."

"You didn't know her at all?"

"No, sir."

"No idea whereabouts she lived?"

"No idea, sir. I'd only just started talking to her, like, when all this happened."

"Did she see all this, too?"

"I suppose so, sir. There wasn't time to say nothing, then the car hit the shop and she screamed and ran away."

"Can you give me any idea what the man and woman who jumped out of the car were like?"

"No, sir. They was too far off. I think the lady had black 'air now I come to think, but there was rather a lot to look at, like, just for the minute, if you get me."

"Quite," said Elliot. "Was there anybody else about at the time?"

"Now I come to think of it, there was a man talking to a policeman outside the shop that was hit. I didn't see them after, perhaps they ran away."

"Policeman," repeated Elliot and his face darkened. "Nothing else you can think of? No? We are very much obliged to you. If you wouldn't mind waiting a few minutes while your statement is typed out and then signing it—thanks very much. This constable will show you where to wait, they won't be long. Good night, and thanks very much. Pleasant evening out, that precious pair seem to have had," he went on as the sailor left the room, "the car thief and his black-haired girlfriend, I mean. One man shot, another burned alive, and another—or possibly two—crushed to death when the car hit the shop. One of them possibly a policeman, which makes it worse. Well, if they think they can get away with that kind of thing in this country, they can think again. Four murders in one night!"

"You may find," said Hambledon evenly, "that that's nothing to what they can do when they really try."

"Constable Allen, sir, has a statement to make," said the Inspector.

"Send him in."

Constable Allen said that he was walking up Commercial Road on his way home when the black saloon car overtook him and slowed down, two people jumped out, and then the rest of the tragedy was played out before his eyes. The two people, man and woman, ran across the road and jumped into a waiting taxi which started at once and came towards him.

"I ran into the road, sir, and shouted to them to stop. They took no notice, only came on faster, so I threw my truncheon at the windscreen. It starred all over, but they drove on."

"Can you give a description of the man and woman?"

"No, sir. They crouched down as they went by and the driver covered his face."

"Get the number of the taxi?"

"CG 3912, sir."

"CG 3912," repeated Elliot. "Good. Not but what I expect it's got another one by now," he added. "Inspector, send a man round to the Knight Taxi people to bring in the driver of a cab with a starred windscreen, number CG 3912, or any other number for that matter."

But there was no taxi with a starred windscreen belonging to the Knight Taxi Company, nor did any of their cabs bear the number CG 3912.

CHAPTER IV

Strange Behavior of a Coffin-Plate

"THE SUPERINTENDENT is not here, sir, at the moment," said the station-sergeant at the Guildhall.

"Detective-Inspector Grogan, then?" asked Hambledon.

"Yes, sir, he's here. I'll send a man up to tell him you want to see him."

"Morning, Grogan," said Hambledon ten minutes later. "I don't want to interrupt if you're busy, but I did feel I'd like to know if you've caught the beggars who bumped off Macgregor the other night. If it's still all secret and confidential," he went on, noticing an exasperated expression spreading across Grogan's face, "say so at once. The last thing I wish to do is to intrude on police procedure, we will turn instead to the subject of bearskin rugs. Do you know at all where I can buy a black bearskin rug in Portsmouth? You know, one of those long-whiskered—"

"I gather," said Grogan, "that you haven't heard yet what happened last night?"

"What happened?"

"Macgregor's house was blown up."

"Please go on," said Hambledon.

"In the small hours of this morning," said Grogan, "there was a violent explosion in Macgregor's house which wrecked it very thoroughly, rendered the houses on either side so unsafe that they had to be vacated at once, and broke every window in the street."

"Dear me," said Hambledon, sitting down on one of the hard chairs, "they did mean to make sure of him, didn't they?"

The Detective-Inspector, less accustomed to violent death than the British agent, looked really shocked, and said, "They got his widow, anyway."

"The devil they did. That makes five."

"Yes, five," said Grogan sourly, "and the police have as yet no evidence to show who did any of 'em. No trace of the yellow taxi, either."

"Cheer up," said Hambledon encouragingly, "it's not so bad as it sounds. It's obvious that this is all one and the same job, done by the same people, so it's only one murder really, isn't it?"

"One case, possibly."

"One case, yes. Cheer up, some ray will soon dawn. No information obtainable from any of the clients at the Café d'Albertini?"

"No. We've checked up on all of them bar two. A man and a girl, sitting at the table near the service door, nondescript young man, and a girl with a penetrating voice."

"I remember them," said Hambledon thoughtfully.

"Not known by the names they gave—or any others—at the addresses they gave, so their descriptions have been circulated. Girl should be easy to find, showy piece in my opinion."

"Oh, you shouldn't be too hard on her," said Hambledon, coming to the conclusion that Grogan had got out of bed the wrong side that morning, "I expect she's a dutiful daughter and kind to her rabbits and all that." Grogan merely snorted so Hambledon went on. "I thought most of the people there looked pretty guilty."

"Yes, but most of their guilt was innocent enough," said Grogan, "at least, it was ordinary enough. The Wax Doll looked guilty because she knew Macgregor and didn't want to admit it, but there was nothing in that. The others were mostly people who were merely supposed to be somewhere else. Talk of a murderer's guilty look, believe me, sir, a man who's caught taking his typist out to dinner looks guiltier than six murderers, and I've seen both."

"I bow to the voice of experience," said Hambledon without a smile. "I think I will go and look for Mr. Bellair."

"He was in Durham Street earlier on," said Grogan, "poking about the wreckage of Macgregor's house and talking to some explosive experts from the dockyard."

"Experts are apt to be a little touchy," agreed Hambledon, who did not like Grogan very much.

"Eh? Oh, I meant they were experts on the subject of explosives."

"I see. Thank you very much, I won't take up any more of your time. Durham Street, did you say?"

"Yes, Durham Street," said Grogan, rising to his feet. "Cross Commercial Road outside here, turn half-right, third left, second right and carry on."

Hambledon followed these directions and came eventually to a barricade across the top of Durham Street supporting the elbows of a continuous line of observers. Behind the front-row stalls were more onlookers, peeping over their shoulders, and Hambledon, to whom Providence had not been generous in the matter of inches, could see nothing. There was a gap in the barricade, guarded by an elderly police-constable whom Hambledon approached.

"May I come through?" he said.

"Excuse me, sir, do you live 'ere?"

"No," said Hambledon, surveying the narrow roadway littered with broken glass, and, in the middle distance, sliding moraines of rubble defiling the street. "I don't think I'm sorry, either," he added. "No, I was only looking for Mr. Bellair, I understand he's here somewhere."

"Mr. Bellair, sir, yes, he's down there. Been there some time. Excuse me, sir, 'ave you a police permit to visit the spot?"

"No," said Hambledon, to whom the idea of asking police permission to do anything was still a novelty, "I didn't think of asking for one. I wonder whether he'll be much longer."

"I'll try and get a message to him that you're 'ere—what name please, sir?"

"Hambledon."

A very junior constable was sent on the errand and came back with the message that Mr. Bellair was coming in just a moment if the gentleman would wait; Hambledon thanked him and stood back among the onlookers.

"Gas-mains," said one. "You mark my words, they'll find it was gas-mains."

"Gas," said another, "as 'ud blow three or four houses to bits is not by no means the same as is laid on to our gas-cooker. Gas-mains, my foot. It's the Irish."

"Ah. It's the Irish all right."

"Irish me eye. Gas-mains."

"What would the Irish want to be blowing up a poor decent corpse as never did them any harm? Lightning, that's what it was, a thunderbolt, like."

"Trust you to stand up for the Irish, Mrs. Leary. But it's no thunderbolt would do the like of that, and nothin' at all left of the coffin but a bit of wood with the plate on it blowed straight through Mrs. Dummer's bedroom windows opposite as she told me 'erself, for when she switched the light on to see if they was all still alive there it was, believe me or believe me not, stuck up on the mantelpiece next her Nellie's photo for all the world as if it was put there a-purpose, and didn't half give her a turn."

"Give her a worse turn if poor old Mac 'ad come froo the window with it," said one of the men with a horse laugh.

"'Ave they found 'im yet?" asked Mrs. Leary in a whisper.

"Well, not altogether, as you might say—"

Hambledon drifted away and joined a group of men who were discussing Pompey's chances for the Cup. Even when he discovered that they were only talking about football he stayed there. He preferred it.

Presently Bellair came up the street with three or four men to whom he was talking confidentially. When he saw Hambledon he left his friends and came to him.

"Morning, Hambledon. Made a nasty mess, haven't they, whoever they are?"

"Quite," said Hambledon as they walked away. "Thorough, these people, very thorough."

"M'yes," said Bellair, and coughed. "My throat's full of lime dust."

"I could prescribe for that," said Hambledon, "will you lunch with me? Splendid, where shall we go?"

"The Queen's grill?" suggested Bellair.

"Sounds good, lead on."

They found a quiet corner in the grillroom at the Queen's since it was almost too late to lunch at all, and over steak and lager Bellair talked of what he had seen and heard.

"These explosive wallahs," he said, "are undoubtedly swells at their job. I showed them my card when they arrived and they kindly let me follow them round and listen to their remarks. To me, you know, it just looked one mess. Macgregor's house is an empty shell, four walls, two with straight edges at the top and two gabled to fit the missing roof. In the space enclosed, a shapeless heap of rubble, plaster, broken glass, timber and furniture. You can tell where the different rooms began and ended because the wallpaper varies and there are traces showing where the party-walls came. On one of the first-floor walls there still hangs that well-known picture of a girl reading a book instead of doing her hair. The artist has caught her at the moment when she's just realized she'll be late for breakfast. It is called, I believe, 'The Soul's Awakening.' It's crooked, but the glass isn't even cracked. I shouldn't have thought there was any trace of anything in that ruin, but the experts nosed around, sniffing, though I couldn't smell anything except gas everywhere. They admitted that they also smelt gas everywhere, but in places the smell had other ingredients besides gas. I took their word for it. They pointed out that the explosion had definitely taken place on the ground floor because the splinters round the walls where the bedroom floor came from, were all pointing upwards." Bellair paused for breath and took a pull at his beer, while Hambledon waited in sympathetic silence.

"There was a police constable passing by at the time the event occurred," went on Bellair, "who said that he smelt explosives. Asked if he were sure it was explosives, real chemical explosives he meant and not gas, he replied that the smell reminded him of the Great War and they didn't have gas laid on in any frontline trench he'd ever been in."

"Did your friends look for stains?"

"They did. They found a hollow in the debris in the middle of the house which looked yellowish, so they borrowed spades and dug. That's when I got my throat full of lime. It was yellower as they went down, so they leaned on their spades and said, 'It was here.' "

"And where was 'here'? Whereabouts in the house, I mean?"

"We went into the next house, still erect though a bit tottery, whence the inhabitants had fled and I don't blame 'em, and came to the conclusion the bomb had been put under the stairs. They all have cupboards under their stairs, those houses—they're all exactly alike—and the gas-meters are in these cupboards. But no gas explosion would do all that damage, of course."

"It looks at first glance," said Hambledon, "as though someone planted the bomb in his cupboard. A time-bomb, of course, delay-action. After the man was brought home two days ago, whoever put the bomb there had no opportunity to remove it."

"Do you mean to suggest," said Bellair, "that there were two separate gangs of assassins after poor old Macgregor, one lot armed with bombs and the other lot with automatics? He must have been very unpopular."

"It's possible that they were separate attempts, but not very likely, not necessarily, either. Suppose for some reason Macgregor had to be silenced before a certain date—before he met me, for example. A delay-action bomb is planted, but there's too much delay and not enough action, so they shot him instead."

"They did leave it till the last second before they shot him," agreed Bellair. "Another moment and he'd have been out of range, another hour and he'd have spilled the beans."

"Yes. That would explain, too, why the bomb was left there after his death. A time-bomb is a chancy thing to handle anyway, but a time-expired one—"

"I don't blame them at all."

"Nor do I," said Hambledon, "except, of course, for putting it there in the first place. Here's a point. I wonder what Macgregor kept in his cupboard. If it were something he wanted every day, the bomb could hardly have been there long. Unless the cupboard was full and the bomb stuffed away underneath things."

Bellair nodded. "Our experts thought of that, too. Mrs. Macgregor was killed in the bomb explosion and I don't know whether any neighbors were intimate enough to know what they kept in their cupboards, that's a matter for the police to find out, no doubt. But we did go into several of the neighboring houses and asked to look in their staircase cupboards, and we weren't made at all welcome. In fact, although we were escorted and introduced by a police inspector in uniform, complete with official card, it was plain we weren't trusted alone with the cupboards. I wondered why till we'd seen three or four, and then I noticed that they all kept their beer there."

"The extensive cellarages of Durham Street," said Hambledon. "The chances are that Macgregor did the same. There may be a message in that for us, but if there is all I can say is that it hasn't reached me. Even the most outsize in beer bottles wouldn't burst with that shattering effect."

"Wonderful propaganda for the teetotallers if it did. I'm so glad I came to Portsmouth, this affair gets more interesting every day."

"That reminds me of something else I meant to say to you. Bellair, I think Portsmouth is a little too interesting to be healthy for you at the moment, I think a strategic withdrawal is indicated."

"Are you taking me off the case?" asked Bellair bluntly.

"Heavens, no. I am only saying that I don't think it's wise for you to go on sculling round Portsmouth on your own just now. Consider Macgregor. Consider the man in the car, whoever he was. Consider those two fellows idly chatting by the paint-shop—consider your car, if you can bear to. Remember Mrs. Macgregor and then tell me if you're safe in Portsmouth."

"Thanks awfully, but I shall be all right," said Bellair, a trifle too politely.

"Oh, don't be stuffy," said Hambledon irritably. "It's no novelty to me to have to bury my assistants, believe me, but it always annoys me."

Bellair laughed, but Hambledon said, "It's not really so funny. I mean it."

"Where do you want me to go?"

"I was going to suggest that you came over to Lynbourne till the situation clears up a bit. What? Reck isn't a bad cook and there's a new lock on the front door."

"D'you really mean that? I'd love to, thanks very much."

"Good, that's settled. Pay your hotel whatever is seemly and just in lieu of notice, and come back with me today. You can pack while I buy a hearthrug."

"So soon as that—oh, all right, I will," said Bellair, meeting Hambledon's eye. "Thanks awfully, it's extremely good of you. By the way, you mentioned the man who was killed in the car, he has been identified."

"Who was he?"

"A man named Smith and as inconspicuous as his name. He was a porter by trade, he worked for Colville. Colville says he doesn't know much about him, he was an average sort of workman, neither outstandingly good nor bad. The only salient fact about him was that he was a member of the British Union of Fascists."

"He was, was he? Heil our Hitler—with—an—M and all that? That's interesting if not very illuminating at present, why should they want to slay a Fascist? One would have expected them to cherish him—or would one? After all, Great Britain has more than one enemy, though I think there's only one so thorough and painstaking as this. But perhaps I'm prejudiced."

Bellair raised his eyebrows but naturally asked no questions. "There's only one enemy that counts in this year of grace, surely," he said. "Germany."

"That's the one I meant," said Hambledon.

"I went to the Empire last night and had a chat with the twins," said Bellair. "Do you remember seeing them at the d'Albertini? Irish girls, exactly alike."

"Considering they aren't blondes," said Hambledon, "I remember them extraordinarily well."

"I told you they knew all about everybody. They threw a queer little glimmer of light on the affairs of Macgregor and the Wax Doll. It appears that once a week regularly, on Wednesdays to be exact, he used to call at the

Empire box-office and buy two tickets for adjacent seats for the second house on the following evening. Every Thursday these two seats were occupied by Macgregor and the Wax Doll. They arrived separately, they left separately, and they never seemed to talk very much. He always bought her a box of chocolates for which he always paid one and threepence, and he seemed to get more pleasure out of watching her eat them than from seeing the show. There they'd sit, perfectly quiet and decorous, laugh at the funny man and join in the choruses, till just before the end she'd get up and go out. He waited till the show was over and went out with the crowd. The twins say that on Thursday nights she was always more quietly dressed than usual. Funny little story, isn't it?"

Hambledon nodded. "One funny little scene from one act of a fairly long play, I imagine. There's a story behind that though I don't suppose we shall ever know it."

"No wonder she looked like death herself when she saw him killed. She didn't scream even then, you'd think a woman like that would scream on the smallest provocation, wouldn't you?"

"Perhaps she was wondering what she'd do on Thursday nights in future," said Hambledon.

"Not go to the Empire, I imagine."

"No, possibly not. Or she might buy two seats and a box of chocolates for herself."

"Eileen suggested that," said Bellair. "But why should she? I should think she'd avoid the place."

" 'And still she wished for company,' " quoted Hambledon. "We're getting morbid, pass the port."

"I can't," said Bellair, "they've taken it away."

"Why?"

"Because it's past two-thirty. Closing time."

Hambledon closed his eyes. " 'England, my England,' " he murmured. "Well, I suppose I shall get used to it."

A naval officer came into the room, glanced round and caught sight of Bellair at the table in the corner. His face lit up and he came quickly across the room.

"Been raking Portsmouth for you, old man. Excuse me, might I just have a word with you, frightfully sorry, sir—"

Bellair crossed to the further side of the room and the officer talked for some minutes in a low tone quite inaudible to Hambledon. When Bellair returned he looked puzzled and angry, and dropped into his chair muttering what Hambledon correctly supposed to be maledictions.

"I gather something unpleasant has happened."

"Yes. You remember the destroyer *Araucaria* sailed on Monday? No? Well, she did. She's sunk now. There was an explosion on board in the small hours of this morning."

"In the small hours of this morning," repeated Hambledon.

CHAPTER V

Wax Doll

THE WAX DOLL drifted up Commercial Road, slanted across the top of Charlotte Street, and entered the saloon bar of the Emperor. Since it was still early in the evening the place was half empty; she leaned against the end of the bar near the door and asked for a gin-and-lime. The barman who served her enquired, by way of conversation, whether she had seen Durham Street.

"Isn't it dreadful!" she said, without answering directly.

"They say it was gas-mains blew up," said the bartender, "but I don't know as I believe that, Mrs. Roberts, do you?"

"Seems a lot of damage for a gas-main to do," she agreed. "A friend of mine told me they thought it was the Irish."

"Ah. Funny people, the Irish, never know what they'll do or why. I'm Welsh myself."

"I've known some very nice Irish people," said Elsie Roberts, with the air of one who must be fair whatever the circumstances.

"Ah, we all have. But that doesn't mean there aren't some funny ones amongst 'em."

"Funny people everywhere, come to that."

"You've said it! Pretty rotten trick, though, blowing up a dead man, don't seem no sense to it myself."

Mrs. Roberts did not wince. "I wonder," she said, "if we ever shall know the rights of it. If they do ever find out, they won't tell people, I don't suppose"—the mysterious "they" to ordinary people signifying an unspecified authority.

"Ah, you're right again, Mrs. Roberts. It's a queer thing, though, that there should be people about among us, in this very town, as are willing to blow a poor widow to pieces for spite, as you might say."

"It's dreadful to think of," said the Wax Doll, to whom the death of Mrs. Macgregor was merely an incident which had not happened soon enough, "poor woman!" She gave way to a dainty little shudder.

"I never knew her," said the barman.

"Nor did I," said Elsie Roberts untruthfully.

"But then I wasn't likely to, since I understand she wouldn't frequent places like this."

"Who's this?" asked a girl who had just come into the bar. "Hullo, Elsie, how's things?"

"Oh, not too bad, Kitty, thanks, how's yourself?"

"Still keeping alive. Who wouldn't frequent these lowdown 'aunts? Gin-and-lime please, George."

"We were talkin' about poor Mrs. Macgregor," said George, reaching up for the lime bottle.

"Oh, her," said Kitty.

"Yes," said Elsie. "A good woman she was, so I hear. Had very strict ideas."

"Almost a teetotaller, like?" said George.

"Almost!" said Kitty scornfully. "Rabid, she was."

"I always respect people," said Elsie Roberts in her primmest voice, "who have strict ideas of right an' wrong, and stick to 'em. But I do not think it right to ram your ideas down other people's throats. Live an' let live is my motto."

"Led 'im a bit of a life, by all accounts," said the barman.

"Couldn't call his soul his own, if you ask me," said Kitty. "A woman as can't let a man enjoy his beer in peace ought to be—well, I don't know. Yet he never said a cross word to her, they say."

A group of men came in arguing about which day of the week it was, some saying it was Wednesday and others Thursday. "'Tis Thursday, ain't it, George?"

"You're a day ahead, sir," said the barman. "Wednesday today, Thursday tomorrow."

"Thursday tomorrow," whispered Elsie to herself, and emptied her glass. She ordered another and carried it away with her to one of the settees along the wall.

After all, perhaps Jenny Macgregor wasn't so far wrong, especially since it wasn't beer she objected to, but whisky. If there had been somebody years ago with enough influence over Donald to keep him off whisky it would have been a lot better for him. He never got it at home, it was when he became an apprentice that he learned to drink whisky, people didn't know what they were doing sometimes when they sent a boy straight from home so young to live in lodgings and mix with all sorts of people, and Donald was always rather easily led, especially into mischief.

There was that dreadful time when he had just finished his apprenticeship and got his first job fixing up beer machines in a public-house in Glasgow. He stole a case of whisky—a whole case!—and of course he was found out. There was the most awful row over it and his old people had to pay out no end of money to keep him out of prison. Elsie was only twelve then but, of course, she heard all about it and anyway Donald always talked to her even in those days. He was a man who always had to talk to somebody in the slow Scots accent which she herself had entirely lost, but which always reminded her of home, and the sunlight on distant hills.

Distant hills and the Clyde. Sometimes they all went for trips across the Clyde to Dunoon, a party of neighbors together; the older women sitting on the long slatted seats bolted to the deck, and talking endlessly of men and children—both tiresome, of marriage and bringing up the family—both disappointing if one could judge by their comments, but Elsie always knew they didn't really mean it, that their caustic words only concealed a pride they were too proud to utter and a love they would have thought it indecent to express. Boys and girls strolled or lounged about the decks, chattering like starlings, giggling and pushing, the older men gathered round the bar or sat about talking either politics or shop, it seemed to Elsie that even during a day's outing they could not really leave the work behind. As a background to all this was the mixed smell of engine-oil, varnish, beer and fried bacon, the cries of gulls circling for scraps and the splash of falling water churned by the thumping paddle-wheels, the cool air on one's face, the long ripples of the wake astern where the water was still as glass as it was sometimes coming up to Kilmun Pier in the Holy Loch among the hills, and crossing the Loch to Sandbank and Hunter's Quay. Great hills going straight up from the sea with only a twisting white road between and small houses dotted along the shores, great hills brown and gold and amethyst, ribboned with little silver streams after rain. "I to the hills will lift mine eyes," murmured Elsie, remembering something she had forgotten for years, "from whence doth come mine aid—" The Shorter Catechism, "What is the whole duty of Man?" "The whole duty of Man is to glorify God and enjoy him forever." So long ago and far away, but the hills were still there just the same, perhaps some day she and Donald would save up enough money to go back, for surely no one would remember them now, and this time they would really go ashore at Strone or Kilmun and walk on those hills, they had always meant to but somehow it had never happened. She'd take the boy up, too, the hills—

"Lumme, Elsie, you do look queer! Seein' ghosts?"

The saloon bar of the Emperor in Portsmouth, blue with smoke, crowded, noisy, and hot.

"Perhaps I was," she said with her mechanical smile.

"Feelin' queer? Have a drink."

"No, thank you, not tonight. I've got a bit of a headache, think I'll go home. Thanks ever so, all the same."

Outside the air was biting, frosty with a bitter east wind, she shivered without noticing it. Fancy going right back like that, forgetting that Donald would never see the hills again.

"Evening, Elsie. All on your own? Come down to the d'Albertini an' have a spot of supper."

"It's ever so nice of you to ask me," she said, "but I'd rather not come tonight. I've got a bit of a headache, I'm going home. Thanks ever so, all the same."

"Going home, are you?" said the man in plain disbelief. "You're walking the wrong way."

"Oh, how stupid of me," she said, tears of real vexation coming to her eyes, "I don't seem to know what I'm doing tonight." She turned round and walked back the way she had come, the man following a few paces behind. She noticed this when they entered a quiet street, and turned on him. "Oh, go away!" she cried, "don't follow me, I can't bear it!"

"All right, all right," said the man. "Be awkward, then. I only meant it kindly 'cause I thought you looked ill."

"I'm sorry," she began, but he walked away in a huff. She forgot him instantly and began to look again at the brightly lighted picture that was always in her mind, the Café d'Albertini on New Year's Eve when the door was opened to let in the New Year and Donald came in instead. He stood for a moment inside the door, then suddenly crumpled up and fell in a heap. A woman at the next table said, "Oh! Look at that horrid man! He's drunk!" but Elsie had known it wasn't drink, but death. She wanted to run to him but didn't like to, it was understood between them that they didn't know each other in public. So she sat and waited, watching the people as she always watched people. The twins from the Empire, wide-eyed, Molly looking appealing and Eileen disdainful. Colville, very white round the nose, trying to light a cigarette but finding it difficult to hold the match steadily enough—it came to the Wax Doll suddenly that Colville also must have known that Donald was dead. A young naval officer opposite who slewed his chair round so that the lady with him should not see anything unpleasant, a nice boy, that, it must be lovely to be looked after like that. Bellair went to Donald at once, and his friend with him, a stranger, never seen him before, he looked the sort of man you'd do what he told you, quick. Bellair was nice, no airs about him, Bellair—

Bellair strolled into the kitchen of East Bungalow, Lynbourne, and found Reck wrestling with the coal-burning kitchen range and cursing in German under his breath.

"Can I do anything to help?"

"You can have electricity laid on to this benighted village and an electric cooker installed in this blasted house. Nothing short of that will be of the slightest assistance, thanks."

"I know I'm no good at that job," said Bellair humbly. "I only thought perhaps I could wash up for you, or something."

"Very good of you," said the mollified Reck, "but there's no need. The Awful Woman does all that in the mornings."

"Oh yes. Is she always like that?"

"Like what?"

"What she was like this morning. Dashing about muttering all the time."

"She was much better than usual this morning. You were new, that gave her something fresh to think about. As for her muttering, I don't understand her so it doesn't matter. Usually she bangs things."

"Bangs things? What with, a hammer?"

"No, no. Just together, like this," said Reck, picking up a frying-pan and beating it on the coal-scuttle.

"She must be mad."

"So I think. But then probably she has had this sort of stove to cook on all her life. It is no wonder if she is a little mad."

"It seems to be going better now," said Bellair, admiring the clear red glow between the bars. "Sure I can't do anything?"

"You could lay the table, if you would care to. Spoons and things in the sideboard. Lay for soup, grilled kidneys, sardines on toast, and cheese."

"Where are the glasses?" asked Bellair, returning to the kitchen ten minutes later. "On the dresser, I see. When d'you expect Hambledon home?"

"In about half an hour," said Reck, glancing at the clock. "The Awful Woman has hidden the curry powder. No. It is here."

Half an hour later they heard Hambledon's car run into the garage, and the master of the house came in rubbing his hands and sniffing the savory smells floating out from Reck's kitchen. Hambledon said that it was cold enough to crack paving-stones, that London was an overrated place especially in an east wind, and that the Admiralty had been specially designed and organized to produce a violent inferiority complex in any mere landsman. He then poured out two glasses of sherry, drank his and dropped into an armchair before the lounge fire saying "Ah!" in a comforted voice. "Your sherry, Bellair," he added. "Reck won't touch it."

"Had a good day?" asked Bellair.

"I have acquired a vast store of information and that's good for the brain, but as to getting on any further with the job in hand, I doubt it." Hambledon leaned back in the chair and closed his eyes, Bellair took the hint, and there was silence till Reck came in with the soup.

After the grilled kidneys Hambledon revived. "These explosions," he began abruptly, "have certain features in common. They only take place on ships which are, for one reason or another, particularly important, and they only happen to ships sailing from Portsmouth. Chatham, Devonport and the rest are immune." He took a long pull at his beer. "Now, the *Araucaria*—"

"Would it be possible," said Reck, "to postpone the *Araucaria* till after the sardines? They, at least, are hot."

"How right you are," said Hambledon, while Bellair wished it wasn't rude to stare, since this was without exception the oddest household he ever was in. To start with, Reck was obviously an educated and cultured man with a past he never mentioned, yet he cooked for and waited on Hambledon like a servant, at the same time addressing him with a freedom which horrified Bellair, who was beginning to discover that Hambledon, apparently so easy in manner when one first met him, became more formidable day by day.

"Resuming the lecture," said Hambledon when the cheese was on the table, "we all know that when Mr. Chamberlain came back from Munich last September bringing peace in our time, he very wisely took steps to ensure it by rearming the country at once. The Navy, in addition to building new ships, has a number of old ones which are being practically rebuilt with all the most modern improvements, and some of these improvements are very modern indeed. Equally hush-hush, of course. Experiments, in fact, are being tried out in range-finders, submarine detectors, A.A. gun predictors, and all that sort of thing. Now by a series of regrettable coincidences—if they are coincidences—nearly every time a ship goes out from Portsmouth Dockyard with somebody's extra bright brainwave aboard, one of these hellish explosions takes place and the experiment fails of its intention."

"I take it," said Reck, "that the fact that new experiments are being tried is known to as few people as possible."

"Of course it is," said Hambledon.

"Then it almost looks as though there were someone in a fairly limited circle who talks."

"Not necessarily," said Bellair. "There are all the engineers and fitters who install these gadgets, they all know something new when they see it."

"The case of the *Araucaria* is even more serious than usual," went on Hambledon. "There were several bright ideas being tried out aboard her, so there were a number of civilian technical experts on board, besides extra observers from the Admiralty, in addition to the normal ship's company. Accounts from survivors make it clear that a terrific explosion occurred in or near the wardroom flat, and the majority of those killed were wardroom officers and the said experts and observers. The same sort of loss occurred in the R 101."

"Was there much loss of life?" asked Bellair.

"Twenty-six out of a hundred and forty-three, the ship stayed afloat for some hours, and the rest were all rescued."

"I know some of the officers on the *Araucaria*," said Bellair thoughtfully, "I saw the Commander and First Lieutenant having dinner at the King's on Sunday night. They were dining with Colville."

Reck came in with coffee and asked, "What sort of ship was she?"

"Destroyer," said Bellair.

"Not aircraft carrier as you might imagine," said Hambledon grimly. "To think that Grogan, the other day, was lamenting that there were five unsolved murder mysteries in Portsmouth, and I told him then that that was nothing to what these people could do when they tried. How beastly true."

"There has been serious loss of life before from these explosions," said Bellair.

"Yes, but they've never had quite such a good bag before, some of those men were irreplaceable. It is a lie," said Hambledon, turning cold eyes on his new assistant, "to say that in death all men are equal."

"You are unusually serious tonight," said Reck.

"Sorry," said Hambledon, finishing his coffee and fishing out the undissolved sugar in the spoon. "But you see, I'm not in it at all yet, and so far I see no way of getting in."

"You think that if only you were in it yourself it would at once become a lot funnier," said Reck incisively. "I haven't the faintest doubt that you are right."

"Nor have I," said Hambledon, "but as to which side would enjoy the joke most, that's another question." He got up and went to the sideboard. "Whisky and soda, Bellair? I'm going to have my nightcap on top of dinner and turn in, it's getting late and I find London exhausting—or is it the Admiralty? Say when."

"When," said Bellair. "I wish we could do something instead of only talking about it. I'd like to advertise:—Young gentleman in search of excitement and entirely without scruples, interested in explosives, desires meet kindred spirits."

"Here's your kindred spirit," said Hambledon, handing him the whisky. "I only wish you could get involved in the game, that would be worth while. Oh, we shall manage somehow, it's just finding somewhere to start. You know, if only we could find that precious pair from the d'Albertini, that might give us a lead. You remember, the conspicuous lady and her boyfriend who gave false names." He put some whisky in his own glass and approached it to the siphon.

"Oh, that's done," said Bellair. "I found her this afternoon."

Hambledon leaned heavily on the lever, regardless of the result, and said, "What? Where?"

"Here. I met her in the village shop. I went in for cigarettes and it was rather dark. I didn't recognize the lady till I heard the familiar carrying voice saying, 'No cork tips? What a bore!' "

Hambledon sat down and sipped the contents of his tumbler. "Strange," he said, "I would have sworn I put some whisky in this."

"You did," said Reck, "only you blew it all out again, pressing on the siphon like that. Much better for you without. I'll get something and clear up the mess."

"Tell me some more," said Hambledon, having readjusted his drink. "Who is she, where does she live, what does she do, where is she at this moment, and how can we be sure of meeting her again since I didn't find her locked in the bathroom?"

"Her name is Bettine Gascon, she lives at Lynbourne House in this parish, she is the governess to the children there, at the moment I expect she is in bed, probably smoking cigarettes and reading a novel, and I am going to have dinner with her tomorrow night."

"One of you is a swift worker," said Hambledon admiringly. "But tell me, did she recognize you?"

"Oh yes," said Bellair, "she said so."

"Then she'll bolt," said Hambledon, getting out of his chair, "unless she's bolted already. I think I'll go up there now and interview the lady at once, in bed or otherwise. Why didn't you inveigle her up here and chain her to the verandah-post?"

"She won't bolt," said Bellair calmly. "She's the governess there, and as regards events at the d'Albertini I'm sure her conscience is free. As regards Macgregor, I mean. She gave a false—"

"Who told you she was a governess? Did she tell you that herself?"

"No, the grocer told me, I went back to the shop after parting with the lady. She won't bolt. I tell you. She's not frightened about anything. I expect she just didn't want to give evidence at the inquest."

"I think you take it much too casually," said Hambledon. "I still think it would be wiser to go up now, we want the fellow's name too, you know."

"I'll get that tomorrow night," said Bellair.

"Do you mean to tell me she took one look at you, said 'Ah! the sheik from the next table at the d'Albertini! Come up to dinner tomorrow night'?"

"There was a little more in it than that," admitted Bellair modestly, "but that's the substance of it."

"You know," said Hambledon, regarding him critically, "there must be much more in you than meets the eye."

"Did the grocer introduce you?" asked Reck. "No? Then she's a hussy. I said so before."

"There's one little precaution we'll take," said Hambledon. "We'll ring up the police and tell them we've located their bird. Bird. Joke."

"It's all right," said Bellair. "I did that on the way home."

"I almost begin to hope," said Hambledon, "that with a little careful education you'll very nearly do."

CHAPTER VI

Superintendent's Daughter

BETTINE GASCON looked out of the hall window at Lynbourne House and saw the lights of Bellair's new car coming up the drive, so she opened the front door for him herself. It is conceivable that it was for this purpose that she was looking out of the window.

"Oh, do come in," she said, "isn't this fun? I've been so bored all day with only the children to talk to."

"Good evening, Miss Gascon. So good of you to ask me. Must be frightfully dull with only kids to talk to all day. Where are they now, in bed?"

"Yes, I packed them off in good time tonight and told them they could read in bed for half an hour for a treat. I must run up at a quarter to and turn the lights out. Hang your coat up here, won't you? Come in by the fire and get warm."

Bellair looked appreciatively round the pleasant room. There was a bookcase behind the door full of schoolbooks and children's books, bright oiled-silk curtains at the windows, a big squashy sofa with a gay chintz cover, a glass-fronted cupboard holding a marvelous assortment of dolls, a doll's house four feet high, and a blazing fire on the hearth. A few friendly inkstains on the walls added a touch of homely intimacy.

"Jolly nursery these kids have got," he said, and gathered immediately from Bettine's expression that he had said the wrong thing.

"I'm not a nurse," she explained, kindly but quite firmly, "I'm a governess, so this is a schoolroom, not a nursery. Excuse me a minute, I must just run up and see those children go to sleep."

"You dropped a brick, James," said Bellair to himself, "evidently there's a social difference between a governess and a nurse. I didn't know."

He strolled round the room looking at things. The mantelpiece bore a pair of brass candlesticks, two china dogs, one brown and one spotted, a very utilitarian clock, a box of matches in a brass case, one china ashtray and one large oystershell used for the same purpose, a small vase containing violets, and a photograph of a determined-looking man in the uniform of a superintendent of police. "There's a certain likeness about the nose," thought Bellair, "I expect that's Pa Gascon. Wonder where he superintends the constabu-

48

lary? And what did he think when his daughter's description was circulated—gosh, yes. Either he didn't recognize his little pet or he wouldn't admit it. Of course, he may be dead." When Bettine came into the room Bellair was obviously looking at the photograph.

"Who's the soldier?" he asked casually.

"That's my father," said Bettine. "He's not a soldier, he's a police superintendent. Will you come in to dinner?"

"Either truthful or clever," said Bellair to himself, "I wonder which? How many little responsibilities have you got here?" he added aloud.

"The children? Three. Daphne's eleven, Jill is nine and Alec is eight. The girls are sweet, but Alec's terribly spoilt. I do hope this soup's eatable," said Bettine, almost before the maid was out of earshot.

"Look out, she'll hear you," said Bellair uncomfortably.

"I don't care if she does," said Bettine frankly, "she can't be more tiresome than she is."

"This is all rather different from the last time we met, isn't it?" said Bellair, to change the subject.

"Yes, isn't it? I like the d'Albertini, don't you? Of course it's a small place," said Bettine kindly, "but the cooking's very good and it's such fun watching all the people."

"Do you often go there?"

"I've only been there that once, with Stafford; when the family take the children to Southsea for anything we generally lunch at the Savoy." Bettine rang the bell and the maid brought the next course. "I hope you like oxtail," said his hostess, "I thought it would be nice on a cold night."

"Who's Stafford? Your fiancé?"

"Oh, no. We were engaged once, but that's all over long ago. We're just friends now."

"Oh, really. I thought he looked rather proprietary."

"Sounds like medicine," said Bettine, laughing. "Yes, he is rather proprietary, that's why we parted. I don't want to be owned by anybody, I want to be free. Still, it was a jolly evening, wasn't it?"

"Rather tragic, ending up like that, don't you think?"

"Oh, that poor man falling down dead, yes, horrid. You went and saw about things, didn't you, was he a friend of yours?"

"Not a friend, no. I knew him, that's all."

"Heart, I suppose," said Bettine in a hushed voice.

"No, not heart," said Bellair, watching her. "He was murdered, Miss Gascon."

"Murdered!" shrieked Bettine. "No, I didn't know, they just said he'd died."

"He died all right—of a bullet through the head. Didn't you see the inquest in the papers?"

"Oh no, I never read the papers, we get the news on the wireless, you know. Who shot him, and why?"

"That's what we want to know," said Bellair, and gave her such account of it as had been made public, suppressing any suggestion that Macgregor's death was connected with the sabotage in the Navy.

"Oh, how horrid," said Bettine, shuddering, "and to think I saw it all and didn't know."

"That's why they took everyone's name and address, you know, because it was murder. They wouldn't have done that if he'd died of heart trouble."

"No, I suppose not, I never thought of that. I've got no brains at all, you know."

"That, of course, is obvious," said Bellair, with a long look which conveyed the exact opposite.

Bettine laughed, looked down and played with her fork, and looked up again at him sideways, under her long eyelashes, with her head a little tilted, just the same look she had given Stafford at the d'Albertini and Bellair recognized it.

"It was so funny, though," she said. "You see, neither Stafford nor I were supposed to be there, he because he's a teacher in a school near Leicester and only had the day off, and I because I'm not supposed to leave the children to the servants when Mr. and Mrs. Bingham are away. So we had a hurried talk in the corner and gave false names and addresses, and I don't suppose the police will ever find out. How can they?"

"They go round to the various addresses and ask."

"But if they don't find you there?"

"They circularize your description all over the country till they find you."

"Oh, nonsense," said Bettine, "I don't believe they'd go to all that trouble."

"But they do, Miss Gascon."

"Well, they haven't found me yet, have they? And oh, please don't call me Miss Gascon all the time, it sounds so cold and formal, doesn't it? I'm sure we're going to be friends, and all my friends call me Bettine."

"Bettine," said Bellair softly. "It's a lovely name and so unusual—it suits you."

"What's your name?"

"James. Just James."

"I shall call you Jimmy, do you mind? I always think Jimmies ought to have brown eyes like yours."

After that the sweet and cheese came and went as in a dream, Bettine and Jimmy returned to the schoolroom and sat side by side on the squashy sofa, looking into the fire. She told him that her father was superintendent at Wellstone, just over the Kentish border; that she was only twenty-three and had been educated in a convent school. He told her that he was born in America though he was a British subject, that his father was an Englishman who had died soon after James was born, so his American mother had brought him up. That he went to school in the States first, with his American cousins, but finished his education in England and Switzerland, and that he was twenty-seven.

"That's the same age as Stafford, isn't that funny?"

"Oh—blow Stafford. Who is the fellow, anyway?"

"You mustn't talk about him like that or I shan't like you," said Bettine, with another of her effective glances.

"Do you like him so much?"

"Oh, very much, you see I've known him for years, he comes from Wellstone too, and whenever I go home he's there, and it's so nice always to have someone to go about with."

"Delightful, I'm sure," said Bellair between his teeth.

"Now you mustn't be jealous, because that's silly. I'm never jealous so why should you be?"

Bellair proceeded to explain and presently found himself, by some process which was never clear to him, holding the lady's hand. He thought that this was enough for one night, so he took his leave and went home to find Tommy Hambledon waiting for him.

"Miss Bettine Gascon," said Bellair at once, "is the daughter of Police Superintendent Gascon of Wellstone, Kent. She is twenty-three, was educated in a convent, and is passionately fond of colored anemones."

"Anemones," said Hambledon. "I know, those hairy-legged flowers which always look as though they'd been dyed. My mother, I remember, wouldn't have them in the garden, she said they looked artificial. The man?"

"One Stafford Wilkins, also from Wellstone, the son of the principal drapery store. He plays rugby, smokes a pipe—not cigarettes, they're sissy—and is terribly particular ab out the cut of his shirts. He teaches in a school near Leicester, didn't get its name."

"Superintendent Gascon will doubtless provide full details. I think we'll run over to Wellstone in the morning."

"I don't think there's anything in it," said Bellair. "They had no business to be out that night, that's why they gave false names."

"Are you still so young," said Hambledon enviously, "as to think that every woman speaks the truth?"

"I never was. But I think it's the truth this time, the girl thought Macgregor died of heart disease."

"Doesn't she read the papers?"

"No."

"Good Lord, what did you find to talk about? Not that I wish to intrude!

Perhaps her father doesn't read either, and that's why he didn't identify the wench."

"Would you identify any woman you knew from a description?"

"Personally I should never be so tactless, but then I'm not a policeman— at least, not now. Anyway, she didn't strike you as being the sort of girl to be mixed up in a dark and mysterious plot."

"Heavens, no. She'd never grasp what it was all about. She's one of those—"

The telephone rang and Bellair answered it. He said, "Yes, speaking. . . Thanks awfully, how nice of you . . . No, not at all, I think it was awfully nice of you . . . Yes, rather, I'm looking forward to it . . . Don't be silly! ... No, of course not . . . No, not tomorrow, I'm afraid I shall be out all day . . No, no idea, probably quite late . . . I'll ring you, may I? Yes, rather . . . Good night, sleep well . . . Thank you, same to you . . . Good night . . . Good night . . . Good night." He rang off, looking a trifle sheepish.

Tommy Hambledon was lying back in his chair with his feet up against the side of the fireplace and the tips of his fingers lightly pressed together. He said nothing and there was a short silence.

"That was Miss Gascon," said Bellair.

"Oh, yes."

"She—er—we'd forgotten to settle something."

"So I gathered. Very awkward, having the telephone in the sitting-room. Always feel I'm eavesdropping."

"Not at all, sir. She only means to be friendly."

"Oh, quite," said Hambledon, and arranged his fingers in a different order.

Bellair fidgeted about, glanced at him once or twice and eventually said, "Well, I think I shall turn in. Good night, sir."

"Good night, my boy," said Hambledon blandly. "Happy dreams."

"Anemones," said Hambledon to himself when he was alone, "anemones. A garish taste," and he too went off to bed.

Wellstone's main street climbs steeply to the ancient gateway which spans the road,. There is the mixture of architectural styles and dates customary in our county towns, and there are three hotels, one large and expensive in the outskirts, one solid and comfortable in the main street, and one commercial, round a corner. In the middle of the road where it widens into a market square there is a tall narrow town hall looking exactly as though someone had chopped thirty feet off one of the wings of Buckingham Palace and run aground with it in Wellstone, outside this there is a memorial of severe design with an urn on the top and, just across the road, a one-story Woolworth's. Hambledon and Bellair lunched at the King's Head in the main street and thereafter strolled up to the police-station.

"Picturesque old place, this," said Bellair.

Hambledon grunted.

"I believe there's a ruined castle somewhere."

"Umf," said Hambledon.

"Anything the matter?"

"Have you ever broken the news to a superintendent of police that his daughter is being sought after by all the other police in England? Not in marriage, either, this time. Curious young woman, it seems to be her fate always to be chased for something. I was just wondering how one began."

" 'Excuse me, sir,' " suggested Bellair, " 'but have you found your daughter?' "

" 'Have you lost your daughter' would be even better."

" 'Because if so, we know where she is.' "

" 'You want the best daughters, we have them.' "

"Slogan for an adoption society. No. Something more severely businesslike is called for. 'In re the murder of Donald Macgregor at 12:05 a.m. on January the first last—how wrong that sounds—the wanted woman is your daughter, did you know?' "

"Too brutally forthright," said Bellair. "I think something more gently subtle is required. 'Tell me, sir, when you read these descriptions of wanted persons, aren't you sometimes reminded of your own family?' "

"Aren't we all? Here's the police-station."

They asked for Superintendent Gascon and were told he would be at liberty in about twenty minutes, but Hambledon had done this sort of thing too often himself to be impressed by it from others. He took out one of his cards, wrote the magic initials "M.I." in the corner, and said, "Take that in to him, will you?"

The constable returned at once and asked them to follow him. Superintendent Gascon rose to meet them, still holding Hambledon's card, Hambledon introduced himself and Bellair, and said he would be glad of a few minutes of the superintendent's time if it was convenient. Although Hambledon's manner was perfectly polite and even gentle, the superintendent somehow got the impression that it had better be convenient. "Certainly," he said. "I take it the matter is confidential?"

"Very," said Hambledon solemnly.

"I think we'll go in my den, if you don't mind. I have a man coming in here to do some work which is rather urgent, and there we shall not be interrupted. Come this way."

He took them to a small room in the residential part of the station, comfortably if rather stuffily furnished, with fly-rods on the wall, silver trophies on a side table, and a large glass container which had once been an accumulator jar but which now housed goldfish. The superintendent found comfortable chairs for his guests and himself sat on an upright one beside the goldfish. Hambledon noted this arrangement with an approving eye, the fellow had a correct sense of what was civil and fitting.

"The matter in question arises out of the murder of Donald Macgregor at Portsmouth on New Year's Eve," said Hambledon. "No doubt you had the circularized description of a man and a woman whom it is desired to interview? They gave false names and addresses at the time."

"Yes, I had them," said the superintendent, "and I may say that if two people had given their names to me as Jane Austin—even with an i—and Thomas Hardy, I should have suspected them at once. The names are not, of course, remarkable in themselves, and no doubt the Portsmouth police—"

"You are a reader, evidently," said Hambledon without enthusiasm. "Otherwise the descriptions conveyed nothing to you?"

"No, sir."

"The woman has been found."

The superintendent felt that something else was coming, and made no comment.

"Both these people are, I think, known to you. The woman was your daughter, Bettine Gascon—"

The superintendent stared, stiffened and turned purple. He made an effort to speak but merely produced noises of the burbling type; even the goldfish seemed to catch the infection of domestic crisis, for the largest among them swam to the front of the tank and stayed there, opening and shutting his mouth in exact imitation of his master a few inches away.

Hambledon waited a few moments before continuing. "It is not thought, however, that she had any knowledge of, or part in, the murder, it was her behavior merely which aroused suspicion—"

"Damned little fool!" exploded her father. "Blasted little idiot! No, I'll lay she didn't even know a murder had been committed right in front of her—"

"As a matter of fact," interrupted Bellair, "you're perfectly right, she didn't."

"She wouldn't," said her sizzling parent, "she'd never notice a little thing like that, she—and I suppose all the police in England have been hunting for my—who found her?"

"I did," said Bellair.

"Has she been interviewed yet?"

"Not yet. When I found out who she was, we decided to leave it to you."

"Thank you," said the superintendent with a gulp.

"In the case of what appears to have been a mere girlish prank," said Hambledon smoothly, "we thought the necessary disciplinary action could best be left to parental influence."

Gascon took his handkerchief out and mopped his brow, which needed it. "Leave it to me, gentlemen," he said grimly, "I'll influence her. Feather-brained little—I beg your pardon. I am really very much obliged to you for—"

"With regard to the man," interrupted Hambledon, "the position is not yet clear and may be more serious."

"I'd forgotten the man," said the superintendent. "Of course there would be a man wherever that wretched girl—who was he?"

"We have his name and we thought you could supply his present address," said Hambledon. "One Stafford Wilkins."

He stopped because he really thought that Gascon would have had some kind of fit. His remarks were, however, much more coherent than they had been on the subject of his daughter, and even the goldfish fled.

"You don't seem to like him," said Bellair kindly, and the superintendent concurred at some length till Hambledon tired of it and cut him short.

"As a lightning sketch of his appearance, habits and ancestry, your remarks are quite helpful," he said. "What we want now is his present address. He can be interviewed by the police on the spot."

"And I hope they roast him," said Gascon viciously. "He is a master at St. Raphael's School, Wigby, near Leicester, and I suppose he's there now. He ought to be. His home address is Highlands, Wellstone, that's about a mile out of the town on the Hastings road. His father runs the draper's shop here in the town, Tibtree and Wilkins, but of course the rooms over the shop aren't good enough for them nowadays."

"I will put the police in touch with Wilkins," said Hambledon, writing both addresses in his notebook, "if you will deal with—"

"Leave her to me."

A bell rang in another room and a constable tapped at the door to say the superintendent was wanted on the phone.

"Excuse me—who is it?"

"Miss Gascon, sir, wishes to speak to you."

"And I want to speak to her. Tell her to hold on—"

"We will leave you," said Hambledon, "to the undisturbed exercise of parental authority. Good-bye, Superintendent."

"Good-bye, sir, and thank you."

Hambledon slowed imperceptibly as they passed the superintendent's office window on their way across the yard, and a gentle smile illuminated his face.

"She was only a p'liceman's daughter," he said, "but didn't he lay down the law!"

CHAPTER VII

Broken Windscreen

HAMBLEDON and Bellair came out of the police-station behind the Guildhall in Portsmouth and crossed the road to the car-park to get out Bellair's Triumph Dolomite which he had bought to replace the Beverley, now a tangle of blackened metal in a scrap-yard.

"Care to drive, sir?"

"Thanks, I should," said Hambledon, "I hate being driven. So, I expect, do you, but discipline is good for the young." He backed carefully out, assisted by a constable who held up a Morris, a Lanchester and a Rolls for him. "Why are there so many cars here today, constable? Why these serried ranks of transport?"

"Some sort of parsons' gathering I understand, sir. Since the Bishop is here it is possibly the Diocesan Conference."

"Dear me," said Tommy, to whom the old-school-tie type of policeman was a new experience. "What do you suggest as a suitable collective noun for a number of clergymen? A pride of parsons? A bevy?"

"Bevy suggests beauty, sir, for some reason, and pride is one of the seven deadly sins. A more ecclesiastical flavor seems to be demanded, what about a halidom?"

"A halidom of parsons calls up a pleasing picture," said Hambledon, but Bellair said, "I thought halidom was a swearword."

"Not originally, sir. A blessing of parsons?"

The Morris became tired of waiting and tried to back away, endangering the Lanchester who blew a long blast of protest. Hambledon glanced in the driving mirror and was horrified to see that he was holding up a procession; saying hastily, "I acknowledge mine offenses," he drove away. "Are there many like that?"

"Quite a lot," said Bellair. "They come from the police college at Hendon."

"I heard of that when I was—was abroad," said Hambledon, "but I'd never met a product before. Which way here? You'd better pilot me."

After Portsdown Hill it is plain sailing up the Portsmouth Road, and Hambledon picked up the conversation where it had dropped.

"Yes, I imagine they're very bright lads indeed," he said, "but they don't get much forrader with the Macgregor case, do they?"

"Isn't there any news of the taxi?" asked Bellair, who had not been present at the first part of the interview with Superintendent Elliot.

"There is, but it's negative. It is definitely not one of the Knight Cab Company's yellow taxis which it so strongly resembled, because they all turned up at headquarters within the hour with windscreens intact. Nor has any glass-cutter in Portsmouth cut a Triplex windscreen for a Fisher cab body."

"And they'd never replace that double-curved top from stock in this country. It's either a taxi from outside the town or a private car painted to look like one. I suppose the man who threw his truncheon at the car took its number?"

"Of course," said Hambledon, "and even in that moment of stress it struck him as vaguely familiar. When they looked it up and found it was one of the Lord Lieutenant's, he knew where he'd seen it."

"So we're still in a dead end."

"Yes, and so was the Bettine-Stafford enquiry. The dashing Mr. Wilkins had no more to do with it than his ex-fiancée, so our trip to Wellstone was a washout."

Bellair suppressed a natural urge to say "I told you so," and remarked, "Never mind, we saw the goldfish."

"Did you notice that too? It was nearly my undoing, I never would have believed a goldfish could look so like a superintendent of police. Well, what do we do now? One of the main functions of an intelligent assistant is to produce suggestions good enough for his superior to adopt. If they're really good he does adopt them—as his own, for thus is promotion attained. Well?"

"If I knew the Portsmouth police were looking for a car with a smashed windscreen, I don't think I'd get it repaired in Portsmouth," said Bellair.

"You couldn't drive it far without comment," said Hambledon. "A smashed windscreen is noticed by the most unmechanical female, let alone the difficulty of seeing through it. It wouldn't break, of course, but it would star and split."

"He needn't drive it in that condition, he could take out the whole frame if he were enough of a mechanic, or get it taken out for him. Those Fisher cab windscreens are not so simple."

"You seem to know a good deal about them."

"I've driven in them in Portsmouth often enough."

"So. Well, to return to l'affaire Macgregor. We now know that the murderer is either a capable mechanic or has a friend who is, and that he's got sense enough not to get his repairs done in Portsmouth on this occasion. We know he drives more than one make of car with equal facility and is a pretty shot with an automatic. Anything else?"

"That his girlfriend is dark," suggested Bellair, "which cuts out Siddall. I can't think of anything else. Putting myself in the cabdriver's place, I should drop the windscreen in the back of another car, with a rug over it, and take it out of town to some such place as this." He indicated the premises of Bodmin Brothers of Waterlooville, which they were passing at the moment.

Tommy slowed down. "Let's go in and enquire," he said, "I'm so stuck I'd try anything. It's more than six weeks since Macgregor was killed and we've done nothing so far."

"As you wish," said Bellair, so Hambledon pulled the car in to the curb and they walked back to Bodmin's and looked at it. "Morris Agents," said an inscription on the windows. "Bodybuilders."

"Come on," said Hambledon, and they went into the office, a spacious room with various Morris models on show and many colored advertisements on the walls. Hambledon told the man in charge that he came to enquire whether they had cut a new windscreen for a Fisher cab since the first of January, and if so for whom. The man stared a little and said he would fetch the manager.

The manager came at once and began to explain that it was not usual to discuss their customers' business, and Hambledon said he quite understood, but that this matter was official, and he showed his card.

The manager said of course that altered the case completely, and what did they want to know? Having had it explained to him he said they had better talk to the glass-cutter himself if they would kindly come this way. He took them behind the counter, down three steps, and through a room full so far as they could see, of tall screens of pigeonholes. Beyond this was a large work-shop full of cars in various stages of completion, and many men were busy upon them.

"The body shop," said the manager. "The glass-cutter has a bench in the corner."

They found the glass-cutter in the act of taking a strip off a piece of Tri-plex glass, and stood back to watch the process. The cutter was an elderly man with a white mustache and little side-whiskers; he moved his work and handled his tools with the careful but unhesitating touch which marks the master craftsman in every trade, and which is of all things in the world the most fascinating to watch. He had a pattern of three-ply wood of the size and shape required; he drew his diamond along the edge of this and a crack in the glass ran after the tool like an eager child. He turned the sheet over on the rubber-covered table and did the same on the other side. This left the filling substance, like talc, between, and since the glass was willing to open a little along the crack, he was able to slip a razor blade into it and cut the filling through. The strip came off in one piece, the edges clean and bright, and

Hambledon found to his surprise that he had been holding his breath.

"I wish I could do anything as well as that," he said, and meant it. The glass-cutter laughed and said that if you'd been doing anything for forty years or so you'd be liable to get rather good at it. He lifted his work off the table, and the tabby cat, who had been sitting on the end of the bench watching the performance, got up, stretched itself, turned round and sat down in exactly the same place again, ready for the next one.

"That old cat," said the glass-cutter, "knows more about glass than what I do. She's always there when I'm working."

"Darby," said the manager, "these gentlemen want to ask you something."

"Anything I can tell you," said Darby, "I will." He laid down his tool and took off his steel-rimmed spectacles.

"I am anxious to know," said Hambledon, "whether you have cut a new windscreen for a Fisher cab body since January 1st, and if so, who it was for."

"I don't think I should know a Fisher cab body if I saw one, sir, it's a new name to me and I don't think we've had one in here."

"It's an American body," said Bellair, fishing a pencil out of his pocket, "it's got a double curve at the top—may I draw on something?"

The old workman handed him an odd piece of three-ply, waited while the little diagram was drawn and put his spectacles on to study the result. After which he said "Ah," and turned to a corner of the shop where a number of three-ply patterns were stacked against the wall. He drew one out and held it up.

"That's it," said Bellair eagerly. "Do you remember who brought it?"

"Didn't see him, sir, the job was left at the office, but it's wrote on here who it belongs to. 'Edwards, Portsmouth Bus Office, to be called for, Jan. 14th.' That's who it was for."

"A very awkward job, surely, cutting those curves?" said Hambledon.

"A bit tricky, sir, a bit tricky. But it come out very well, I was pleased with that job I remember. It was the first job I done with that Corlex glass I remember, some new stuff come over from Belgium and I wondered how it would work. Wasn't too bad at all, and the mark fitted in well."

"The mark?"

"The trademark, sir, a five-pointed star with 'Corlex' round it. Here's some of it. You see, the mark should come in the bottom corner to look right, and sometimes we has to cut the glass to waste no end to get it to come right. But this one come jus' right first time."

"That is all you can tell us about it?" said Hambledon.

"That's all, I'm afraid."

"I am very much obliged, that is an immense help. Er—they aren't open at the moment, but when they are—"

"Thank you very much, sir, you're welcome, I'm sure."

"Perhaps," said Bellair to the manager, "the man who was in your office at the time can remember something about it."

"We'll ask him," said the manager. "We'll take this pattern along, it may remind him."

But nothing salient or memorable about the windscreen's owner had impressed itself upon the clerk in the office, though he turned up the records which showed that the stranger had paid in advance for the job, the carriage to Portsmouth, and the crate. "We'd rather have the crate back, though," said the manager. "We got the money for it, true, but there's the trouble of getting another made."

Hambledon agreed, expressed their thanks, and led the way to the car again.

"Back to Portsmouth," he said. "Let's see if the bus office has anything to tell us."

The bus office remembered that the glass was called for by a youth whose manner was regrettably impertinent, that was how he came to be remembered, but his name was unknown. However, a bus conductor who happened to be in the office at the time said that the shop next door would probably know, as they had had trouble with this same youth wangling their slot-machines to obtain cigarettes for which he had not paid, and they had taken the matter to the police.

The shop next door provided the name of Leonard Biggs, an address only two streets away, and a brief summary of the youth's appearance, manners, and probable destination which made up in vivacity for what it lacked in charity.

"We go from strength to strength," said Hambledon. "Now for Leonard Biggs."

Young Mr. Biggs turned out to be the eldest of a large family ineffectually presided over by a harassed mother in a sacking apron. She opened the door with one hand, pushing in hairpins with the other, and stared at her visitors with plain mistrust. Children of all sizes pushed and elbowed in the passage behind her.

"Does Leonard Biggs live here?"

"Oh Lord, what's 'e bin doin' now?"

"Nothing," said Hambledon soothingly, "at least, nothing that I know of. I only want to ask him a few questions, is he at home?"

"Milly, go an' tell your brother there's a gentleman to see him," but the child merely stood and gaped. "Go on now," added her mother, giving her a sharp push, "for goodness' sake do as you're told sometimes if it's only to make me wonder what's the matter with you. Don't know what's come over children nowadays," she went on as the child trotted away, "I know if I'd carried on with my mother like these kids do to me, I'd ha' got the stick good and proper."

Hambledon made a suitable reply, the woman did not ask them to come in, and the conversation wilted somewhat till Milly returned.

"Len says who is the gentleman because if it's anuvver spot of bovver he's out."

"Tell your brother to come down at once," said Hambledon authoritatively. "He has nothing to fear if he comes at once, but if he keeps me waiting he will be sorry. I only want to ask him a question about someone else."

The child nodded and ran off again and the woman said that was just like Len, awkward he was born and awkward he'd been ever since and would be to the grave. Hambledon, who was becoming annoyed, said that in these cases a little wholesome discipline had often been known to work wonders, and suggested, as a cure, the Army.

"Oh, he wouldn't do that," said the woman. "He don't hold with all this dressin' up and marchin' about bein' shouted at."

Presently the child ran back, leaned against the doorpost without speaking, and smiled at Bellair, who fished twopence out of his pocket and gave it to her. A few minutes later heavy footsteps were heard on the stairs and Leonard pushed roughly through the children and leaned against the doorpost himself, a shambling youth with a cap on his head and a cigarette adhering to his lower lip. Hambledon looked him over with distaste, and the boy stared back.

"Good morning," said Hambledon sharply.

"Afternoon," said Len.

Hambledon disregarded the impertinence and said, "I want to ask you something. On January seventeenth you called at the Portsmouth bus office to collect a crate marked 'Glass, with care' for a Mr. Edwards."

"Well, what about it?"

"Who is Mr. Edwards and where does he live?"

"An' why should I tell you?"

"Because I think you would rather tell me here than come to the Guildhall and tell the police. They might remember that you'd been there before, you know."

"It's no crime to earn a honest penny fetchin' a parcel," began the boy, but Hambledon cut him short.

"No, but it is a crime to refuse to assist justice. Where did you take the glass?"

"Justice," broke in the woman, eagerly leaning forward, "was the car stole, mister?"

"No. Where did you take that glass?"

"No business of yours."

Hambledon turned to the woman and said in a low tone, "Send those children away a moment, I have something to tell you." She looked at him anxiously for an instant and then obeyed by the simple expedient of pushing Len out on the step, the other children back into the hall, and shutting the door between. "Now," she said, holding the door handle, "what is it?"

"You will keep this to yourselves for your own sakes. This is a murder case. Now will you answer?"

The woman gasped, the boy turned perfectly white and said, "I didn't—I don't know nothin', I—"

"I know you didn't. I only want an answer to my question. For the last time, where did you take that glass?"

"To Mr. Newton, sir."

"That's better. Address?"

"Buckland Mews, off Grove Road. It's a garage."

"Buckland Mews. Thank you, that'll do. Keep this to yourselves and you'll be all right, otherwise— Another time when you're asked a question, answer civilly at once. Good morning."

Hambledon and Bellair turned away, leaving mother and son gaping on the step, and reentered the car.

"You can drive this time," said Hambledon kindly. "Guildhall, I think, don't you? It may be unworthy to enjoy telling the police you've done something they couldn't, but it's very human. You know, when you meet things like Leonard Biggs you do feel there's a lot to be said for conscription."

"Or infanticide," said Bellair.

Superintendent Elliot was still there and they were shown up to him at once.

"The broken windscreen from that yellow taxi," said Hambledon cheerfully, "was replaced by Messrs. Bodmin Brothers of Waterlooville for Mr. Newton, a garage proprietor of Buckland Mews, off Grove Road."

"Glad to hear it," said Elliot, and touched his bell. When a constable answered it, the superintendent said, "Send me in somebody who knows all about Buckland Mews, off Grove Road, and turn up to see if we've anything on a man named Newton at that address. I can't remember anything about him myself."

Inspector Grogan came in and said, "I know Buckland Mews. They are a block of old-fashioned stables converted into lockup garages by a man named Newton, who has a workshop and garage of his own there. He does minor repairs, washes cars and keeps a car or two for hire. The rooms over the lockups, which used to be coachmen's quarters, are let off in flats now."

"Anything known against Newton?"

"I don't think so, sir."

"Nor do I, but I'm having him looked up. Newton it was, Grogan, who got that broken windscreen repaired."

"It was, was it?"

"Who lives in the flats over these places of Newton's?" asked Bellair.

"Four different lots, I can turn them up for you in the directory," said Grogan. "I only know one offhand, the fellow who has the flat over Newton's own garage. Siddall, the hairdresser from the Leviathan stores."

CHAPTER VIII

Permanent Wave

"SIDDALL," said Hambledon as they were driving home, "I seem to remember your pointing out Siddall at the d'Albertini on New Year's Eve. Wasn't he the black-haired fellow with the gorgeous blonde? Of course, everyone inside the café was automatically provided with an alibi, since Macgregor was shot from outside, though they may have been accompl—"

"Siddall!" said Bellair, thumping the steering-wheel, "but he wasn't inside. He left earlier."

"So he did. I think we might look at him a little more closely, both at home and at business. Have you had any experience of breaking-and-entering?"

"A little, but I should be better with more practice under expert tuition. As regards his business, I think I can manage without illegality."

"How?"

"He is a hairdresser, and I know a girl who really needs a permanent wave. You know, Bettine Gascon."

"Heaven knows she does," said Hambledon, "but do you know her well enough to tell her so?"

"These things can be inoffensively worded," said Bellair. "Besides, I do know her fairly well now."

"I had noticed that you have had a good many evening engagements lately. Take the advice of a man old enough to be your father, and keep 'engagements' in the plural."

"I mean to. I thought it might be a good idea to arrange for her to have a perm and take her there myself. I know Siddall slightly, and if I am hanging about for three hours he can't very well leave me blushing and swithering in the ladies' underwear department, which is just outside. I can't sit in the cubicle all the time, there isn't room and I should be horribly in the way. Where else can he plant me? In his office, of course."

"Where you improve the shining hour while he's curling Miss Gascon. Quite a sound scheme, go to it."

"Thank you," began Bellair.

"Thus combining business with pleasure. I suppose it is a pleasure?"

"Sir?"

"Squiring the lady about. It must be or you wouldn't do it, as it can't be considered part of your duty, Bellair. Of course, things have been rather quiet lately—"

"Do I understand you have an objection to the lady?" said Bellair rather stiffly.

"Come off it. I have had to remind other men before you that ours is a job for bachelors. I do mean that. As a form of light entertainment between courses, Jim, there is much to be said for women, but don't take 'em too seriously. The job is the thing, and in my poor experience it's quite trying enough without adding avoidable complications."

Bellair laughed a little uneasily, and Hambledon went on in a lighter tone. "Looked at as a bit of local color in a box at the Empire or a table at the Queen's, she's wonderful. I said, color, does she wear red socks when you take her out?"

"That's what I thought about her," said Bellair eagerly, "as a useful bit of camouflage to take about, I mean. I can go almost anywhere and stay almost any length of time without arousing comment if I've got Bettine as an excuse, and if I want to talk to a man quietly anywhere I can park her in a box with cigarettes and chocolates and anyone would swear I was still in the theatre."

"Doesn't she mind?"

"She moans a bit sometimes, but that's all. There's nothing to equal dangling after a decorative girl like Bettine to make people think you're a fool."

"How right you are. I was even beginning to think so myself," said Hambledon.

Accordingly, a few days later Bellair and Bettine walked up the baroque staircase of the Leviathan Stores to be confronted at the top with the whole dazzling sweep of the lingerie section. Bellair shied like a startled pony, but Bettine strolled on quite unperturbed, looking about her and making comments while her embarrassed escort tottered along behind. The hairdressing department was on their left, a long row of a dozen cubicle doors with the manager's room at the far end. Siddall emerged from it as they approached, and came to meet them.

"Afternoon, Siddall, how are you? Ages since we met. This is Miss Gascon, who is brave enough to entrust her hair to your tongs and machinery."

"Delighted to see you, Mr. Bellair," said Siddall, looking as though he would like to shake hands if he dared, "it's very sporting of you to bring Miss Gascon along. We'll do our best to make sure she doesn't regret it."

"Oh, I'm sure I shan't," said Bettine, "Jim has told me how frightfully clever you are, but I'm afraid my hair is very dull. Such awkward hair, it never will go as I want it to," and she smiled sweetly at him.

"It is the way it grows," explained Siddall, "it is unusual and interesting. I should like to design a style specially for Miss Gascon," he went on to Bellair, "it should take advantage of the natural forward sweep over the ears and frame her face. What method would you like for the waving? Eugene's is a safe and well-tried process, though the apparatus is a little cumbersome. Have you ever tried the Jamal or the Cadex wireless methods? Just little fittings on the head, with the hair wound round them, none of this being tied up to a machine which some ladies find so tiresome."

"Sounds like magic," said Bellair lazily. "How do they do it?"

"The heat is produced by chemicals instead of by electricity. It is very safe and easy, if Miss Gascon would care—"

"Oh, I'd like that, it sounds such fun! And I do hate being tied up by the head like a pony, I always wonder what would happen if the house fell down or something."

"We should rescue you first of all," said Siddall, emphasizing the pronoun. "Now, if you'd just go in here, Miss Davis will get the first stages over while I make a few sketches. Miss Davis, the Jamal process for Miss Gascon. Come into my office, Mr. Bellair, and I'll try to show you what I think would suit Miss Gascon."

Bellair had to admit to himself, with some surprise, that Siddall not only had every detail of his trade at his fingertips, but was an artist at it. "Miss Gascon has a long oval face. Charming, but one must not overemphasize it. On the other hand, one must not dress the hair too low or that will distract attention from the eyes which are her best feature. So I propose—" and so on, illustrating his remarks with little pencil sketches. "There's no doubt," said Bellair to himself, "the fellow really is a hairdresser, in which case we're probably barking up the wrong tree, for who could imagine a barber blowing up battleships? Murder, yes, there was Sweeney Todd—"

He returned from his thoughts to find Siddall asking for his approval of one style in particular, and gave it since he really didn't care much one way or the other. Let the fellow get on with the job and leave him to go on with his.

"You will be calling back for Miss Gascon, no doubt?" said Siddall, getting up.

"Oh, I think I'll wait. Got nothing on this afternoon and I'd rather like to see you working the magic. Don't mind if I look on, do you?"

Siddall implied that the entire establishment was Bellair's to play with, and they went along to the cubicle where Bettine's hair, having just been washed, was being carefully dried by the deft Miss Davis with warm air from a sort of hose-pipe. Bettine's soft hair blew about in a brown halo, falling over her face, and she smiled in the glass at Bellair behind her.

"I look like a Skye terrier," she said.

"You do, rather," he agreed.

"What happens next?"

"Oh, they merely tear it out by the roots and replant it in symmetrical clumps," he answered, but Bettine threw the hairdresser one of her more than adequate glances, and said, "Jimmy, you are horrid, I'm sure Mr. Siddall wouldn't do anything so dreadful." The drying process, which was not unbecoming in a wild, gypsyish way, came to an end, and the process of combing her hair and dividing it into small squares followed. This performance is definitely trying to the most perfect features, and Bettine very naturally became fidgety when she saw in the glass that Bellair was watching with absorbed interest instead of going away. He was so absorbed as not to notice how much he was in the way; poor Miss Davis, who was far too polite to tell him to go, had to dodge round him and reach past him at every moment. Bettine saw this and came to the rescue.

"Oh Jimmikins darling, do go away and come back later. Miss Davis can't move for you."

Miss Davis smiled wanly, Bellair apologized fluently and was in the act of withdrawing when he was startled by the sudden opening of a shutter at the end of the cubicle beside the mirror, and a girl looked in.

"Mine's a lager," said Bellair before anyone else could speak.

"Jamal sachets," said Siddall, and the head disappeared.

"Oh, I thought it was a buttery hatch," said Bellair in a disappointed voice, and Siddall laughed.

"No, there's a passage behind there by which a messenger can bring us all the gadgets we want," he explained.

"You run along somewhere and have your beer, precious," said Bettine.

"How can I? They're not open," said Bellair, and drifted disconsolately out.

Five minutes later he was back again, a trifle flushed.

"Frightfully embarrassing place, this," he said. "Most extraordinary things outside here on stands, some with lace on them and some without." He tried to perch on the edge of a small wheeled trolley which promptly ran away and bumped loudly against the door. A little upright line appeared between Bettine's brows and Siddall saw it.

"Come along to my office," he said, "you'll be more comfortable in there. Would you like tea? Good, I'll have some sent up to you."

"So he took me along to his office," said Bellair to Hambledon that evening, "and parked me there. A girl came in with tea, again to see if I'd got everything I wanted and again to take the tray away, and Siddall himself kept popping in so I didn't get a lot of peace. But I managed to have a look round."

"Find anything?"

"He's a real hairdresser, he showed me a book of press-cuttings about the celebrated Mr. Siddall and his works, he seems to be quite an international figure and has won medals and whatnot at exhibitions in most of the capitals of Europe. Seems to run in the family, too, one of his forebears was court hairdresser to George IV."

"Then why hasn't he got his own shop in Bond Street instead of a little sideline in a not quite first-class provincial departmental store?"

"He says, because it amuses him. He likes to take over a place that's not doing too well, and work it up till it's a flourishing concern; when he's done that he loses interest and goes elsewhere. He says he's done that in Glasgow, Sheffield, Newcastle and Bristol, and what's more the press-cuttings endorse it."

"Press-cuttings can be forged."

"Yes, I know. But I made notes of the dates of some of them and they can be verified in the files of the papers concerned."

"It shall be done. Anything else?"

"He told me he was in the Army in the last war and showed me a regimental group to prove it. You know these regimental groups, it might have been he and equally well might not. But I'm willing to bet that if you turn up the records you'll find Rodney William Siddall there at the specified date."

Hambledon nodded. "I notice you don't really believe it. What makes you doubt him?"

"I've got a hunch, that's all, his background is really too perfect. So is his English, it's excellent, but he never takes those little liberties such as we all take without noticing it. None of his desk drawers were locked, but there was only business correspondence there. The only significant thing at all was that he had two or three dictionaries on a bookshelf, and they all started with German. German-French, German-Italian, German-Swedish."

"Oh. What other books?"

"Mainly reference books, Bradshaw, Portsmouth directory, and so on. One or two French novels, a copy of *Gone with the Wind* from Boots' Library. Nothing old."

"Looks as though we shall have to look round his flat," said Hambledon. "Either he's all right or he's no fool."

"Oh, he's no fool," said Bellair with emphasis. "About his flat, he was very friendly indeed and asked me to drop in one evening for a drink. As a matter of fact, I was impressed by his little pencil sketches and asked if he ever did anything more serious, and he said he sometimes painted in watercolor, he'd like to show me some. I can talk fairly intelligently about watercolors if I really try, so I accepted. All right?"

"Excellent. You can at least study the lie of the land, I don't suppose you'll be given the faintest chance of doing more than that."

"No. I'll run down the day after tomorrow, I think—in the evening, of course. I wonder why he asked me."

"Keep your eyes open," advised Hambledon, "It is, of course, just possible that he likes you."

Bellair intended to go down alone to Portsmouth, but shortly before he was due to start Bettine rang him up as usual. By this time it had become an established custom for her to ring him up at least once every day and sometimes oftener, a performance which infuriated Hambledon, who hated listening to long one-sided conversations. He used to pick up his cigarettes whenever one of these colloquies began and stroll, with an exaggerated sigh, out into the garden. At frequent intervals he would look in at a window where Bellair could not help seeing him, and walk away again if the call were not finished. On one occasion he answered the telephone when Bellair was out.

"Oh! Is Jimmy there, please?"

"Sorry, Diana, he's out."

"Is that Mr. Hambledon?"

"It is."

"Oh. Why do you call me Diana?"

"Because I think the name suits you, that's all."

"Why, is it a favourite name of yours?"

"I had the privilege of a classical education," said Hambledon noncommittally. "Any message I can give?"

"No, thanks, I don't think so."

"Good afternoon," said Hambledon, and put down the receiver.

The next time Bettine met Bellair, she said, "Oh Jimmy, do you know anything about Diana?"

"Diana who?"

"In the classics."

"Diana the moon goddess?"

"I expect so. What did she do?"

"All sorts of things. She was a huntress."

"Oh, was she," said Bettine thoughtfully, and the telephone calls were less frequent for nearly ten days.

However, on the evening when Bellair intended visiting Siddall, she rang up and asked what he was doing that evening.

"I'm terribly sorry," said Bellair, "but I've got to go out and see a man."

"Out where, darling? Portsmouth?"

"Yes."

"Can't I come with you?"

"Afraid not, it's a business matter."

"Oh darling, and I'm so bored! Couldn't I just come with you, just for the run, I wouldn't be any trouble to you, would I?"

"You'd be more bored than ever," said Bellair, "because I couldn't take you in with me."

"I could sit in the car and wait for you, precious, I wouldn't mind that a bit."

"But—"

"Then we'd at least have the run there and back together, angel, wouldn't that be nice?"

"Yes, but—"

"I'm sure you wouldn't like to think of me spending the whole evening moping in that dull schoolroom I've been shut up in all day."

"Of course not—"

"Do let me come, sweetness! It's so lovely when we're together, isn't it?"

"Oh, very well," said Bellair, giving up the struggle, for really Bettine was very appealing when she was pleading for something; of course hers was a dull life and it was very pleasant to have someone desiring one's company so earnestly. "I'll pick you up in twenty minutes, can you be ready?"

"I'll be on the doorstep," she said joyfully, and kept her word.

They found Buckland Mews with some difficulty and several wrong turnings. It was a very quiet corner, a backwater from a cul-de-sac, and the few streetlamps merely filled it with shadows. Bellair looked about him and said, "I think I'll run the car on to this yard of his, then I needn't leave the lights on all the time, my battery's none too good. This is where he washes cars, evidently. Cigarette, m'dear? Golly, this is our last match."

"Perhaps I've got some," said Bettine, searching. "No, I haven't."

"Never mind, make that one last as long as you can and I'll scrounge another box off this fellow. You won't mind being here for a bit, will you?"

"No, of course not, but don't be long, sweetheart. I'll just sit here and think about you."

"You're rather a pet. We might go to the d'Albertini afterwards, shan't be long."

Bellair found the right door without difficulty since Siddall had described the place to him, it was just across the yard and round a rather dark corner. Siddall himself opened to him and took him upstairs. Bellair was surprised to find how comfortable the flat was, and with what good taste it was furnished. The rooms were small but not overcrowded, the few things standing about on mantelpiece and table were good, and the owner's watercolors, in plain frames on the cream walls, were worth looking at. Siddall offered a rather exceptional variety of drinks from a cocktail cabinet, and Bellair spent a pleasant half-hour or so till he remembered Bettine and rose to go.

"Sorry to rush away," he said, "but I've got an appointment and it's later than I thought it was. I had some trouble in finding your place, wasted quite a lot of time driving round in circles."

"Come straighter next time," said Siddall genially, "and stay longer. I won't attempt to keep you if you must go, but this has been a great pleasure, I hope you will come again."

"Thanks, I mean to," said Bellair truthfully, and Siddall came downstairs to open the door for him. The darkness outside was baffling after the lighted rooms upstairs, and Bellair took two steps forward and hesitated.

"If you'll shut the door," he said, "I'll just stand for a moment till my eyes get—"

Something soft but heavy hit him on the back of his neck, Siddall jumped forward to catch him as he fell, but the man who had hit him was quicker still.

"There," he said, "easy as kiss me hand. Now what?"

"Put him in the back of his own car," said Siddall, "and drive off. Go along the Esplanade to the end and bear left for Ferry Road, do you know it? Runs along the side of Eastney Lake." The man nodded. "Drive along to a place where there's a slope down to the water, turn the car to head into it, put her in gear and jump out when she's moving. Then you walk back to Eastney and get a bus home."

"Suppose the road's full of courting couples?"

"Drive up and down, they'll think you're plainclothes police, and go away," said Siddall. "I will lend you a hand carrying him to the car."

Bettine had got very tired of waiting in the dark without even a cigarette to pass the time, and what was more, it was really a little eerie in that shadowy deserted place with only the distant sound of traffic in Grove Road to keep her company. She heard the door open when Bellair came out, and the sound of low voices, but the corner of the garage prevented her from seeing anything. Presently a shapeless little group came round the corner towards her and she made out that it was two men carrying a third, was Jimmy ill or— horrible thought—drunk? She became afraid, and cowered down in the seat.

One of the men told the other to open the car door, he spoke in a gasping voice, for an unconscious man is heavy. The rear door opened, and the men grunted with effort as they lifted their burden.

"Pitch him in," said another voice, "head first, anyhow, he won't grumble."

Bellair, however, uttered a protesting groan, and the first man said savagely, "I told you you didn't hit him hard enough. Get a move on, now, or you'll have him waking up before you get there."

"He won't wake up after," said the second man, and slammed the door.

Bettine was paralyzed with terror. Next moment they would open the front door and find her, and then—at that instant Bellair's arm slid over the back of the front seat and his hand touched her neck. She writhed away, opened her mouth, and screamed at the top of her voice.

CHAPTER IX

Miss Gascon Drives the Car

INSTANTLY the two men turned and fled, Bettine could hear running footsteps across the paved yard. Her one idea was to get away before they came back to finish off Jimmy and probably herself too, and she made panic-stricken efforts to remember what Jimmy did when he started the car. After one or two attempts she got the engine running; backing was beyond her but she put the car into low gear and managed to swing it round in the yard at the expense of a bent wing and a long streak of paint off the garage door. Once in the road she drove off at random, turning to left and right alternately with some confused idea of baffling pursuit, till she was completely lost. At the third corner a policeman shouted at her, she distinguished the word "lights" and switched them on, headlamps and all. After which she felt better, because it is reassuring to have plenty of light on one's road; she even ventured to change up into second, and the diminution in the roar of the high-speed engine was a further encouragement.

"I wish I'd gone on with those driving lessons," she said plaintively and changed up again into third. This alarmed her because she seemed to be going so fast, but frequent applications of the brake restored her courage and she never noticed a Belisha crossing. Happily the pedestrians upon it were all active young men.

She rounded another corner rather too fast and came upon Mr. Wall, an elderly man, a hawker by trade, who was moving from his room to another three streets away; he was not overburdened with furniture and a couple of trips with the barrow would do it. This was the second trip, and having with him a curtain-pole, two rolls of linoleum, a tin trunk, a folding bed and mattress, a basket chair, three pots, two kettles and a frying-pan, an old-fashioned gramophone with a large horn and a picture of Cherry Ripe, Mr. Wall was a little overloaded. He could not dodge quickly enough.

Bettine saw the barrow almost too late and just managed to miss everything except the end of the curtain-pole. Unfortunately this was underneath everything else and was made of brass so it didn't break. It acted as a lever instead, and the other contents of the barrow merely fell overboard or else flew up in the air and came down upon Mr. Wall.

Bettine, more terrified than ever, took two corners on the wrong side, giving a heart attack to an elderly chauffeur driving a Daimler and causing a policeman on a bicycle to leap for his life. The chauffeur stopped his car and the policeman, duty spurred by personal feeling, took Bettine's number.

"Did you see that?" gasped the chauffeur.

"Did I hell! More's going to be heard of this," and the policeman dived for a telephone box.

In the meantime Bettine emerged into Milton Road opposite the Marine Barracks, which she recognized. She sighed with relief, at last not only did she know where she was, but she knew the way out of Portsmouth too. She relaxed a little and began to worry about Bellair. She knew he was not dead because she heard him say something inarticulate several times, notably whenever she tried to change gear, but he must be terribly uncomfortable on the floor of the car, he might even get apoplexy or something if he were lying head downwards. It never occurred to her to ask the police or anyone else in Portsmouth for help although she drove straight past the hospital, her one idea was to get home, away from this dreadful place.

When she passed the police box on Portsbridge somebody waved a light and shouted, but it did not occur to Bettine that the signal was for her. She drove on up the London Road and dodged across the bows of a bus trying to turn into Cosham High Street, but halfway up Portsdown Hill a car drew level with hers and a uniformed policeman leaned towards her and shouted, "Stop! Pull in to the curb."

Bettine obeyed at once, finding an immense relief in the sight of the familiar uniform, here at last was someone dependable. The police car pulled up just ahead and the sergeant got out and walked back.

"I didn't pass the traffic lights," said Bettine breathlessly, "they were green."

"Nobody said you had, miss," said the sergeant, turning his torch on the car, "it's about the only thing you haven't—what's all this?"

"That's Mr. Bellair," explained Bettine. "He was set on by robbers in Buckland Mews and stunned, so I'm—"

"Where?"

"Buckland Mews."

The sergeant turned towards the police car and called. "Wilson! Come here." The constable came, the sergeant said a few words in a low tone and Bettine heard Wilson say, "Good Lord." After which they both returned to the Triumph, one each side, opened both rear doors and bent over Bellair.

"Is he much hurt?" asked Bettine anxiously, and scrambled round in her seat to see. The sergeant lifted Bellair's head and shoulders, whereupon the victim stirred, half opened his eyes and said, "Can't change gear—for toffee." Then he relapsed again.

"Lift him up on the back seat," said the sergeant, and helped to do it.

"Only stunned, miss, I think," he added cheerfully to Bettine, and went on to tell Wilson he, the sergeant, was going to drive Mr. Bellair home and Wilson could follow in the police car to bring the sergeant back to Portsmouth. The constable said something about the city boundary, but the sergeant said, "Hang the city boundary. Must take this fellow home."

Then he turned to Bettine and said, "I think you'd better let me drive now. Do you think you could sit in the back with Mr. Bellair? You could steady him, perhaps."

"Oh yes, please," said Bettine, and slid out of the car to find that her knees were trembling so violently that she had to cling to the door-handle. The constable said, "There now," and helped her into the back seat where she covered herself with confusion by bursting into tears.

"There, there," said the sergeant, "take it easy. You've had a trying time but you're all right now. Ever driven before?" he added, to distract her attention.

"Only tw-twice," sobbed Bettine, "and I—I haven't got a d-driving license."

"You sit quiet," said the sergeant, "and don't worry." He got into the driving seat, said a few words to Wilson, and put the car in motion.

"You see," said Bettine between sniffs, "I had to get away, they might have come back and killed us both. Two horrible men—"

Bellair rolled over and came to rest against her shoulder. "Good girl," he said, in one of his conscious intervals, "can't change gear. I'll teach you t'morrow." He sighed heavily and collapsed once more.

The sergeant drove them direct to East Bungalow, Lynbourne, with Wilson patiently following behind in the police car. It seemed to revive Bellair to find himself at home with his friends about him, and he managed to protest that there was no need whatever to put him to bed and send for the doctor. Nobody took any notice of his remarks; while Hambledon and Reck undressed him and tucked him up, the sergeant took a statement from Bettine and the constable Wilson sat in the corner and took notes.

"Name, please, miss?"

"Bettine Gascon."

"Address?"

"Lynbourne House, Lynbourne." She looked across at Wilson and something about him struck her as familiar.

"Surely I've seen you before somewhere?" she said, with that air of personal interest which was her principal charm.

"Yes, miss," said Wilson stolidly.

"Were you ever one of my father's constables? He is Superintendent Gascon of Wellstone."

"No, miss. I was taking notes at the d'Albertini Café on New Year's Eve."

"Oh, were you," said Bettine in a deflated tone, and Wilson permitted himself to look faintly amused. The sergeant had not the key to the joke and pursued his enquiries.

Bettine told him as much as she knew of what had happened, and the sergeant asked if she would be able to recognize either of the two men.

"Oh no. I was much too frightened to look, besides, it was dark."

"You didn't happen to hear either of them mention the other one's name?"

"Oh no, I'm sure they didn't. I think, though," she hesitated, "one of them was rather a rough sort of man by the way he spoke."

"And the other?"

"The other had rather a nice voice. It reminded me—but that's absurd, of course."

"Reminded you of somebody?"

"Yes, of Mr. Siddall. You know, the hairdresser at the Leviathan Stores. Of course, I know it wasn't Mr. Siddall, but it was someone who talks very like him, if that's any help. I'm afraid I'm not being very helpful, but really I don't know any more. I'm so sorry." Tears filled her eyes as reaction set in again, and the doctor chose that moment to announce his arrival by a loud knock on the door just behind her. Bettine sprang from her chair and burst into sobs.

"Dear me," he said, as Wilson admitted him, "is this my patient?"

"No," said Hambledon, coming out of Bellair's room, "he's in here if you'll come. Please don't upset yourself like that," he added to Bettine, "it's all right now."

But Bettine sat down in Hambledon's own armchair and continued to upset herself.

"Oh dear," said Hambledon helplessly, "I do wish you wouldn't, it's all over now. What does one do?" he asked, and the sergeant diffidently suggested some form of restorative, if available.

"Oh, ah," said Hambledon, and hastily opened the sideboard. He poured about three fingers of whisky into a tumbler, added a splash of soda, and patted Bettine on the shoulder to attract her attention. "Here, drink this," he said, "this'll do you good. Put a kick in you."

"I should think so," murmured the sergeant to the constable. "Lay most people flat, a dose like that, what does he think she is, a Royal Marine?"

However, Bettine sat up, sipped the restorative, mopped her eyes and thanked Hambledon prettily for being so sweet to her. "This is just like what Daddy gives me when I'm upset," she said.

"Daddy," said Hambledon indignantly to himself, "I'll give you daddy—oh well. I suppose I am getting on in years. Cheer up, little girl," he added, in a tone intended to be fatherly. "You've done very well tonight, don't go and spoil it all by crying."

"I'll try not to be silly," said Bettine submissively, and smiled bravely at him through her tears.

"A very gallant little lady," said the sergeant in a tone intended to be just audible. Wilson unkindly reckoned to himself that Bettine would stand five foot seven in her socks, but it is not part of a constable's duty to provide unasked-for comment, so he held his peace.

The doctor came out of Bellair's room and said, a trifle sourly, that there did not appear to be much harm done, and that if his directions were followed the patient could expect complete recovery in the course of the next day or so. He looked at the two Portsmouth policemen with plain curiosity but rather pointedly asked no questions, said good night to Bettine and Hambledon, and walked out. Reck appeared in the bedroom doorway and leaned against the doorpost to watch his departure.

"One could almost think," said Hambledon, "that something had annoyed the gentleman."

"One would be right," said Reck. "He asked how the accident happened and Jim said he hit his head on the ceiling. The doctor asked how he managed that, and Jim said he stood on a chair. He asked no more, but he seemed to think we mocked him."

"Do you think," said the sergeant, looking from Reck to Hambledon, "that Mr. Bellair is well enough to make a statement tonight?"

Bellair evidently heard this remark, for there was a somewhat muffled reply from the bedroom, and Reck, looking over his shoulder, said, "All right, old chap, they shall. He says, 'Please come in.'"

"I'll come too," said Hambledon. "You sit quiet," he added to Bettine, "and drink your whisky. You'll soon feel better, and then I'll drive you home." He turned to the sergeant and said, "If I might suggest, it would perhaps be as well if you came in alone, Mr. Bellair can't be feeling very fit, and the fewer visitors he has, the better. Besides, it's a very small room."

The sergeant raised his eyebrows slightly, but made no objection, and they went into the bedroom with Reck, leaving Bettine and Wilson outside. As soon as the door was shut, Bellair, still looking rather white, beckoned the sergeant to him and said slowly, "Look here, I can't possibly tell you anything tonight. Will you be so good as to tell Superintendent Elliot that Mr. Hambledon and I hope he will be able to see us at eleven tomorrow morning. We have something to tell him which bears on the Macgregor case."

"Very well, sir."

"And thank you very much for bringing me home, and all that. Decent of you."

"Not at all, sir."

"Oh, and tell Elliot it might be as well to keep an eye on Siddall, you know, the hairdresser chap at the—at the—can't remember names tonight."

"Leviathan Stores, sir. Miss Gascon said—"

"Leviathan Stores. What about Miss Gascon?"

"She said that one of the men who put you in the car had a voice like Mr. Siddall's."

"Oh, did she? That's interesting, because she didn't know I was going to see him. I mean, she didn't know Siddall was the man I—oh, hell! I can't think any more."

"Don't try, Jim," said Hambledon. "I don't—there's the telephone. Excuse me."

He went into the lounge to answer it, Bellair lay back with his eyes shut, and they could all hear the voice of Hambledon saying: "Yes, thank you, he is. ... Not too bad, got a bit of a headache. ... Yes, he had a friend with him who drove him home. ... I quite understand. ... Very good of you to ring up. ... Yes, rather. ... Thanks very much, I'll tell him. He's in bed now. ... Oh, be all right after a night's rest, no doubt. ... Yes, thanks. ... Good night."

"That, believe it or not, was Siddall," said Hambledon, having returned to the bedroom and shut the door again. "It appears he heard a bloodcurdling scream—doubtless Miss Gascon giving tongue—followed later by a crash as of mudguards. It struck him as odd, because as he rightly says, one usually hears the crash first and the scream afterwards. He dashed downstairs to see if he could do anything, but the car was out of sight. Later on, the police rang up to ask if he knew anything about an attack on you in Buckland Mews—"

"How did the police know?" asked Bellair, still keeping his eyes shut.

"Miss Gascon told us you'd been stunned by robbers in Buckland Mews, and I told Wilson to inform headquarters on the phone before he followed us here," said the sergeant.

"Oh."

"Siddall says," pursued Hambledon, "that he is horrified to think you should have been sandbagged on his doorstep as it—"

"Sandbagged," said the sergeant, "I never said sandbagged, my mind was running more on a blow from a club or something like that."

"A blunt instrument," prompted Hambledon.

"Just so, sir. I made an examination of Mr. Bellair at the time—"

"So how did Siddall know he'd been sandbagged?"

"Exactly, sir."

"I did tell you, didn't I," said Bellair wearily, "to tell Elliot to keep an eye on Siddall?"

After Bettine had said a few kindly words of thanks for their assistance, the police went away, and Hambledon said that if she was feeling well enough to move he would get the car out and take her home.

Bettine thanked him delightfully and said that she was now feeling completely recovered as a result of all his kindness, and could perfectly well walk, it was only about a mile.

"Nonsense," said Hambledon, and went out to start the car. Reck remained leaning thoughtfully against Bellair's bedroom doorpost with his hands in his trouser pockets—his favorite attitude. Bettine rose, collected her hand-bag, threw a glance at Bellair's room, adjusted her coat collar in the glass over the fireplace, patted her hair, glanced at Bellair's doorway again, and powdered her nose. Reck remained in the doorway looking at nothing in particular, and did not speak. Bettine finished her preparations and looked straight at Reck this time.

"I'll just say good night to Jimmy," she said.

"He's asleep," said Reck firmly.

"I'll just take a peep at him to see how he is," she said, advancing.

"You can't possibly do that," said the scandalized Reck, "he's in bed." He took one hand out of his trouser pocket to shut the door and then leaned against that instead of the doorpost.

"Oh," said Bettine in a pained voice, "I do think you're unkind."

"I daresay you do," said the champion of the proprieties, "but your mother would thank me, I'm sure."

"My mother knows she can trust me," said Bettine angrily.

"No doubt your mother knows you better than I do," said Reck ambiguously, and Bettine was still thinking it over when Hambledon called her from the porch. She went without saying good night.

When Hambledon returned he found Bellair's door open again and Reck in the kitchen making soup and toast for him. The two old friends looked at each other and laughed quietly.

"An enterprising young lady," said Hambledon.

"And at present Jim's her enterprise."

"I gather you gave her no encouragement."

"Were you looking through the window?" asked Reck, turning the toast.

"Of course. I was admiring your impersonation of St. Anthony—the one who discouraged houris."

"I don't like any women much," said Reck frankly. "I think they're generally silly and always tiresome. But of all the sorts of women I've met, I dislike the forward ones most."

"You think a man ought to do all the chasing," said the amused Hambledon.

"Well, yes. But I wouldn't have minded if she'd been a nice girl, since he's been hurt. I just don't like Miss Gascon, that's all. A girl like that does get a following, I suppose?"

"Dozens of 'em," said Hambledon cheerfully.

"Pack of young fools," said Reck, stirring the soup.

" 'Set her up on Tinto's top,' " quoted Hambledon, " 'the wind'll blow a man to her.' "

"It would take a very special hurricane," said Reck, "to blow me."

CHAPTER X

Episode at the Empire

"I REMEMBER coming down the stairs from Siddall's flat," said Bellair, "but, to be quite truthful, the next thing I remember is hearing Miss Gascon changing gear. It woke me up effectively. One must be fair and say that she has only had two lessons in driving, and that was a year or two ago, I understand."

"I think she did very well, considering," said Superintendent Elliot handsomely. "She didn't hurt anyone or even damage anything except your gears," for Mr. Wall had not thought it worth while to complain to the police. "But she didn't see you struck down."

"No. And I don't know if I was hit inside Siddall's front door, or the moment I stepped outside, or after he had shut the front door and started upstairs again."

"So we have really no evidence against Siddall," said Hambledon, "except Miss Gascon's remark that the voice of one of the men sounded like his. We can't rope him in just to ask how he knew Bellair was sandbagged."

"Were you expected that evening?" asked Elliot.

"No. He just asked me to drop in some time."

"Did he leave the room at all while you were there?"

"Did he—yes, he did. He was absent for a few minutes, once, I thought nothing of it."

"He could have got into touch with the other man then, provided he were on the premises—where is his telephone, did you notice?"

"In the sitting-room I was in. He didn't use that."

"So if one of the men was Siddall, the other was also on the premises."

"Hambledon's right," said Bellair. "The only evidence against Siddall is Miss Gascon's remark, and she may well have been mistaken. There's nothing particularly noticeable about Siddall's voice."

"It's a pity," agreed Elliot, "but he gets away with it this time, if it was he."

"He rang up this morning," went on Bellair, "that's the second time, he talked to Hambledon last night. I answered him myself this morning, he was delighted to hear I was so little the worse for the dastardly attack; some day when I am quite recovered, we must have an evening out together, during which he hopes to wipe out the unpleasant memory associated with our previous meeting. He talks rather like that."

"Yes, and I wonder precisely how he proposes to wipe it out," said Hambledon. "With wine and roses, so to speak, or a large hammer?"

"I think there's only one way to find out," said Bellair, "and that's to go and see. I have accordingly made a date with him for next Tuesday."

On Tuesday evening, Tommy Hambledon strolled into Bellair's room while he was changing.

"You know," said Hambledon abruptly, "I should be happier in my mind if I were going with you."

"Can't be done," said Bellair. "At present the nefarious gang don't know you're associated with me, at least, I hope they don't. We don't want to tell them, for I have a horrid feeling they suspect me."

"I know all that. Well, keep a good look out."

" 'In vain is the net spread,' " quoted Bellair, "in the sight of this bird, anyway."

He met Siddall by appointment at the d'Albertini; Jim noticed, with an amusement he did not show, that there was no suggestion from his host of another visit to the flat in Buckland Mews. "Keeping that till last, perhaps," he said to himself, and felt with satisfaction the compact weight against his thigh of a small automatic in his trouser pocket.

"How does Miss Gascon like her hair style now she's used to it?" asked Siddall.

"Oh, fine, I believe, except that she thinks it's a trifle sophisticated for the country," said Jim. "By the way, I have a message from her, she wants to make an appointment with you about doing it again or something, I expect you know what she means."

"Wash and set," said Siddall professionally. "Any particular day?"

"Friday, if you could manage it?"

"Friday afternoon I could. Five-thirty too late?"

"I don't suppose so, if it is she must let you know. I'll make a note of it."

Siddall asked, of course, whether anything had been discovered about the attack on Bellair at Buckland Mews.

"Absolutely nix," said Bellair cheerfully. "Between ourselves, I don't suppose there ever will be. What? Imagine their feelings, all set to go quietly through my pockets, pinch the car and drive—I imagine—westward to some unfrequented spot. Then they'd pitch me out and drive on. Probably they've got a garage and workshop in some remote place where they dish up stolen cars till their own chauffeurs wouldn't know them. They change the engine numbers and all, you know. In fact, it's my own theory that they didn't mean to attack me at all, only I barged in at the wrong moment and they lost their heads and batted me. Then they got me all safe and comfy in the back and opened the driver's door and at that nervous moment the lady who was with me went off like a burglar alarm. She said they ran away, I think they're probably running still. After all, it's only a week ago, what's that to a fine athlete?"

"The two men are now rounding Cape Wrath," said Siddall, "neck and neck."

"Square four," said Bellair, watching the other man's face. "They got my wallet, of course."

Siddall was looking down at that moment, but his eyes flashed wide open with astonishment before he could control his expression. "What rotten luck," he said slowly, "was there much in it?"

"Twenty-five quid," said Bellair bitterly.

"Do you know the numbers of the notes?"

"Of course not, I got a tradesman to cash a check for me and he just took the money out of the till. No, that's gone."

"Oh, hard luck," said Siddall sympathetically. "I am shocked to hear that."

("And I'll say he was too," said Bellair, recounting this episode to Hambledon. "You could see him wondering just where his hired assassin had put it across him. Wonder if he's paid him for the job yet?"

"There may yet be unkind words about it," said Hambledon hopefully. "You didn't lose anything, actually, did you?"

"Not a thing, strange to relate. No, I only said it to see what would happen—it happened all right.")

After coffee, Siddall suggested a visit to the Empire, so they drove the Triumph there, parked the car, and strolled up to the foyer bar behind the dress circle, collecting Eileen from the box-office on their way. Her twin was already there, putting her chocolate tray in readiness for the interval.

"What's the show like this week?"

"Nothing very special," said the disdainful Eileen. "There's a band that's rather good and some dancing that's rather awful, and the usual comics, you know."

"There's the conjurer," said Molly.

"The trouble with you," said Bellair to Eileen, "is that you see too many shows. You're blasé."

"Oh no, I don't think so, but I do like turns to be really good."

"The conjurer—" began Molly, but Siddall interrupted. "Eileen has the critical faculty highly developed," he said.

"You can tell that from her eyelids," said Jim Bellair.

"Oh, nonsense," said Eileen. "There was a turn on last week, a slack-wire act, now that was clever."

"Eileen, you know the conjurer's good," said Molly. "Of course one knows they're all tricks, but they are amazing, really they are."

"Don't like conjurers," said Eileen. "I like people who really do things, not just pretend to," and Siddall agreed with her so heartily that Bellair began to think he'd found out why they had come to the Empire.

"You don't really want him to shoot a ribbon right through a lady, do you? You bloodthirsty wench!" he said.

"Jim, you know I don't mean that!"

"Here's the band," said Molly. "Last turn before the interval, I must go."

"We shall see you later, shan't we?" said Jim.

"Six Nestlés, two Black Magics, three peanuts," she said, counting her store. "Yes, I expect so, I'm coming back here afterwards. Six nut chocolate, two motoring—" She moved away, still reckoning up.

"Care to see the band?" asked Siddall, and they went to lean over the barrier behind the seats, for a modern swing orchestra is a thing to watch as much as hear. When the interval came they drifted back to the bar, but found it so hopelessly overcrowded that they passed through it into the staff bar beyond. Here were some of the show people themselves renewing their energy with various prescriptions, and among them a little man with a tired face who was playing with three tumblers.

He stood them all in a row bottom upwards, took two of them and set them the right way up. He took two again, and turned them, yet another pair and turned them also. When he had finished all three were standing the right way up.

"What's all this?" asked Bellair, and the man looked up with a smile.

"It's quite simple," he answered, "no trick about it. It's only to have three of anything, tumblers are handy. You start with 'em all the same way up, doesn't matter which way, turn them two at a time," he demonstrated, "like this, and in three moves they're all standing up the other way." They were, too.

"But that's mathematically impossible," said Siddall. "It can't be done."

"Oh, surely," said the conjurer gently, and did it again.

"Here," said Bellair, borrowing three wineglasses, "let me try. Two at a time; again; and yet again. But they aren't."

"You aren't doing it right," said the little man. "Look carefully." He did it slowly and openly, and finished with all three glasses reversed. "Mine's a Guinness, miss, please."

"That's on me," said Bellair instantly. "What's yours, Siddall? You try."

"Haig, please," said Siddall. "I tell you this is impossible, look." He was quite right, it was, but by this time most of the dozen or so people in the crowded little bar were trying it too.

"I've done it!"

"No, you 'aven't. That's the same way as you started with."

"No, it isn't."

"Yes, it is, Bill, really. Try again."

"Bottom upwards, for a start. Over. Over. Well, I'm—"

The conjurer leaned back on the plush seat, sipped his Guinness, and watched all these attempts with the placid satisfaction of a nurse who has found a really good game for the children.

"It can't be done, gentlemen," said the bartender. "Give it up."

"Show us again!"

"Can't be done, Charlie?" said the conjurer. "Look. Over—and over—and over. There."

"Dammit, he's done it again," said Siddall.

"You know," Bellair said to him, "it looks as though there was more in this conjuring business than you seem to think."

"Nonsense," said Siddall testily, and commandeered Jim's three wine-glasses. "I told you it was impossible and"—failing to do it—"I was right."

"I think you're rather an annoying person," said Bellair, with a laugh, to the conjurer.

"Come and shoot me, then," he answered.

"A little more of this," said Siddall after another attempt, "and I should feel like doing so."

"Well, you can. I call up a member of the audience to come up on the stage and shoot me, and it might just as well be you. Where are you gentlemen sitting?"

"We haven't got beyond the bar yet."

"Sit in the stalls," said the little man, "then when I call for a volunteer you can just come up on the stage and do it."

"What do we do?" asked Bellair. The interval had come to an end and the bar was empty except for the three of them. "Have another?"

"No, thanks," said the conjurer, "I've had my ration. It's very simple, the shooting trick. I've got a .303 rifle and some cartridges, and I pass a cartridge down to the stalls and ask some gentleman to mark the bullet. Then I load the rifle with it, get somebody to shoot it at me, and catch the bullet in a little box I hold. You hear it fall in, and when the box is opened there's the marked bullet."

"Substitution, I suppose," said Siddall in a tone of merely polite interest.

"Of course," said the conjurer. "The bullet which is actually fired is made of graphite and dissolves into dust. I pull the marked bullet out of the cartridge case and hold it against a sprung slit in the side of the box. When the rifle is fired I let my muscles jerk, as they naturally do at any sudden noise, and the bullet drops in the box."

"Very clever," said Bellair. Siddall said nothing and his face, Bellair felt, would have expressed boredom if he had not been too polite to show it.

"Oh, it looks all right from the front," said the conjurer. "I must go, I think, two more turns and I'm on. Shall I see you gentlemen in the stalls?"

"You will," said Jim. "I'm going to have that shot at you even if it is only graphite."

When the conjurer came on the stage he was accompanied by his assistant, an extremely pretty girl dressed in pink satin pajamas with, for some reason, gold epaulettes. With her silent but well-drilled help he produced unexpected objects from empty glasses, materialized white doves from the insubstantial air, and finally stood the lady in front of a target and fired a ribbon at her. The end of the ribbon scored a bull, passing through the lady on its way, and she walked gracefully towards the conjurer along the ribbon as a threaded needle slides along the thread.

"If I had a delicate stomach," said Siddall, "that performance would make me feel sick."

"It doesn't seem to worry Belinda," said his guest. "What comes next? Oh, our shooting."

The conjurer told his audience what he was going to do, and the bullet was marked by a naval petty officer in the front row of the stalls. A volunteer to fire the shot was called for, and Bellair got there first. He made some display of aiming carefully and fired, there was a clatter in the box the conjurer held, and the marked bullet was duly found inside. Applause.

"You are clapping," said the conjurer, "because you think this is a very clever trick. I am going to show you that it is nothing of the sort by asking another member of this splendid audience to come up on the stage to fire the gun, and perhaps this gentleman would hold the box?" Bellair nodded. "Thank you, sir. Now, if another gentleman would come up—I myself will just load the gun and then go down and sit in the stalls and make magic in comfort for once. Thank you, sir," as a stocky man came deliberately up the steps at the end of the orchestra pit. "Are you a shot, sir? Shooting gallery? Very good practice, too. Only twice? Not so good, but perhaps you have a natural gift for it, as the cow said to the margarine. You know how to aim, don't you? I'm sorry to be so fussy, as the hen said to the incubator, but you can't expect the bullet to go in the box if you don't hit it, can you? Get the tip of the foresight just in the vee of the back sight, and both on the middle of the box. Right. Splendid. Now let me load it for you."

Bellair stood waiting while this was done with a lot more patter, and exchanged a sympathetic smile with the girl in the pink pajamas, who was standing in a graceful but detached attitude at the back of the stage waiting till she should be wanted again. A nice girl, he felt, and the conjurer was a nice fellow, too, quiet, decent old stick, funny to find a quiet little man like that making his living on the stage, you'd expect him to be a bank clerk, or a salesman in an ironmonger's shop.

"Now you, sir, with the box," said the conjurer, crossing the stage to Bellair. "Don't balance it on the palm of your hand, sir, please, or the bullet will just knock it off. Hold the box very firmly, with your hands on the sides, so (here's the bullet," he added in a whisper, his back momentarily to the audience, "and here's the slit)—well up in front of you. Oh, splendid. I shall have to go out of business if I get all this expert competition, anyone'd think you'd been a conjurer all your life."

Bellair, who was beginning to think that this was a thoroughly jolly evening, raised a laugh by trying to hide as much of his person as possible behind a box ten inches square, and then raised another by striking an attitude noble but resigned, holding the box steadily before him for his opposite number to aim at. The conjurer crossed the stage, went down the steps into the auditorium, and sat down in the stalls.

"Now, sir," he called to the man with the gun, "whenever you're ready."

The stocky man took careful aim, there was a sharp report, and Bellair dropped the box with a crash and clutched his right arm with his left hand.

"He's been shot," said the stage-manager at his post in the wings, and immediately gave the signal for the curtain to be lowered, but the electrician in charge of the lights was quicker still, he instantly threw a switch over, covering the stage with darkness, and the curtains fell and swung together. The conjurer sprang from his seat in the stalls, ran up the steps to the stage and dodged behind the curtain.

Instantly there was a buzz of excited talk from the auditorium which was only hushed when the stage-manager appeared in front.

"Ladies and gentlemen," he said in an actor's silky voice, "I am sorry to say there has been a slight accident. Is there a doctor in the house?"

A tall man in the stalls rose gradually to his full height, clutching at a raincoat and his wife's box of chocolates with one hand and holding up the other like a schoolboy in class.

"Thank you," said the manager. "If you would come round—the attendants will show you the way. Thank you. Ladies and gentlemen, the accident was only a slight one and the program will be resumed in just a moment. Thank you."

Molly hurried round behind the dress circle to the doorway at the head of the stairs, found the two commissionaires outside talking together quite unaware that anything was wrong, and blurted out: "Oh! isn't it dreadful! Jim's been shot."

"Who's Jim?"

"Mr. Bellair."

"How on earth—"

At that moment the attendant from the stalls appeared at the foot of the stairs and said: "The doctor to be taken round behind."

"I'll take him," said Molly, and hardly waiting till the tall doctor had reached the head of the stairs, she seized him by the hand and ran him round behind the circle, through the foyer bar and the staff bar to the head of the staircase leading down to the dressing-room behind the stage.

"Really," gasped the doctor, disengaging himself, "my dear young lady—"

"Quickly!" she said, capturing him again, and rushed him down to the bottom where the stage-manager was waiting.

"Thank you," he said. "So good of you. Must start the show going again. Take him to number six, Molly."

Bellair had been taken to number six because it happened to be the nearest, though officially it was occupied by a lissome young woman who did Plastic Poses. Molly, continuing to tow the doctor, rushed in to find Jim more or less surrounded by ladies of striking appearance and kindly disposition, all trying to be helpful. The conjurer's assistant, still in pink satin pajamas, was holding up his right arm to discourage bleeding, the plastic lady was dabbing eau-de-cologne on his forehead, an extremely pretty girl with a mop of black hair was helping him to drink a glass of water, and a large motherly woman in a violently flowered wrap was unpacking the contents of a first-aid box. Jim Bellair sat in the middle, looking pale but interesting, he glanced round as Molly came in.

"Hullo, m'dear! Sorry to be such a nuisance."

"Are you much hurt?" she gasped.

"Don't think so—" he began, but the doctor asserted himself firmly.

"If all you good people would very kindly go away," he said, "we'll soon see what the damage is. You," he added to the conjurer's assistant, "can go on holding his arm while we get his coat off. The rest of you run along."

"I can't," said the plastic lady, "I've got to change and this is my dressing-room."

"Golly," said Bellair nervously, "I'm frightfully sorry, I—" He attempted to rise but was skilfully balked by the doctor.

"Please don't worry, I've got a screen here," said the lady, unfolding it swiftly and retiring behind it. Only her head showed over the top while rustling sounds continued out of sight, and Molly and the others were shooed into the corridor to be joined a moment later by the conjurer's girl.

"I dare say he's a good doctor," she said, "but doesn't he order about! 'Now then,' he says, 'you hop it, thank you very much,' he says—"

Molly wandered away and stood alone in a quiet corner, everybody doing things for Jim except her, though of course she'd got the doctor there in double-quick time. She listened to the various noises incidental behind the scenes when a show is in progress; the steady rhythm of the orchestra and the rattle of a tap-dancer's feet on the stage, a babble of talk and laughter from a dressing-room farther along, how could they laugh like that, perhaps they hadn't heard about it, the lowered voices of two scene-shifters discussing canary-breeding, the scurrying footsteps of somebody hurrying along the passage, but no sign or sound from number six. Of course it would take some time. She drifted disconsolately away and heard a voice she recognized in a dressing-room at the foot of the stairs, with the door unwisely ajar.

"—all carefully worked out, and then you go and make a muddle of it," said the voice angrily.

Siddall, scolding someone, of course he often came round behind, but why—

"Wasn't my fault," said another man's voice, "it was Newton's job. Where was Newton?"

"I told him to be there," said Siddall, "I had to stay with Bellair, I couldn't be in two places at once, could I? If you'd had the sense—"

"Then why didn't you do the job yourself when Newton didn't turn up? Don't expect me to produce him out of a top-hat, do you?"

"It was just damned bad luck," said Siddall rather more mildly, "getting probably the only man in the stalls who couldn't hit a haystack at five yards—"

"Then why come and row me about it? It's you that's made the hash of things, not me."

"The —'s got nine lives, I think," said Siddall bitterly. "What the boss will say to this I don't know."

"That's your funeral—"

Footsteps approaching along the passage and a glimpse of pink pajamas round a corner. Molly turned and bolted up the stairs like a rabbit. At the top she met the callboy.

"Who's in number four at the bottom of the stairs here?"

"Signor Maggiore."

"The conjurer."

"That's him. Why?"

"Only wondered," said Molly.

CHAPTER XI

A Spot of Burglary

BELLAIR ENTERED East Bungalow, Lynbourne, late that night with a sheepish expression and his arm in a sling. He had rather hoped the household would be in bed, but there was a light in the lounge and Tommy Hambledon drowsing over a book before the fire. He rose slowly to his feet and surveyed his assistant.

"Dear me," he remarked, "in the wars again. What is it this time?"

"Only a flesh-wound, it's nothing really. It'll be a bit stiff for a few days, that's all."

"How did you get home?"

"They started me off with a driver, but I dropped him at Horndean and came on."

"Is Siddall dead?"

"No, why?"

"Only wondered. You'd better get off to bed, you can tell me all about it in the morning. Can you manage, or shall I call Reck to help you?"

"I can manage, thanks," said Bellair between his teeth. "Good night, sir."

"Good night," said Hambledon, and picked up his book again. "Blasted young idiots we do get nowadays," he growled to himself, "can't think what the service is coming to. Look at Jim, supposed to be one of their bright lads and can't spend an evening in Portsmouth without getting chewed up. Dammit, these boys want nursemaids."

He came to breakfast in the same disgruntled mood, which was not dispelled by a letter he found lying beside his plate. It enquired politely whether he would like further assistance, as matters did not seem to be progressing. Reck heard him murmuring to himself in German and said, "Whatever is the matter?"

"Have you seen our young guest this morning?"

"No. Why?"

"He came home from Portsmouth last night with a bullet-wound through the upper part of his right arm. Oh, only a flesh-wound, it's of no consequence. I heard about it from Superintendent Elliot, over the phone, so I waited up to see Jim come in. He looked a bit sheepish, I'll say that for him. I was not, I fear, particularly sympathetic."

89

"What happened to Siddall?"

"Nothing. Bellair, no doubt, had a preconceived idea that Siddall would invite him to the flat again and set about him there, and that consequently he was quite safe in his company anywhere else. When will these damned young fools learn that you're never safe in the enemy's company? So he thought it was quite all right to stand up on the stage of the Empire in full view of the audience and let a total stranger take a potshot at him with a rifle at about ten yards' range. Blasted idiot."

"Why wasn't he killed?" asked Reck mildly.

"I can't think. I can only suppose that the man who shot him just couldn't believe it was so easy. He must have thought there was a catch in it some-where and that unnerved him, I don't wonder, it would me. He was probably wondering whether the gun would burst when he pulled the trigger, or whether he was going to be shot from the wings before he got so far. How the devil should I know? These bright boys make my head ache."

"Have some coffee," said Reck sympathetically.

"As though that wasn't enough, here's a letter from the department," said Tommy, banging his fist on it as it lay on the table, "asking kindly whether I'd like any further assistance in the matter of those infernal explosions, as progress seems to be a little slow. Slow!" he repeated, and hit the table again. "There, now I've broken a plate. Don't fuss round picking up the bits, there's a good fellow, or I'll throw them at you. My faith, I expect the department think I'm in my dotage and if there's much more of this I shall be."

Reck tactfully withdrew, to return a few minutes later with kidneys and bacon, hoping that Hambledon would have cooled down a little in the mean-time. Hambledon, however, was still sizzling.

"I don't know whether German intelligence is about six times better than it used to be, or whether we're all over blue mold," he said. "I hand it to this fellow Siddall, though, he deserved success, I'd like to sympathize with him. Damn bad luck, I call it."

"How did he work it?"

"Again I don't know, no doubt Bellair will tell us all about it."

"Why so savage?" asked Reck curiously. "You've had mistakes made—and made them yourself—before now, without getting so worked up over it."

"I'm disappointed," said Hambledon frankly. "I expected better things of this lad, somehow."

"He's got pluck," suggested Reck, "going off to meet Siddall last night like that."

"Got pluck, yes, but what's the good of that? It's no good having pluck if the other side is going to run rings round you, laughing at you all the time, it's intelligence you want."

At that moment Bellair came out of his room, said good morning and apologized for being late. Hambledon glanced at him, noticed that his tie was crooked and that he had cut himself in several places while shaving, and said no more. After breakfast he asked for an account of what had happened and Bellair gave it.

"What happened to the conjurer?"

"The police interviewed him and he explained, with many apologies for his carelessness, that he must have muddled changing over the cartridges. It seemed true, for the graphite bullet was found in the box."

"So he gets away with it," said Hambledon. "Where was Siddall all the time?"

"Sitting in the stalls. He came round behind after it happened, and did everything he could."

"Short of stabbing you with a property dagger. Did he offer to drive you home?"

"He did, but I got out of that."

"You would probably have been perfectly safe, but perhaps you were wise."

"You know," said Bellair, "it was very well done. It was I who made friends with the conjurer, Siddall said he didn't like 'em and spent the evening making eyes at Eileen Trotter—the twin in the pay-desk. In fact, I came to the conclusion that that was why we'd come to the Empire. Besides, when the conjurer explained how the trick was done, I couldn't—"

"Explained the trick?"

"Yes."

"That's where you should have smelt a rat. Conjurers don't, as a rule, explain their tricks to anyone, let alone a casual acquaintance in a bar. What were you thinking about, to swallow that?"

Bellair bit his lip and said nothing.

"Oh well, doubtless you'll live and learn—if you live. You didn't think of collecting Siddall's fingerprints, by any chance, did you?"

"I cleaned the door-handle on the passenger's side of the car with that idea, but about sixteen people have pawed it since Siddall touched it."

Hambledon nodded. "It'll have to be done some other way. They may be useless when we've got them, probably are, but the routine must be gone through."

"I do really wonder," said Hambledon to Reck, when Bellair had gone down to the village ostensibly to buy cigarettes but actually to get out of range of Hambledon's critical eye, "I do wonder how he got that reputation I heard about. He had a couple of years in Spain, I believe, and did rather well, but either the Spaniards must be a credulous and confiding people, or else he had an amazing amount of luck."

"Haven't much to go on in this case yet, have you?"

"Precious little. Let me run through the affair again for a moment, perhaps

something will transpire. On New Year's Eve Macgregor was shot by someone in a car outside the d'Albertini. That lets out anybody who was inside,
though I remember remarking that a man named Colville, at the next table,
had something on his mind. That, of course, proves precisely nothing, he
may have been expecting the bailiffs, or an enraged wife, or he may merely
have had indigestion. In the car—which was Bellair's so it's no good chasing that—were a man and a dark woman who eventually disappeared in a
faked taxi. The taxi's windscreen was damaged and repaired to the order of
one Newton, a garage proprietor of Buckland Mews." Hambledon paused.

"And Buckland Mews is where Siddall lives."

Hambledon nodded. "And Siddall has made two murderous attacks on
Bellair, though we can't prove either of them."

"Can't the police do something with Newton?"

"They wanted to, but I persuaded them to let him alone for the present. No
doubt he would have some convincing story we couldn't disprove, but what
is more important, we don't want the small fry, we want the principals. Because this case is not really a question of who killed Macgregor, but of who
is arranging these explosions. There has been rather a lull in them lately, but
I fear that is less due to our efforts than to the fact that the Admiralty consid-
ers Portsmouth unhealthy for experimental stuff, and sends it elsewhere. Well,
that's as far as we've got. Siddall undoubtedly has a finger in the pie, but I'll
eat the bearskin rug if he's the principal. There's no connection between him
and the Navy so far as I can see, and the man who puts the bombs on board
has a very close connection indeed."

"Wasn't there another man in Bellair's car," said Reck, "a man who was
killed?"

"Yes, an employee of Colville's. And Colville was jumpy that night. But
they killed him, which doesn't suggest that he was a friend of theirs, so
there's no reason to suppose Colville was, either. In fact, I don't think Colville
comes into the picture at all."

"What does he do?"

"He's a naval wine merchant," said Hambledon and repeated thoughtfully,
"a wine-merchant to the Navy. Yes, but there's no suggestion that he even
knows Siddall."

"There's the conjurer," said Reck.

"Who has told a perfectly good tale and is going to stick to it. Again,
there's no suggestion that he knows Siddall, either. No, it's all a dead end at
present; you see, in this country you can't pull people in and make 'em talk
when they don't want to."

Reck suggested, rather vaguely, the Habeas Corpus Act.

"Yes. That's the worst of a free country. Where the people are free, the
police are chained."

"As one of the people," said Reck, "I think that's an extremely sound idea. I had enough of unchained policemen in Germany. But what, if anything, are you going to do about it?"

"I will tell you," said Hambledon. "Tonight, you and I are proceeding to Portsmouth, and we are going through that garage and flat in Buckland Mews with a fine-tooth comb."

"Not with me," said Reck firmly. "Since Jim is *hors de combat*, you can borrow a policeman."

"I don't want a policeman—"

"You won't get me."

"I don't want a policeman," repeated Hambledon dreamily, as one beholding visions. "I want a man who is bold and resolute, whose soul is set on noble deeds, whose sense of duty is his guiding star—"

"All policemen are like that—in Portsmouth."

"Whose daring initiative is untrammeled by petty rules, and you can't say that about the police. I want a man who in moments of stress will say to himself, 'Agincourt and Cressy, Poitiers and—' give me another British victory, quick."

"Bannockburn and Sidney Street."

"Flodden, Assaye, Torres Vedras—"

"Hastings."

"Hast—oh, shut up. No, honestly, Reck, I only want somebody to stand outside and keep watch in case Siddall comes home too soon."

"What, precisely, is Siddall supposed to be doing while you burgle his flat?"

"Today is Wednesday," said Hambledon, "and every Wednesday Siddall goes to town to address a hairdressers' convention on subjects like Dandruff and Its Effects on Married Life. He doesn't get back to Portsmouth till after midnight."

"Newton, then? The garage proprietor."

"Newton's best car, with himself driving, has been hired to take some happy people to Corfe Castle. He won't be home till one a.m. at earliest, they'll see to that."

"Then the place will be all locked up."

"Leave that to me," said Hambledon, and produced three keys out of his pocket.

"Somebody isn't trammeled by petty rules, I notice," said Reck. "I won't ask who."

"I'm afraid it would be all the same if you did. You see, it's so easy. All we do is to unlock two or three doors, have a good look round and come out again, relocking the doors after us."

"After you, you mean."

"Got any gloves?"

"I believe so, what for?"

"We mustn't leave fingerprints if we can help it. Take a torch too."

"I thought I was only going to stand outside and keep watch," said Reck, weakening.

"I should hate you to catch cold," said the considerate Hambledon. "Besides, it will be so dull."

They reached Portsmouth soon after nine, left the car in a quiet street, and walked round to Buckland Mews. In two of the flats over the garages there were lighted windows, but Siddall's flat and Newton's business premises below it were dark and silent. It was a moonless night, and in that shadowy corner the two men in their rubber-soled shoes moved like ghosts. Reck, like Bettine before him, found the place rather eerie, and said so in an appropriately low tone. "Creepy spot, this," he remarked.

Hambledon disregarded this as unworthy of a descendant of the men who fought at Agincourt, and merely said, "The garage first, I think." He produced the three keys from his pocket, and opened the garage door; the two men went in and locked the door behind them.

Once inside, Hambledon switched on an electric torch and had a look round. The garage had that vacant air usual in garages when the big car is out, a large bare space, with a patch of oil in the middle, surrounded by jacks, tool-boxes, lengths of hose and unspecified sundries against the walls. Across the end of the garage were high folding doors of matchboard with a small postern door at one side.

"Siddall's private lockup," said Hambledon, "is beyond that partition. I see nothing here to interest the most suspicious, the fellow hasn't even got a desk. Two books here. Bookings for hire runs. Mrs. Tulip wants her car washed, oiled, and greased on Friday morning. Mr. Boggust, car to station; Thursday 4:15. Any notes at the end? No. Not guilty. The other's his petty cash book or whatever he calls it. Equally innocent."

"He'd keep anything private at home, of course," said Reck. "Where does he live?"

"In a street near by, I am not much concerned with him at the moment. Let's go on and see what's through here."

Hambledon opened the small door, held the torch down so that Reck should see the step, and then swung it up.

"Hullo," he said. "Hullo again."

He stepped through the doorway and began to examine closely the car which was inside. It was painted yellow and had an excellent model of the head of a knight in armor on the radiator cap.

"Behold the elusive taxi," he said. "At least, I think so, I think so. Let's look at the windscreen. If it's got 'Corlex' in the corner, we've won this trick."

In the bottom corner on the driver's side was a trademark in the glass, a five-pointed star with the word "Corlex" encircling it.

When the train drew out of Guildford Station and gathered speed again, the blonde girl in the corner loosened her furs and smiled at her companion.

"Once more we're lucky," she said. "I did think the worried lady in the red hat was going to get in."

"The train isn't particularly full," he answered. "We probably shouldn't have got a carriage to ourselves either earlier or by the last train. This one's too late for the daily-breaders and too soon for the revelers."

"Too early for you, darling, I'm afraid—and for me too, when we're together."

"So long as we are together, it doesn't matter what the time is, does it?"

"You are funny, darling—come and sit closer to me."

"Why funny, Doris?" He moved across the compartment to sit beside her and she slipped her hand into his.

"It's only the way you said that. You always say nice things as though you grudged having to say them."

"I have no right to say nice things to you."

"Why not?"

"I'm not your husband."

"You needn't bother about him," she said scornfully, "he doesn't bother about me. He doesn't care what I do so long as I put in an appearance when I'm specially asked to."

"I can't believe that—"

"Rodney, it's true, do believe it! There's nobody in all the world for me but you."

"But you married him."

"There was a reason for that and it had nothing to do with love. Love and Leonard don't go together, though they start with the same letter—he doesn't know what it means. I can't afford to sneer at him, though, I didn't either till I met you—"

She leaned forward to look into his face, but the train slowed down for the stop at Haslemere and she drew back into her corner and stared angrily out of the window. Siddall's face showed no expression at all, and when the train moved off again, still leaving them alone, he started another subject.

"Bit of luck seeing the Boss at Waterloo," he said, "and still more lucky he didn't see us. I should have been in the soup if he'd called round this evening and found me out."

"He must have changed his plans," said Doris. "I am sure he didn't intend to come back tonight. Still, it doesn't matter now, you'll be in plenty of time."

"I suppose so," said Siddall moodily. "There was an earlier train."

"Yes," said the girl impatiently, "but it was such a slow one, it doesn't reach Portsmouth much earlier than this. Besides, it was fun seeing that Mickey Mouse, wasn't it?"

"Quite good."

"Oh, you are afraid of him, aren't you?" she burst out. "I believe you care more about his opinions than mine."

"Don't start that again, for goodness' sake. I shouldn't be much good to you if I was dead, should I?"

"Please—"

"And you know what happens to people who double-cross him, don't you? Well, I don't intend it to happen to me, that's all."

"But—"

"No buts about it. So long as I'm under his orders I'm being a good boy and doing what I'm told; if he says 'Be at home tonight, I may want you,' I stay at home. But I'm not going to stand it much longer," he went on, his voice rising, "I never bargained for all this business and it gets worse and worse. I'm getting out and he can find someone else to stare down with those cold eyes of his, they give me the shivers. Damn it, I'd rather live in Wigan."

"And leave me?" she said, clinging to him. "Look at me, Rodney darling, you wouldn't have the heart—"

Hambledon, carefully gloved, made a thorough examination of the yellow taxi, but entirely without result.

"These people are too tidy for words," he said.

"Look at this," said Reck.

"What have you found, a cupboard?"

"Yes, of a sort. Look what's inside."

"A ladder nailed to the wall, and it leads to the floor above—to Siddall's flat, in fact. How very interesting indeed. I suppose there's a trapdoor at the top. I'm going to climb up and push it, just to see what happens," said Tommy, clambering up the perpendicular ladder. "How very Castle of Otranto, or am I thinking of the pantomime?"

"It'll be bolted down from above," said Reck pessimistically.

"It's quite likely not to be if they want to keep it secret," said Tommy Hambledon, gasping slightly. "I am not—ugh—a gymnast." He paused near the top for a rest and looked down at his old friend. "A bolt in the middle of your drawing-room floor is apt to attract attention, besides, it wears out the carpets." He braced himself firmly, put one hand on the boarded ceiling above him and pushed.

"It might be countersunk," said Reck, "the bolt, I mean. Try the other end."

"That's left-handed," said Hambledon, and tried it. "It moves a bit, there's probably something standing on it."

"Just a moment," said Reck, and went in search of a pole of some kind. He returned with the garage broom and between them they heaved up the trap-door. When it reached an angle of about thirty degrees there was a slither overhead and a crash, and the trap continued much more easily.

"Crockery, by the sound of it," said Hambledon. "Now, I wonder what that was?"

"One of those pots with ferns in it, I expect—look out!"

But Reck was too late, for a thin stream of water ran over the edge above them straight down Hambledon's neck and splashed on to Reck's upturned face.

"Not fern-pot," gasped Hambledon, trying to avoid it, "flowerpot. Cut flowers, in water." He gave a spring and disappeared from sight, all except his legs.

"Sitting-room," he reported, "and this is a sort of alcove. Coming up?" The legs also vanished; when Reck got up he found Tommy prowling round the room with a torch.

"I don't like to switch the lights on," he explained. "Someone might be interested if we showed lighted windows and he might wonder who'd drawn his curtains for him if we have to leave in a hurry."

"Better tidy up this mess," said Reck, referring to a pool of water on the floor from the jar they had overturned, a tall blue glass pot full of willow branches tasselled with catkins. "There should be a rag of some kind in the kitchen."

"Refill the thingummy with water, too," said Hambledon, throwing a momentary light on it. "My hat, a tumbler two feet high, what a nice long drink! Here's his desk, bureau or writing-table, this is where I get down to it."

Reck cleared up the mess and replaced the willow while Hambledon opened drawers and ran hastily but thoroughly through their contents, muttering to himself all the time.

"Do I shut down the trapdoor?"

"Yes, of course. Nothing locked up, nothing. What a memory the man must have!"

"Why?"

"Because he doesn't need to keep notes. Here are some private letters."

"How do we get out if he walks in on us, if I shut the trapdoor?"

"He won't. You must shut it, we can't leave traces like that. One adoring letter from D. whoever she is, the rest trivial. Only one from D. and it obviously isn't the first, he must have destroyed the others. What do you deduce from that, Watson?"

"Sensible man," grunted Reck.

"Oh, quite, also that most of the affection is on her side."

"What shall I do now?"

"Come and hold a torch for me, I shall be much quicker using both hands. There, that's as he left—what's that?"

"Key in the door," gasped Reck, "he's coming."

"Into the bedroom, quick," said Hambledon, and they retired hastily. Reck dived under the bed but Hambledon pushed the door almost shut and stood behind it. The farther door in the lounge opened, there was a click, and the other room was flooded with light.

There followed a short pause as though the newcomer were looking about him, then a muffled exclamation which sounded impatient, and sounds of someone moving about the room.

Opposite to Tommy Hambledon there was a mirror on the wall in which was reflected a view of the lounge; it was a very narrow, upright strip of view because the door, behind which Hambledon was standing, was nearly shut. He watched this strip intently, expecting to see a vertical section of Siddall pass across it; to his surprise when a figure did pass it was not Siddall at all. In place of the tall and rather too elegant figure of the hairdresser, there was a glimpse of a short man, rather stout and considerably bald.

Hambledon was so intrigued that he tried to make the view wider by opening the door a little further, but it showed a tendency to creak and he desisted. Noises from the lounge proclaimed that the stranger had opened Siddall's cocktail cabinet and was helping himself to a drink. There was the hiss of soda-water from a siphon, and the man picked up his glass and crossed the room with it in the direction of the bureau. To Hambledon's exasperation, every time he passed within sight his face was turned away. More small sounds from the other room, the snap of a cigarette-case, the scrape of a match, the glass being set down on a hard surface. Quite suddenly a chair was pushed back, there was a footfall on polished boards, the further door opened and the light clicked out. The door closed again decisively and there were sounds of further departure culminating in the slam of the front door at the foot of the stairs, and the whine of gear-changing from a car outside.

"Now tell me who the devil that was," said Hambledon aloud. He switched his torch on and saw Reck behind the bed rising like Aphrodite from the wave.

"Wasn't it Siddall?"

"No. Fat little man with a bald head."

"Oh. See his face?"

"No, he kept it turned away all the time, blast him. I'll have the glass he used, though, that might tell Elliot something," said Tommy and walked across to the bureau. On it, in a conspicuous position, was a slip of paper with a message in a particularly neat hand. "Ring me as soon as you come in," it ran, and it was unsigned.

"I'll have this too," said Hambledon, and put it in his wallet. "Sorry to upset their arrangements, but my need is the greater." He swathed the tumbler carefully in his handkerchief and looked at Reck who was wearing, as usual, a shabby drab mackintosh.

"Got a pocket you can put this in?"

"Give it to me," said Reck, and stowed it away.

"Now we will get on with our job," said Hambledon. "What's he got in his cocktail cabinet? Quite a cellar. All the usuals, plus Cointreau, vodka and Van der Hum. Dash it, I've cut my wrist on his John Haig, there's a chip off the bottom of the bottle. Nothing behind here—what are you doing?"

"Only arranging a line of retreat," said Reck, opening a window in the bedroom. "There's a nice stackpipe outside this one, I'll leave it open."

"You get more like d'Artagnan every moment," said Hambledon.

CHAPTER XII

Love Laughs at Stackpipes

"I THINK we've looked at nearly everything," said Hambledon, completing a brief but exhaustive tour of bedroom, bathroom and kitchen. "I don't think I've ever seen an establishment which had so few secrets in it. That's suspicious it itself, nobody could possibly be so innocent as this fellow appears. We've had no bag at all except one mysterious visitor."

"You haven't looked at his books," said Reck, pointing out a bookshelf beside the fireplace. "It's true they don't look very interesting."

"They might provide us with some evidence as to whether his name always was Siddall," said Hambledon, pulling out one or two. "Some of these might almost be schoolbooks, Gardiner's History, for example. If we find R. W. Siddall in childish round-hand—"

"If you don't," said Reck sardonically, "either his name was different when he was young, or else it'll be the name of the fellow who sold it to the secondhand dealer Siddall bought it from. I think I prefer cookery, it's a more exact science than your trade."

"Here's Liddell & Scott," said Hambledon, unheeding. "What would a hairdresser want with a Greek Lexicon? It's even heavier than usual, it—look here."

Liddell & Scott opened in one place only because all the other pages were stuck together. The insides of the pages had been cut out so that the Greek Lexicon was more box than dictionary. Inside there lay a small German automatic.

"Well, well, well. I hand it to you, Reck, you suggested looking at the books. A perfectly good Mauser, what a warlike hairdresser. Now I wonder if that's the weapon that killed Macgregor?" Hambledon put his hand in his pocket and fished out a duplicate. "Always carry one myself, I got so used to it in Germany that I'm not at home with any other. Now if we swop these two over, I think Siddall's would make a nice present for Superintendent Elliot, don't you? I want another handkerchief, have you got a spare one?"

"No, but you can have this one," said Reck, handing it over. Hambledon carefully wiped all possible fingerprints off his own automatic and put it in the book instead of Siddall's, which he wrapped in the handkerchief and dropped into his pocket. The Liddell & Scott went back in the bookcase.

"Now I think we can go," said Hambledon. "Is everything tidy? Put that chair—"

"Ssh!" said Reck, and sprang for the bedroom door. Hambledon stared for an instant and then heard what Reck had heard, footsteps on the stairs. There were straight curtains hanging to the ground on either side of the alcove, he slid behind these since it was plain there was no time for two men to climb out of a window and slither down a stackpipe before they were heard. In fact, faint scrambling noises from the bedroom only changed into scratching noises ending in a thump as the door opened and Siddall and the blonde Doris walked in.

They switched on the lights, Doris said "Ugh! it's cold," turned on the electric fire and knelt in front of it. "Draw the curtains, darling, and let's be comfortable. I'll make some coffee in a minute, when I'm warm, have you got any sausages?"

"I think so," answered Siddall, "anyway, there are some rashers." He pulled down the window-blind, drew the curtains across it, and come to Hambledon's hiding-place. He took hold of the curtain within six inches of Hambledon's nose, and added, "Anyway, there are tomatoes, a bottle of Bismarck herrings, and some olives. Also cheese and biscuits." He drew the curtain that side and the other, and Hambledon relaxed slightly. "Why did you want curtains over this alcove?"

"To make the room look cozy," she said. "It's a silly alcove anyway, with nothing in it but a flower-vase. It ought to be one large built-in cupboard."

"Not a bad idea," he said, drifting across to the fire, "make the other exit a trifle more private too, wouldn't it?"

"Come and sit down on the rug," she said, holding out her hand to him, "goodness knows we don't get much time together these days."

Hambledon could, of course, see nothing of what was happening, but he gathered from a soft thump and "There's a dear," from Doris, that Siddall had done what he was told. Hambledon himself was not at all happy. He knew that the last incomer was Siddall, because he saw the man quite plainly when he drew the further curtain over the alcove, but who the lady was Tommy could only guess. Presumably she was either the blonde or "D" or possibly both if they were the same person, in any case since this was Siddall's own flat there seemed no reason why he should go out again that night at all unless he took the lady home to wherever she came from. But by the way she talked about frying sausages it did not seem as though she were in any hurry to go, and for all Hambledon knew she might be staying the night there. In which case it was difficult to imagine how and when he would be able to slip out unobserved, and indeed he was beginning to wonder how much longer he could stand there without making a sound, already the calves of his legs were beginning to ache. Besides, like most fairly heavy smokers, Hambledon had an habitual cough, and the mere fact that he knew he mustn't set his throat tickling. If only they'd go into the kitchen, turn on a couple of taps and make a cheerful clatter with pots and pans, he would make a dive for the bedroom and Reck's road to freedom—

"Howling draft in this room tonight," said Siddall, interrupting an aimless but pleasant exchange of small talk, "feels as though the bedroom window's open. It can't be, though, I remember shutting it."

"Oh don't move, Roddy darling, I'm so comfortable."

Hambledon shuddered. The situation was quite bad enough without this precious pair starting to make love in his presence. However, Roddy darling was firm.

"We'll soon get comfortable again," he said, "but at the present moment I've got icicles growing down my spine. Just a minute, beauty girl."

There were sounds of movement, footsteps across the room, and then Siddall's voice from the bedroom. "Damn funny," he said in a puzzled voice.

"What's funny?"

"The bedroom window's wide open, and it's not the one I generally open. It's the one that sticks when you try to shut it."

"Queer," said Doris. "Never mind, darling, perhaps Mrs. Oompoof, or whatever the charwoman's name is, left it open. Shut it and come back, I want you."

"She wouldn't do that," said Siddall's voice, and there were sounds of struggling with an obstinate sash. Eventually he shut it and the next time he spoke his voice sounded nearer though he had not walked across the lounge, Hambledon could picture him standing in the bedroom doorway looking worried. "And if he's half as worried as I am he has my sympathy," said Tommy to himself.

"Wonder if the Boss has been here," said Siddall.

"Darling," said Doris in an exasperated tone, "if he had, would he open your bedroom window for you? Do be reasonable. If he'd been here he'd have left a note, he always does. There's no note, so he hasn't been."

"Well, somebody has."

"Probably the window-cleaner. Come back, Rodney dear, and let's go on being happy."

"I think I should find it easier to be happy if I wasn't so infernally hungry," said the voice of Siddall, advancing across the room.

Doris sighed audibly, but Hambledon heard her get up. "All right, I'll go and fry ham or whatever there is. Come and talk to me while I cook."

Hambledon risked a glance between the curtains when he was sure they were both walking away from him. His guess was right, this was the blonde girl he had seen at the d'Albertini, but he could not remember whether Bellair had ever told him her name. It didn't matter, Jim could tell him later if she was likely to be the D. of the adoring letter, and in any case that was of no real importance. What was important was that she was undoubtedly in the game too. She knew all about the trap door, therefore she probably knew all about the yellow taxi at the bottom of the ladder. If she knew that she probably knew who killed Macgregor, and that he was shot because he had something to say about the *Araucaria* and her unhappy predecessors. And, finally, if she knew Siddall knew, in fact the net was closing round the clever hairdresser from more than one point. If the Mauser in Hambledon's pocket fired the shot which killed Macgregor, Siddall could be pulled in at any time. But who was behind Siddall, this boss of whom he was so much afraid? Of all the things the blonde girl knew, that was the most important.

In the meantime, there was the question of getting out. The bedroom window was out of the question since Siddall had shut it, because reopening it would make far too much noise. The true exit door of the lounge was in full view of the two in the kitchen so that was no use. There remained only the trapdoor he was standing on. This unfortunately projected beyond the curtains into the room, not much, six inches or so, but quite enough to astonish the most careless observer if it were gaping instead of closed. Besides, one couldn't open that silently, either. No, there was nothing for it but to stay where he was till Siddall and his guest went away, and in the meantime one might as well be comfortable.

Tommy Hambledon, with infinite precautions against noise, lowered himself carefully to the floor, stretched out his legs and leaned his back against the wall, prepared to wait if necessary for hours, and hours, and hours.

The delicious smell of fried bacon and hot coffee came to remind him that the evening meal was about three hours overdue, and that again reminded him of Reck. What was Reck doing, he wondered, probably he'd walked back to the car and gone to sleep. A very sound idea, too. Tommy closed his eyes.

He opened them quickly ten minutes later, because Doris and Siddall were returning to the lounge with supper.

"I'll carry the tray," said Siddall.

"Let's have it in front of the fire," said the girl. "I'll get that little table." She came close to Hambledon's alcove and said "Hullo!" so suddenly that he started nervously.

"What's the matter?"

"This carpet's sopping wet."

"Why? Do bring the table over, this tray's heavy."

"Why?" she repeated. "(Here's the table.) How should I know? Unless somebody's upset the vase."

"It wasn't upset just now," said Siddall, while Hambledon said to himself,

"Oh dear, oh dear. Now they'll pull the curtains—I wish I hadn't come—"

Nonetheless, when they did pull the curtains they found a harmless-looking little man sleeping peacefully, with a gentle smile just hovering about his lips. He was so sound asleep that even Siddall's loud exclamation did not disturb his even breathing, his head was tilted a little to one side and his hands were lightly clasped across a comfortable waistcoat.

"Good gracious!" said Doris, "who's that?" Hambledon mentally handed her a bouquet for not screaming, but Doris was not of the screaming kind.

"No idea," said Siddall uneasily.

"He's asleep," said Doris, and Hambledon took his mental bouquet away again for making obvious remarks.

"He's probably drunk," said Siddall. Tommy encouraged this good idea with a timely snore. "I'll stir him up and kick him out."

"No, don't do that, he may have stolen something. Ring up the police."

"As you wish. No, you ring them while I keep an eye on him."

"All right," said Doris, crossing the room. "What's the number?"

"No number. Just call the operator and say 'Police.' "

Doris did so, but it nearly disturbed Hambledon's peaceful slumbers to hear himself described as "a horrid-looking old man, probably drunk." She replaced the receiver and said, "They'll be here in ten minutes, we are to keep him here till they come."

"Oh, I'll keep him all right," said Siddall grimly, and Hambledon was horrified to hear her say, "Mind that thing doesn't go off. I don't trust those Belgian revolvers, shall I give you the other one?"

"No thanks, this one'll do. I say!"

"What?"

"Where was he when I drew the curtains?"

"Oh, under your bed, I expect," said Doris lightly. "He must have come across here while we were in the kitchen."

"You're a cool hand, I must say," said Siddall. "You don't turn a hair."

"Well, I don't think he's very alarming, and as for turning a hair, I'd better not, had I?"

Hambledon was so indignant at this that he had difficulty in maintaining the even rhythm of his snores. This girl really was the limit, he liked women who took things placidly and didn't make scenes, but this inhuman calmness was rather terrifying. He was far from realizing that Siddall thought so too.

"Cigarette, darling?" said Doris. "Let me light one for you."

"Thanks."

An electric bell rang in his kitchen and Doris said, "The police, I'll go." She went, and in a few moments could be heard explaining matters to two sets of heavy footsteps coming up the stairs. Tommy thought it artistically correct to be rendered a little restless by all this, so he groaned slightly, rolled into the corner, and settled off again.

"That's it," said Doris, pointing a slim white finger at the culprit. One of the constables advanced on him, took him by the arm and shook him.

"Wake up," he said loudly, "and come on."

Hambledon opened with difficulty eyes apparently heavy with sleep and looked vaguely about him. Then his wandering glance fell on Doris and his face lit up.

"There she is," he said warmly. "Boo'ful lady."

"What are you doing here?"

"Unhand me," said Hambledon, with dignity marred by a convincing hic-cup. "Came to see boo'ful lady. You go 'way."

The policeman shook the arm he held, and the hand at the end of it waggled helplessly. "Come on out of this," he said. "You'll be sorry in the morning."

"Why?"

"How did he get in?" asked Doris.

"How did you get in?"

"Climbed up shtackpipe into the window. Ushed do mountaineering when I wash young. Mont Blanc, 'n' all that."

"Goof," said Doris not unkindly.

"The bedroom window was open," said Siddall, "and there is a stackpipe outside it."

One of the constables went with Siddall into the bedroom and opened the obstinate window. He came back a few minutes later and looked at Hamble-don with a marked increase of respect.

"It's quite true," he said in a surprised voice. "You can see marks on the pipe." Doris also seemed impressed.

"You'd never think it to look at him, would you?" she said.

Hambledon drew himself up with as much dignity as is consistent with sitting on the floor while everyone else is standing up. "There'sh no need to be rude about it," he said. "Love shimply laughsh at shtackpipesh."

Doris burst into peals of laughter, and one of the policeman asked her if she knew the prisoner.

"Never seen him in my life before."

"Oh. He seems to know you, madam."

Doris shrugged her shoulders and said that no doubt the funny little man had seen her about somewhere without her ever having noticed him. She added kindly that she did not want too much fuss made of what was probably a harmless drunken prank, and that so long as he had not stolen anything he could go free so far as she was concerned. The elder constable said that that was not a matter for him to decide and that the prisoner would be searched at the station, so if the lady would ascertain if there was anything missing, it could be sought for among the things found on the prisoner. He then took names, addresses, and a short statement from Doris and Siddall, and removed the body of the prisoner down the stairs and out of the front door. Siddall came to show them out; they could hear him shooting bolts and rattling a chain as they walked away.

Hambledon waited till they were out of earshot from the door, and was just about to speak when one of the constables flashed his torch on a bicycle standing by the curb, and said to the other, "That's yours, where's mine?"

His companion suggested, without much hope, that it had been put round the corner for a joke, and the bereft one looked round all the adjacent corners without success.

"My new Raleigh," he observed bitterly.

Hambledon said in perfectly distinct and sober tones that he thought it quite probable they would find it parked outside the Guildhall, and suggested going there at once.

"Don't you worry about the Guildhall, nor making jokes about a stolen cycle," said its embittered owner. "You're coming along to the station in Albert Road. Come on, quick march."

"I am certainly not going to be marched through the streets by two uniformed constables," said Hambledon coldly. "Will you be so good as to call a taxi?"

"Here," said the other constable, "I thought you were supposed to be drunk."

"Exactly. I was supposed to be drunk, and what Elliot will say when I tell him that neither of you even thought of smelling my breath, I'd hate to think."

The two constables looked at each other.

"I am going to the Guildhall to see Superintendent Elliot," continued Hambledon. "I know him well and I have something to tell him. As for you, you know perfectly well that if an arrested person wishes to hire a taxi, he has every right to do so. Now, please call one."

"I'll go and telephone," said the constable whose bicycle was still there. When the taxi came they went together to the police station in Albert Road, the second constable cycling behind. Hambledon repeated to the station-sergeant there his demand to be taken to Elliot at the Guildhall.

"I will ask him in the morning," began the sergeant, but Hambledon cut him short.

"You will be so good as to telephone to him at once. Tell him that I am here—Mr. Hambledon—and that I wish to see him as soon as possible."

The station-sergeant looked at him with distaste, picked up the receiver and gave the Guildhall number. He then asked to be put through to Superintendent Elliot and went on: "This is the Albert Road Station speaking. A man has been brought in here charged with breaking and entering premises at Buckland Mews—" He broke off as the telephone proceeded to emit what reached Hambledon as a long series of squeaks and crackles, but which was evidently plain to the sergeant, for an expression of pained astonishment crossed his face and he took the receiver away from his ear and looked at it reproachfully.

"Yes, sir, name of Hambledon ... very good, sir. He was asking to see you ... I said, he was asking to be taken to you ... Oh! ... yes, sir, certainly. At once." He put down the receiver. "Is that taxi still outside?"

"No, sir, I sent it away."

"Why?" asked Hambledon incisively. "I told him to wait."

"Get another," said the station-sergeant balefully and the constable fled.

CHAPTER XIII

Enter Franz

HAMBLEDON was accompanied to the Guildhall by the policeman whose cycle had been stolen; when the taxi drew up at the door there was a very new Raleigh propped up by the curb.

"That your bike?" asked Hambledon, indicating it with a jerk of his head.

"It is one very like it, anyway, sir," said the man doubtfully.

"I told you so, didn't I?" said his omniscient prisoner, and swept into the Guildhall with his chin up. He was taken upstairs to Elliot's room and found its owner marching up and down with his hands clenched at his sides, and Reck sitting on a chair in the corner with his knees crossed and an expression of sardonic amusement on his face.

"Evening, Elliot," said Hambledon. "Hullo, Reck, as soon as I heard the cop's bicycle was missing I thought I should find you here. It was you who pinched the new Raleigh, wasn't it?"

"Not pinched, borrowed. It's outside."

Elliot shook his fists in the air and went on pacing up and down.

"What's the matter, Elliot? You seem upset."

"Upset, no. I'm never upset."

"You look even more like a Border laird resenting a Sassenach foray than usual. What's the trouble?"

"You. First I hear of you breaking-and-entering, then you're caught and charged with being on enclosed premises, with being drunk and disorderly, with burglary too for all I know—"

"I'm quite guilty of that," said Hambledon cheerfully, "but I don't think it's been discovered yet and when it is I'm darned sure they won't complain."

"Your assistant here has had a comparatively innocent evening, he merely stole a policeman's bicycle—"

"Not stole," repeated Reck patiently, "merely borrowed. It's outside, I said so just now."

"Did you give him the glass?" asked Hambledon.

"No. I started to tell him all about it, but he seemed so annoyed that I thought I'd wait till you came." Reck fished the glass out of his pocket, still wrapped up, and Hambledon put it on the superintendent's desk.

"Exhibit No. 1. I am glad, Reck, that it didn't get broken when you slid down the stackpipe."

"Were you in the flat too?" asked Elliot.

"Yes, but I didn't get caught," said Reck triumphantly. "I've ruined the left knee of my trousers, though." He uncrossed his legs and displayed a large three-cornered tear.

"Oh, is that why you were sitting like that? I wondered. Look, Elliot, at exhibit No. 1. This glass bears the fingerprints of the Master Criminal—or one of 'em. The man behind Siddall, anyway. Here is a specimen of his handwriting. He is a short, rather paunchy man with a bald head."

Elliot left off pacing up and down and stared at Hambledon. "Your regrettable methods undoubtedly get results," he said. "Ever seen him before?"

Tommy shook his head. "Didn't see his face. From the back he is completely indistinguishable from five thousand other men of the same type in Southsea alone. Nor did I hear his voice except in a noise like 'Tchah!' expressive of impatience. He let himself into Siddall's flat with a latchkey presumably, I didn't admit him. He walked into the lounge and switched on the lights—of course I thought it was Siddall, I was behind the bedroom door—then he went across to the cocktail cabinet and mixed himself a drink. Oh, very much at home. But when I caught a glimpse of him in passing, it wasn't Siddall but another. So I souvenired his glass, that's it."

"He went away again, did he?"

"Certainly, all in one piece. I did not slay him and put the corpse in the dustbin, I thought you wouldn't like it. He wrote that little note, left it on the bureau, and departed. So I took the note also. Exhibit 2."

"I'll have these looked into," said Elliot. "Fingerprints and writing too. Did he use Siddall's paper?"

Hambledon nodded. "Tore a sheet from the telephone pad."

"So it's no use looking that up, but I'll have the rest seen to at once."

" 'But this when thou hast done, thou hast not done,' " quoted Hambledon, " 'for I have more.' " He produced Siddall's Mauser from his pocket, unwrapped it and laid that also on Elliot's desk. "Exhibit 3. It would be interesting to know whether that is the weapon from which the shot was fired which killed Macgregor."

"God bless my soul," said the superintendent, "where did you find that?"

Hambledon told him and Elliot said, "If he misses this he can't make a case of it, he had no business to have it at all. He may be suspicious, though, when he finds it's gone."

"He won't," said Hambledon, "unless he's got a note of the number, I left him mine instead. It's exactly like this." He went on to give an account of what had happened after Siddall came in, with special mention of the references to "the Boss." "That's why I assume it was the Boss who came in earlier, he certainly behaved in a boss-like manner. Who's the blonde, do you know?"

"One Doris Baker."

"Oh. I thought perhaps her name began with a D, she writes him loverly letters."

"You went through his private correspondence too, evidently," said Elliot wistfully. "You know, you break all the rules and will probably land in jail, but you do get results. There are times when I wish I was in your department instead of in the police."

"If we could make that girl talk," said Hambledon, "we might get somewhere. She knows about it all, she knows, she knows. Omar Khayyám, more or less. By the way, could my car be brought here by some garage body? It's unobtrusively parked in Merton Road—Bellair's long-nosed Triumph, I forget the number."

"It shall be done," said Elliot. "With regard to this Baker woman, couldn't you hypnotize her or something?"

"What, at my age?"

The Triumph was delivered at the Guildhall, Hambledon and Reck took their leave of Superintendent Elliot and went downstairs. On their way through the entrance hall they met two policeman carrying a stretcher with an unconscious man on it. Reck walked past with the uninterested air of a man who never expects to see anyone he knows, but Hambledon glanced at the occupant of the stretcher and uttered a loud exclamation of surprise.

"What's the matter?"

"Look who's here. Put that stretcher down a moment, men, where on earth did you find this man?"

"On my soul," said Reck, "it's Franz."

"You know him, sir? He came running like mad up Ridge Street from the Unicorn Road way, and just as you turn into Spring Street he ran slap into the side of a car and fell down. Wasn't the driver's fault, I saw it myself, the car was hardly moving, but he seems to have stunned himself. Anyway, we couldn't get him round so I sent for a stretcher and we brought him in."

"More like collapse from exhaustion, poor old chap, I think," said Reck. "He looks ill."

The station-sergeant emerged from his cubbyhole behind the glass window. "Friend of yours, sir? I'd better get the doctor, hadn't I?"

Reck, stooping over the stretcher, said Franz's color was returning a little, and Hambledon asked if there was any brandy available. Elliot came through on his way home and said: "What is all this?"

"This is a man who was my servant for many years when I lived abroad," said Hambledon, "though what he's doing here and how he got into that condition I can't imagine."

The constable repeated his account of the affair, and Elliot said the unfortunate man looked as though he had been starving and sleeping in cellars.

"That may well be," said Hambledon grimly, "such things happen where he comes from. Moreover, it may be partly my fault. Isn't that brandy ever coming?"

The superintendent looked round impatiently and the brandy materialized as though by magic. Franz showed signs of returning consciousness as Hambledon slipped one arm under his servant's head and poured a little into his mouth.

"Not too much," said Elliot, bending forward with his hands on his knees, "you'll choke him."

Franz opened his eyes and stared blankly at the superintendent facing him. "There now," said Elliot encouragingly, "you feel better, don't you?"

"*Danke schön,*" said Franz feebly, and turned his head to see who was holding him. The moment his eyes fell on Hambledon's face, he turned a greenish white, uttered a weak cry of terror and fainted.

"Dear me," said Elliot, "the sight of you doesn't seem to reassure him. Did you say he was your servant?"

"I'd forgotten for the moment that he thinks I'm dead," said Hambledon. "In fact he attended my funeral. Franz, old chap, it's all right, I'm quite real. Have another drink, come on."

"Better let me see to him for the moment," said Elliot, pushing Hambledon aside. "He may be able to bear the sight of you more bravely when he feels better. Get out of his line of sight a moment. Now then, old chap, drink this up. It's all right, you're among friends."

"He won't understand a word you say," said Hambledon in a low tone.

Franz opened his eyes again while Elliot drew a long breath and gathered himself for a great effort. "*Trink hier,*" he said carefully. "*Du bist*—er—*inter kameraden. Allen ist bon.*" He subsided, and Franz actually smiled. One of the constables stood forward and said that he could speak German after a fashion, so Elliot, with a sigh of relief, told him to carry on.

"Are you feeling better now?"

"Thank you," said Franz. "Much better. Where am I?"

"Portsmouth police-station."

"Police," whispered Franz, turning pale again and struggling to sit up.

Elliot caught the word "*politzei*" and guessed what had alarmed the stranger. "Tell him it's all right," he said, "we aren't man-eating tigers, not 'less he's done something wrong."

The constable translated and Franz looked reassured. "I have done nothing wrong," he said, "at least, nothing you would think wrong. May I get up now?"

They helped him to his feet and he stood up, swaying, and steadied himself. He turned to thank Elliot, and over his shoulder saw Hambledon again. Franz uttered a startled cry and instantly bolted for the door, to be gathered in by a large policeman there and held firmly.

"Franz, old man," said Hambledon in German. "I am not dead, my old friend, I am very much alive. I was not killed at Danzig. Look, here's Mr. Reck too."

Franz left off struggling and turned to look at him. "But you were honorably interred," he said. "I was there."

"Somebody else was, not me. We arranged that," said Hambledon, advancing towards him, and this time Franz did not run away. "Take my hand, it is flesh and blood. We bolted, that's all. I was always sorry I could not let you know."

Franz took him by the hand and looked into his face. "This night," he said unsteadily, "pays for many things. After so much sorrow and so much terror, I stand in a free country at last. As though that wasn't more than I dared to pray for, almost the first person I see is you, my—" his voice failed.

Hambledon, little less moved than Franz, patted him on the shoulder. "Buck up, old chap," he said. "Reports of my death are usually unreliable. I am damned glad to see you."

Reck came up to join in the reunion, and Franz said, "You know, sir, there was one point which always made me wonder whether there was a doubt about your death. Mr. Reck was never found, alive or dead."

"Careless of us," said Hambledon, "I must remember that next time. Wonder if anyone else noticed it."

"Dr. Goebbels, sir, was enquiring repeatedly whether there was any news of Herr Reck."

"The devil he was. And don't call me 'sir,' Franz, the time for that is past."

"Very good," said Franz with a smile, "but what is your Excellency's name these days?"

"Hambledon. What's yours?"

"Von Krug."

"Ask him what he was running away from," said Elliot.

Hambledon translated the question and Franz answered, "The Gestapo."

"The devil!"

"The same thing, sir—er—Hambledon."

"I know you're right. But what are the Gestapo doing in Portsmouth?"

"Oh, that running away. That was from two men on the ship, I heard them talking to somebody who came on board to meet them. I was on the skylight, you understand. Then my knife slipped out of my pocket and they heard it. I thought it better to run away, it was not the sort of conversation one wishes to have overheard, you understand?"

"Oh, quite. What were they talking about?"

"Battleships. The man was to put something on board to damage them."

Hambledon uttered a yell of joy. " 'Come to my arms, my beamish boy! O frabjous day! Calloo! Callay!' "

"I beg your pardon," said Franz, baffled by the sudden gush of English, and Elliot said, "Here! What's all this?"

"I think the place to continue this little conversation is in your office, Elliot, with the doors locked."

"Come up," said Elliot, but Reck said, "Don't you think Von Krug would feel more like talking if he had something to eat first?"

"How right you are, Reck—when did you have a meal last?"

"Three days ago, in Hamburg, since then, chocolate and biscuits only. I stowed away, you understand."

"Heavens above, man. Could somebody go to the d'Albertini—"

"I'll send a man," said Elliot.

"May I use your telephone? I'll order something."

Chicken en casserole and a half-bottle of Heidsick restored the color to Franz von Krug's face and the animation to his voice. Hambledon, Elliot and Reck sat round him in the superintendent's office and waited till he had finished before they would let him talk. When at last he pushed back the empty plates and asked what exactly they wanted to know, Hambledon began to question him, translating for Elliot's benefit as he went along.

"The men were in the cabin and you were looking down at them through the skylight?" Franz nodded. "How many were there?"

"Three. Two came on the ship from Hamburg and one came aboard to meet them here."

"Where's the ship?" asked Elliot. "And what's her name?"

"I don't know the name of any place here," explained Franz. "I did not know this was Portsmouth till the policeman said so downstairs, I was not even sure this was England. The ship is the *Hulda von Gronau*, of Hamburg."

Elliot made a note and Hambledon went on. "You would know these men again?"

"Certainly I would. They had the light on in the cabin, I was only waiting till it was a little darker to slip ashore."

"What happened, exactly?"

"I was creeping along the deck to reach a place where I could jump down to the quayside, looking about me and listening, eyes and ears all out on stalks, you understand, when suddenly I hear voices from the cabin below. I stop at once for fear they hear my step overhead, also I want to know if they are likely to come up at once."

"Could you hear what they said?"

"Most of it. Evidently the man from here had only just come aboard, for he apologized for being late. He said he had had to wait for somebody who had not come."

"Did they mention any names?"

"Not once."

"Wise men. What did they say?"

"They congratulated him on having such an uplifting influence on the British Fleet, and they all laughed. I would not have known what they meant, only one of them said 'Pouf!' and threw his hands up—like this, and they all laughed again. I thought this so interesting that I listened longer. No business of mine, you will say, but I have been for so long in the habit of collecting useful information that it seems I cannot stop." Von Krug paused while Hambledon translated, and continued: "Then the visitor said, 'Have you any more orders for me?' One of the Germans said, 'Yes, you are to continue the good work as and when instructions reach you.' The visitor said, 'I am running short of the—er—uplifting influence,' and again they laughed. The German said, 'Have no fear, we have brought you plenty to go on with.' I got the idea they would not talk much longer, they did not really settle down, you understand, as though time were short, so I thought I had better go. But as soon as I moved my knife slipped out and clashed on the glass. I saw them all look up with angry faces, so I jumped ashore and ran—and ran—"

Franz leaned back as though even the memory exhausted him. "Only one more question," said Hambledon, "then we will go home and you shall rest in safety. Can you describe these men?"

"We can get the Germans' names from the ship's papers," put in Elliot, and Hambledon nodded.

"Or the names they go by at the moment. Carry on, von Krug."

"The Germans. One was a big dark man, fat, middle-aged, hair thin on the top, fat neck, oh you know, the overfed bullock type. Signet ring on left hand, dueling scars—both the Germans had those—he had had his nose broken at some time." Franz waited while Elliot took down particulars. "The other one was the stubby sandy-haired type, gold-rimmed spectacles, blue or gray eyes, nose thick at the tip, deep lines round his mouth. He was wearing a dark scarf with white spots on it, I think he had a cold, he coughed a good deal." Franz paused again. "The Englishman—so to speak, I mean the visitor—I did not see so well, he was directly below me. I can't say what his height was, but was inclined to be stout. Brown hair turning gray, thin on top, in fact very thin. I only saw his face at the last moment when he looked up, and I was in a hurry then. A very ordinary man, so ordinary that I can't describe him, but I think I might know him again. He looked like a better-class tradesman, but quite undistinguished in any way."

"Nothing that we can do for you," said Hambledon, "can ever repay what we owe you for this information."

"There is one matter which is rather worrying me," said von Krug, looking doubtfully at Elliot.

"What is that?"

"I have no papers, I had a passport once but it expired years ago—"

"Don't worry about that, we'll see to it. Will you do me the honor of being a guest in my house, for the present at any rate? I don't think Portsmouth is a very healthy spot for you, at least till the *Hulda von Gronau* has gone again, and her passengers too."

"The honor will be entirely mine," said Franz. "I am in your hands. Shall I have the pleasure of meeting again the gracious Fräulein Rademeyer?"

"Not at present, dear old Aunt Ludmilla is on the Riviera with Frau Christine Beckensburg, who has been ill. Aunt Ludmilla found England in November rather trying, so I packed her off to the sunshine. I thought she was getting bronchial."

Von Krug nodded. "I shall hope to see her again some day. You know it has only just struck me, you must be an Englishman. Half German, I suppose?"

"Not even half," said Tommy Hambledon. "I am entirely English. Fräulein Rademeyer adopted me when I was like a lost dog—it's a long story, I'll tell you all about it tomorrow. Let's go home now, you must be tired and it is very late. Good night, Elliot. You'll see about those German fellows in the morning, no doubt."

"I shall give instructions for the ship to be watched now, before I go home, and go aboard first thing tomorrow morning. I shall see you again soon."

"Yes, tomorrow night possibly, I'll see. Ring me up if there's anything urgent."

"You know," said von Krug as they went downstairs, "I was wondering what was different about you and I have just discovered what it is. You have lost your scars."

"I went to a surgeon who specializes in facial improvements. The motive of his clients is normally beauty, but my face is merely one of those nice kind ones you can't do much for. I went to preserve my anonymity. I felt such a modest shrinking from recognition as would do credit to any violet, however lowly. So he did a spot of skin-grafting, and made a very good job of it, I think."

"They gave you a very distinguished appearance, I thought," said the German.

"So did I," said Tommy dryly. "That's why I had 'em removed."

CHAPTER XIV

Deserted Lady

DURING the afternoon of the following day, Albertini the younger telephoned to Bellair to say that Molly Trotter, one of the twins from the Empire, had rung up the Café d'Albertini to ask whether they knew if there was any likelihood of Jimmy's coming to Portsmouth that night. If so, she would like to see him as she had something to tell him.

"Umf," said Hambledon, when this was repeated to him. "Intelligent young women, those two. If I were you I should go."

"I will. I was thinking of going down tonight anyway. I'll drop in at the Empire and arrange to see Molly somewhere as soon as she can get away. It depends how long the story is, perhaps she can tell me there."

"I'll drive you down," said Hambledon. "You don't want to use that arm of yours more than you can help for a few days."

"Oh, thanks awfully, but don't bother. I shall be all right."

"No bother at all, and I know more about bullet wounds than you do, I expect."

"No doubt you do, but this one's trivial. I don't want to be a trouble to anybody."

"I'll see you aren't, but I think I'll drive tonight, all the same."

"It's extremely good of you," said Bellair, rather awkwardly, "but I was going out tonight in any case."

"So was I," said Hambledon calmly. "I want to see Elliot. I was going to ask if I might borrow your car, but as you also want to go, it's simple."

Bellair opened his mouth and shut it again. "Don't do that," said Tommy, "it reminds me of Superintendent Gascon's goldfish."

"Would you mind very much," said Bellair politely, "if we had another passenger?"

"My dear boy, why ask my permission? It's your car, isn't it?"

"Yes, but—"

"Subject to the requirements of the service, you were going to say. Of course you're perfectly right, but I can't see the slightest objection to Miss Gascon coming with us. I don't anticipate any trouble tonight."

"I didn't say it was Miss Gascon," said the baited Bellair.

116

"But it is, isn't it?"

"Yes—"

"Then why not say so?" said Hambledon blandly. "I am sure there is no necessity to apologize for the presence of anyone so noticeably charming."

"I wasn't going to—"

"And I cannot believe—a reasonable and proper pride forbids it—that you find it necessary to apologize for mine."

Bellair looked at him. Hambledon was standing on the hearthrug, rocking gently on his feet, with a completely placid expression on his face, but there was something in his eyes which effectively forbade reply. Bellair muttered something inaudible and drifted out of the room.

Reck, who was sitting on a corner of the fender, broke into a low chuckle and Hambledon smiled in reply.

"You can be very trying when you like," said Reck.

"When I find it necessary," amended Hambledon.

"I thought 'noticeably charming' a little cruel."

"Listen. He's a good cub, but he's only a cub and wants licking into shape. If I wish to go to Portsmouth or Pimlico or Pernambuco, we go, and no hesitations about cars or girls or anything else. He's got to learn that if the department wants him he doesn't own a car or a girl or an immortal soul either. See? Where's Franz?"

"Gone out for a stroll. He says it's such a wonderful feeling to walk about just as you like and not even wonder whether you'll be arrested."

Bettine had at first been rather too obviously surprised to find Hambledon was coming too, but he insisted on her having a glass of sherry before they started and unexpectedly provided chocolates and cigarettes for the run down. She was quite incapable of being distant with any man who had so many of the right ideas, and a somewhat deflated Bellair found himself occupying the back of the car alone while Tommy Hambledon babbled and Bettine laughed in the front seats. Eventually the car stopped in the Guildhall Square and Hambledon got out.

"I simply hate to leave you," he said, "but I have to go and see a man about another man. I hand over to you, Jim, with unbounded confidence. Where shall I meet you?"

"Where, Jimmikins darling?"

"At the d'Albertini?"

"Splendid," said Hambledon. "Au 'voir." He moved away into the crowd and instantly disappeared. Bellair, after a momentary pause, got over into the driver's seat.

"Where shall we go? Like to look in at the Empire?"

"Anywhere you like, sweetness," said Bettine, who was suffering from a slight attack of conscience. Bellair turned the car round in the square and drove back in silence to the Empire.

"Jimmy darling."

"Yes?"

"You aren't annoyed with me, are you?"

"Of course not, don't be silly."

"I believe you are."

"Here we are. Will you run up and ask one of the commissionaires to find you a box while I put the car away? I won't be a minute."

"The commissionaires don't find people boxes, darling, the girl does that."

"Then ask the commissionaire to ask the girl to find you one," said Bellair, feeling that if he had another ten seconds of this he would shake her. Why the devil had he ever promised to bring her, anyway, dangling round after a girl like that while Hambledon went off on his own and reaped all the laurels. Bellair was still restive under the recollection of having spent the previous evening saying more to Bettine than he had ever intended, while Hambledon apparently just walked in and out of people's houses as he liked and solved more of the problem in one evening than Jim Bellair had done in six months. Finally, Hambledon had occupied that evening's drive in demonstrating how easy he would find it to detach Bettine if he thought it worth while. Bellair ground his teeth, parked the car and walked back to the Empire. Enough of this idiocy, he had got to get Molly's story, not spend the evening meditating on the vagaries of a governess with scarlet fingernails. He had a particular objection to red fingernails anyway.

He stopped and metaphorically shook himself, realizing that he was working himself up into a rage; that the next thing he would do would be to snub Molly and spoil the story, whatever it was. Dear laughing Molly, always so ready to do anyone a good turn and never expecting to be taken out to dinners and shows as a reward. Besides, this was the job, the real thing, and nothing else really mattered. He figuratively picked up Bettine, threw her out of his mind, and strode back to the Empire whistling "Lullaby of Broadway."

Bettine was waiting for him in a box, and he found it quite easy to sit beside her through a couple of turns and entertain her as though she were a necessary stranger. After that he disregarded Bettine's puzzled expression, excused himself, and strolled round to find Molly. He met her in the gangway at the back of the dress-circle.

"Hullo, Molly! How are you tonight?"

"Very well, thank you, Mr. Bellair. How is your arm?"

"Practically all right again, thanks, it was nothing really. But why—"

"Oh, I'm so glad."

"Very nice of you. But why the formality? What have I done to deserve 'Mr. Bellair'? You always used to call me Jim."

"Oh, I don't know, I just thought—"

"Come on, out with it."

"Well, I—I thought perhaps Miss Gascon wouldn't like it."

Bellair's irritation reawoke at once.

"Will you tell me precisely why what Miss Gascon likes or doesn't like should make the faintest difference to you and me?"

Molly blinked her eyelashes with surprise. "Really, needn't it? I thought you were engaged, I did indeed."

"Well, we aren't, and I've no intention of being. But even if I were—even if I married the lady, which heaven forbid—that's no reason why my other friends shouldn't be just the same to me as they always were."

"All right," said Molly pacifically, "I won't do it again. And if she looks at me as though—as though—"

"What?"

"As though I'd got a hole in my stocking or hadn't washed my neck or something—"

"Don't take any notice," said Bellair, laughing.

"I won't. I—did you get my message?"

"Yes, thank you very much for it. Nice of you."

"No, it wasn't. But there's something I heard which I think you ought to know. I talked to Eileen about it and she thinks I ought to tell you."

"Can't you tell me now?"

"No, it's rather a long story, besides, we're sure to be interrupted, somebody's certain to come in—there are some people now, I must go. I'll be back in a minute."

She ran away to show three sailors and their girlfriends into seats at the left, and Bellair leaned his elbows on the rail and looked about him. He noticed that Bettine in her box was not watching the stage but was looking towards him, the surveillance annoyed him and he made no sign of recognition. When Molly returned he leaned towards her and said: "What would you like me to do about it?"

"Oh—well, I was hoping you'd come along to our flat for a little while after the show. Mother would be so pleased, and we shouldn't be interrupted there, besides, nobody would overhear us." She glanced round, it was true that there were several people within earshot if they chose to listen. "But you won't be able to manage that now, will you?"

"Of course I shall. Look here, I'm taking Miss Gascon to supper at the d'Albertini. When you leave here, drop in there on your way and tell Albertini you've gone home. Then he can come and tell me I'm wanted on the telephone, and there you are. I shall reach your place—where is it?"

"I'll wait for you outside the café," she said, "it's simpler to show you. It's not very easy to find."

"Splendid, that's settled. Now come and have a drink, I'm thirsty if you aren't."

When Bellair returned to the box he half expected Bettine to be annoyed with him, but she was charming instead. "It is nice of you," she said, "to come and sit with me. It's such fun here, but it's much nicer with you to talk to."

Bellair looked at her, suspecting sarcasm, but the brown eyes were as clear and trustful as a spaniel's. Apparently the wench actually meant what she said, and Bellair relaxed gratefully. Not in an imperious mood tonight, evidently, all the better since he would have to leave her alone again later on. Towards the end of the performance he said, "Well, d'you want to see the rest of this, or shall we go and have something to eat?"

"Not awfully funny, is it? Perhaps I am getting hungry."

"If only she were always like this," thought Bellair, forgetting how bored he would be if she were, and they went into the d'Albertini. The place reminded Jim, as it always did, of Macgregor and the puzzle he had left behind him; while they were waiting for their mixed grill Bellair became immersed in thought about what Hambledon had told him of last night's doings. The unromantic figure of a fat man with a bald head, so like ten thousand other respectable citizens in appearance, so malevolent in fact. The yellow taxi in the garage under Siddall's flat; the automatic hidden, of all places, in a Greek dictionary; Siddall's dazzling blonde who looked so decorative and knew so much. Finally, Siddall himself—

"By the way," said Bellair, suddenly breaking a long silence, "you've got an appointment with Siddall for hairdressing, haven't you? When is it, now?"

"Tomorrow at five-thirty," said Bettine, who was beginning to think the sweetness pose a mistake. Men merely took advantage of meekness to become inattentive. If Jim thought he could just sit and gaze into vacancy instead of entertaining her, steps would have to be taken.

"Will it take long?"

"Half an hour—three quarters perhaps. Why?"

"Only wondered," said Bellair, who was really wondering if it would be advisable for her to go. On the face of it, it seemed ridiculous to object, even a man like Siddall couldn't do anything harmful to a lady customer in a crowded shop during business hours. On the other hand, he was undoubtedly dangerous, a man who probably arranged that little shooting affair at the Empire in front of a large and attentive audience was capable of anything; and Bettine was known to be Bellair's friend. If the fellow got the idea she had been sent there for Bellair's purposes—after all, she was on the first occasion—besides, she was in the car the night of the first attack, Siddall might have known her and think she had recognized him.

"Do you really want to go?" he asked abruptly.

Bettine stared, as well she might. "Of course I do, darling. Why?"

"Thought you might like to go somewhere else for a change, that's all. That's not the only hairdresser's in Portsmouth."

"But I've made an appointment. You made it for me."

"You can make an excuse to cancel it."

"But why, Jimmikins? You are strange tonight."

"No stranger than usual, believe me," he said lightly. "I'd rather you went somewhere else, that's all. You'll do that if I ask you, won't you?"

But Bettine was a little vexed. First he left her alone to go and talk to a chocolate girl, next he sat in moody silence when he ought to be entertaining her while they waited for their meal, and finally he only broke that silence to make this preposterous demand. Ridiculous.

"I'd do anything to make you happy, you know that, angel, but I do think this is rather absurd. If only you gave me some reason it would be different, but you won't. You don't mean to tell me you're jealous of Mr. Siddall," she said archly.

Bellair, however, was not in a mood to be arched at. "If you must, you must, I can't stop you. No, I am not jealous of Siddall. I merely ask you, to please me, not to go there tomorrow, that's all."

"But why?"

"No reason."

"There you are again. Oh, don't be so tiresome, Jimmikins darling, you're spoiling our evening. Give me a good reason and I won't go."

He made no reply and she went on. "Besides, I don't want to be rude to Mr. Siddall, I think he's such a nice man, and so attentive. Why, what's funny about that?"

"Nothing," said Bellair. "Of course he's attentive, it's his job."

"Then why laugh?" said Bettine reasonably. "Darling, you're in a horrid mood tonight, I don't like you one little bit."

"I'm sorry. So you'll keep your appointment tomorrow at five-thirty."

"Yes, of course I shall. I'll see you afterwards, shan't I? Couldn't you meet me at the Leviathan?"

"I'm not sure, I'll let you know tomorrow. I don't know yet what Hambledon will be doing."

Bettine raised her eyebrows but said no more, and the conversation lapsed as their mixed grill arrived. She amused herself by watching the people in a mirror facing her, for they had the same table at the end of the room at which she and Stafford had sat on New Year's Eve. Bettine saw a dark girl come in at the door, say a few words to Albertini and go out again; it occurred to her that the girl was very like that young woman at the Empire to whom Jim had been talking that evening, but there was no trace of interest or recognition on his face so she concluded she had been mistaken. A moment later Albertini came up to the table.

"Excuse me," he said to Bellair, "you are wanted on the telephone."

Bellair threw down his napkin, apologized to Bettine, and disappeared behind the central staircase.

Bettine finished her mixed grill and sipped the Braunberger which had been the result of a private conference between Jim and Albertini at the beginning of supper. She smiled indulgently at the foibles of men who loved to make a mystery out of a simple thing like ordering wine, but Jim was always like that. Albertini came to her with the menu and suggested that she might like to choose a sweet, Mr. Bellair had said she was to carry on.

Bettine selected Pêche Melba and said that she supposed Mr. Bellair would come back now, it had been a very long telephone call already.

Albertini, who should have been in the diplomatic service, said he understood there had been a little difficulty; Mr. Bellair had, by some accident, been cut off and there was delay in reconnecting. Doubtless Madame knew how it was with these long-distance calls, all too often.

Bettine said that she had sometimes been driven to suppose that the telephone operators did it on purpose to annoy, but Albertini said he could not really believe that, although undoubtedly occurrences did sometimes bear that appearance.

"Can't he come and sit down till the call comes through again?"

"I understood him to say that the connection might be made at any moment, so it was hardly advisable."

"He seems very keen about it, doesn't he, I suppose it's about that play he's writing."

There was the faintest flicker of Albertini's eyebrows. "Possibly, madame."

"Oh, have I let the cat out of the bag? I thought somehow you might know about it."

"I had an idea Mr. Bellair was engaged upon some sort of literary work, but I did not know of what nature."

"Then please forget what I've said. It was very stupid of me to mention it, he is so funny and secretive about it. Even I don't know what it's all about."

"Most writers have their peculiarities, madame," said Albertini. "Excuse me, I think I am wanted." He left Bettine to enjoy her Pêche Melba alone.

After a time she began to think about that evening when she had first seen Jim Bellair. She had been sitting at this very table with Stafford Wilkins when Jim came in with Hambledon and Reck. She had thought then what a nice expression he had, but soon afterwards that poor man was shot and there was all that fuss about names and addresses. What a ridiculous uproar Father had made over that, as though it mattered what names they gave. To be scolded as though they'd done something disgraceful—Bettine's expressive face assumed so indignant a look that a young man at the next table, who had been trying to catch her eye, hastily desisted.

Presently it came back to her, thinking over that New Year's Eve, that when the police constable had telephoned she had heard his voice quite distinctly, though not what he said. It was odd she couldn't hear Bellair's now. At that moment, as luck would have it, the telephone bell rang and she spun round in her chair in time to see Albertini hurry across the room to answer it. She listened and found she could hear his voice perfectly well.

So Bellair probably had not been telephoning at all.

So Albertini had told her a pack of lies, doubtless prompted by Bellair.

So probably the girl who came in just before this sham phone call, whom Bettine had thought so like the chocolate girl from the Empire, really was the chocolate girl from the Empire. . . .

When Hambledon strolled in some twenty minutes later, he found a Bettine white and trembling with anger. She was very charming indeed to him, so charming, in fact, as to alarm Hambledon, who had no intention of being promoted to Bellair's place in her life. But there was a sparkle in her eyes and an energy in her usually traînante voice which suggested that Hambledon's personal attractions were not solely responsible. He felt that if he were not careful, he would be used to show Bellair where he got off. "She was too sweet for words," Tommy said to Reck afterwards, "but alas! 'twas not for me. Smoke was coming out of her ears, I saw it."

CHAPTER XV

Conjurer's Assistant

BELLAIR left the d'Albertini by the further entrance, not the one Bettine could see in the mirror, and found Molly Trotter waiting for him outside. He slipped his hand through her arm and said, "This is nice. Now where do we go?"

"This way, it's only about two hundred yards. Were you in the middle of dinner?"

"No, I'd had all I wanted, thanks."

"We'll have to be quick," said Molly, hurrying.

"Why?" asked Bellair, hanging back. "It's a pleasant evening for a stroll."

"Oh, you are silly, you know Miss Gascon is waiting for you, and she'll get annoyed and then there'll be a row."

"She's all right," said Bellair placidly. "She's got a mixed grill, followed by Pêche Melba if I know Bettine, and a bottle of Braunberger, what more does a girl want to make her happy? Albertini's got instructions to go and soothe her down if she gets fidgety, and I expect Hambledon will be back soon—she likes Hambledon," he added crisply.

Molly glanced at him but made no further comment, and soon Bellair found himself being led up a narrow stair to be greeted by Eileen and her mother at the top.

"This is a great pleasure to us to have you in our house, Mr. Bellair— Molly, go and see if the sitting-room fire is burning properly. Come right in, and are ye sure you noticed the way ye came, for I hope we'll often see you here. You'll drink a glass of wine with us before you and Molly start your business—Eileen, get the glasses out, darling, and bring them in. Come this way, Mr. Bellair, will you put down your coat on the settle there? No, you'd much better take it off or you'll not get the benefit of it when ye go out again, which I hope won't be for a long time, these nights are cold for all it's May. Molly, put some more on the fire, darling, sure we don't begrudge the warmth. Take the big chair by the fireplace, Mr. Bellair dear, you'll be more comfortable there—Eileen, push it up for him, darling. Now we'll have a glass of wine together—Molly darling, don't interrupt when your mother's talking— will you care for a biscuit with it? Molly, get the biscuits—"

Eileen took Mrs. Trotter by the arm and shook it. "Mother, do listen. Mr. Bellair's in an awful hurry—"

"Eileen darling, that's no way to talk and him only just entered the house, where's your manners? Take this glass to Mr. Bellair, and he'll have a cigarette too, I wish my husband was here but he's out tonight. He joined this balloon business, Mr. Bellair—"

"Mother," said Molly, loudly and firmly, "Mr. Bellair has got a lady waiting for him."

"A lady waiting for him, then why didn't he bring her too? Sure we should have been pleased—"

Bellair rose above as it were the flood and said that he hoped he would be allowed to come again another time, but that on this occasion it was unfortunately true that he had got people waiting for him. He hoped therefore, that Mrs. Trotter would not think him rude if he and Molly went through their little business and then he would have to run away, but she could depend upon it that it would not be long before he was in Portsmouth again and perhaps they could all go and have a little dinner somewhere. Mrs. Trotter said that of course she understood perfectly and he should have his talk with Molly at once. She then swept Eileen out of the room, as though she had been causing all the delay, and shut the door after them, and silence descended.

"Mother's always so pleased to have people to the house," began Molly.

"I think she's a darling," said Bellair. "I like that Irish hospitality—she is Irish, isn't she?"

"Oh yes, and father's Irish too."

"I'm going to meet your father too, one day soon," said Bellair, who was wondering whether father came into the story. Apparently he did not, for Molly did not pursue the subject. She fidgeted about, refilled his glass and poked the fire.

"Nice place you've got here," said Jim.

"Oh, do you like it? We're very comfortable here."

Again the conversation lapsed, and Bellair began to wonder what in the world she could have to say which was so difficult to start. He tried another tack.

"What sort of show will it be next week?"

"Oh, quite good." Molly ran through some of the items, with comments. "A better show than this week's, I think."

"But no conjurer, eh?"

"No." Molly paused, and added with a rush, "He'd got a new assistant tonight, did you notice?"

"No, didn't see the turn. What's become of the lady in pink pajamas? Run away?"

"She's dead."

"What! Run over or something?"

"No, she committed suicide. Gassed herself."

"Good Lord! Why?"

"I don't know," said Molly rather undecidedly.

"But how horrible. She seemed a nice kid, and there didn't seem anything wrong with her on Tuesday night. She was very kind when I was hurt."

Molly nodded. "I've spoken to her a few times, but I didn't really know her. I thought she was nice."

"How beastly for her people. Where does she come from, d'you know? Somewhere miles off, I suppose."

"No, she was a Portsmouth girl, as it happens. Her name was Newton, her father keeps a garage in Buckland Mews."

Bellair said, "Does he really," in a perfectly calm voice, but his mind was racing with the implications of this surprising piece of news. Molly, however, once started, went on.

"She knew Siddall too—I don't think she liked him but she had to see him. Eileen says she met them once walking on the common, he was saying; 'But it must be done. Understand? It has got to be done,' in such a horrible voice. Eileen says she was looking awfully miserable and he had such a hard cruel expression; then all of a sudden he saw Eileen and was all smiles as usual. I think he's a horrid man and so does Eileen."

"I don't think him particularly charming myself," admitted Bellair. "In fact I could carve something much more lovable out of a small piece of damp soap. It was awfully good of you to tell me this, it does begin to look as if there was something funny about that accident of mine, doesn't it? Because Siddall pretended he didn't know the conjurer when we all met in the staff bar. Was that what you were thinking?"

"Oh, it wasn't an accident at all," cried Molly. "All that about Dulcie Newton wasn't what I was going to tell you, there's something much more important. You know when you were shot the manager asked if there was a doctor in the house and I showed him the way round behind, do you remember? Yes, well, when he turned us all out, I hung about for a few minutes in case anything else was wanted, and heard two men talking in the last dressing-room at the foot of the stairs. One of them was Siddall, I knew his voice." Molly repeated what she had heard Siddall and the conjurer saying, and added: "Siddal was in a frightful rage about it and I think he was frightened, too, his voice went up and down. You see, they said Newton ought to have done it, I didn't know who Newton was and I didn't even know Dulcie's real name was Newton, she called herself Neville in the profession. It was only after she died and everybody was talking about her that I heard who she really was."

"So you think her father was supposed to pop up and shoot me?"

"I don't know what to think. I suppose it might be some other Newton, it's a common name. But Jim, why should they want to shoot you?"

"Perhaps Siddall's got a rich uncle in Australia who's made a will leaving all his money to me," suggested Bellair, but Molly was not amused.

"I see," she said. "It was silly of me to ask."

"My dear Molly, nothing that you do is silly. I'm afraid I can't tell you any more about it, that's all. Have you spoken to anyone else about this?"

"Only to Eileen. I didn't know what I ought to do about it, so we talked things over and she said I ought to tell you at once. I didn't know how to get hold of you, so I rang up the d'Albertini—"

"You did perfectly right, but in future when you want me my address is East Bungalow, Lynbourne, and the telephone number is Lynbourne 23. Don't, of course, say one word to anybody about any of it—the affair was a complete accident. See Eileen doesn't either, will you?"

When Bellair got back to the d'Albertini, expecting squalls, he found instead an entranced Bettine hanging upon every word that Hambledon uttered. When she did notice his arrival she smiled politely and said: "Darling, how quick you've been."

"Good," he said, "I was afraid I'd been away rather a long time—longer than I meant to be."

"It didn't seem long to me," she said kindly, and turned her whole attention to Hambledon again. Before long, however, the lowering of a few lights tactfully indicated to the company that the Café d'Albertini desired to close its doors and go to bed; Tommy cut short an intentionally boring anecdote of his childhood, and the three went out to the car. Hambledon opened the front door of the car and handed Bettine in with some ceremony. He then got into the back of the car, extended himself over most of the seat, and said to Bellair: "You drive. If you don't go too fast I may get a little rest. Tell me if I snore." He wrapped himself carefully in a rug and took no apparent interest in the subsequent proceedings.

Bettine made no comment and complete silence was preserved till they were over Portsbridge. Jim was just beginning to wonder how long she would keep it up when she said it was a lovely night.

"Beautiful," he said enthusiastically, "beautiful. So—so moonlit."

"One misses the stars, though. They don't show much when the moon is so bright."

"They don't, do they? Still, one can't have everything."

"Why not? If they'd been made a little brighter they would all have shown at once."

Jim felt that under the circumstances this was overdoing it. When two hearts beat as one, he thought, it doesn't matter what the voice says, but when they emphatically don't, to talk nonsense is just nonsense. He therefore held his peace, and presently a slim hand was slipped under his arm.

"Jimmy."

"Yes?"

"You aren't annoyed with me, are you?"

"Heavens, girl, no. Why should I be?"

"I told you a lie, Jimmikins."

"Did you?"

"I said it didn't seem long while you were away this evening. It did, it felt like years."

"I'm sorry," said Bellair, feeling rather remorseful. After all it is rather over the mark to take a girl out for the evening and leave her alone half the time while one talks to another girl, and as for talking to Hambledon on the way down, she was sitting next him so she had to. Bettine had just cause for being annoyed and it was rather sweet of her to take the initiative in making it up again. He took one hand off the wheel to enfold the slim one which offered itself, and repeated: "I'm sorry, I am really, I had to leave you for a time—matter of business—but I didn't mean to be away so long. Things crop up, you know."

"I know," said Bettine sympathetically, and there was peace for a time. She had not forgotten the sham telephone call, but this was not the moment to deal with that, one could always bring it up later if desired. The sheep must be returned to the fold first. The drive was very pleasant till Bellair said: "Nearly home now. I'll see you tomorrow evening, shan't I?"

"Oh, will you meet me at the Leviathan, darling? How lovely!"

"Are you still going?" he asked in a flat voice.

"But of course, sweetness. I promised."

"A business engagement isn't a promise."

"But why put it off? Mr. Siddall might not be able to see me for another week."

"I don't want you to put it off. In plain English, I would rather you didn't go there any more, if you don't mind."

"But Jimmikins darling, why?"

"I can't give you a reason, I just ask you not to go."

"But listen, dear. When you've just had a perm done, it's usual to go back to the same place for the first wash and set afterwards, especially when anybody's taken so much trouble over it as he did. It's almost rude to go anywhere else; what will he think?"

"Does it matter what he thinks?"

"I think it does," said Bettine stubbornly.

"What about what I think?"

"Darling, you mustn't be unreasonable. Only tell me why you don't want me to go."

"Listen. You're always saying how lovely it would be if we were engaged"—Tommy Hambledon in the back seat pricked up his ears, but Bellair had forgotten he was there—"but the first time I ask you to do something without telling you the reason, you jib. Don't you trust me?"

However, Bettine, who sometimes seemed to have no will of her own at all, could at other times turn completely mulish. "Of course, if it is anything important, I'd do what you say without hesitation, but this is so trivial. What does it matter where I get my hair done? I don't want to bother you to take me, either. Mrs. Bingham is going up to town tomorrow and back by the late train to Mark. I'll go in to Mark by bus in the afternoon and go by train to Portsmouth. If I get back to Mark at about the same time as Mrs. Bingham's train, the car can take me home with her. It's all so simple."

"Quite," said Bellair.

"Darling, don't be stupid and jealous. Mr. Siddall—"

"Damn Siddall!"

After which silence prevailed till the car stopped at the gates of Lynbourne House. "Good night," said Bettine, "and thank you very much for taking me out."

"Not at all," said Bellair politely. "It was very kind of you to come."

Bettine waited a moment, but Bellair, with a murmured apology, only leaned across to open the door for her. She jumped out of the car, slammed the door violently behind her, and ran off up the drive.

"Good night, Miss Gascon," said Hambledon's amused voice from the back seat. Bellair started violently and drove away.

Reck had gone to bed when they got home, but Franz von Krug was sitting before the lounge fire keeping coffee hot against their return. His long ugly face lit up with pleasure when Hambledon entered.

"Glad to see you back," he said. "Had good hunting?"

"Not at all, speaking for myself," said Hambledon. "We drew blank. What about you, Bellair?"

"One or two trivial indications of a lead in the right direction. The conjurer's assistant is Newton's daughter—was Newton's daughter, I should say. She committed suicide last night. Newton was supposed to pop up on the Empire stage and shoot me, but for some reason he didn't turn up and they got a stranger who couldn't shoot a sitting haystack. Siddall was very angry about that and said the something unspecified—that's me—had got nine lives and the boss would be ever so cross. He and the conjurer, a Signor Maggiore I believe, had quite a row about it in one of the dressing rooms at the Empire with the door ajar."

"This Siddall is certainly second-rate," said Franz thoughtfully.

"He's not too bad usually, but he was careless that time," said Hambledon. "Why did Miss Newton commit suicide, Jim?"

"That's a mystery so far. What happened at your end, Hambledon?"

"Elliot went aboard the *Hulda von Gronau* early in the morning—this morning of course. The two Germans on board are the Herren Linde and Holz, they did not attempt to come ashore. It appears that the Herr Linde has had an illness and was recommended a short sea voyage to recuperate, the Herr Holz is his next-door neighbor and just came along to bear him company like the skipper's little daughter on the *Hesperus*. Holz is the sandy one, Linde the big dark man. The *Hulda von Gronau* sailed again at noon, having discharged such part of her cargo as was intended for Portsmouth, so it was hardly worth while for the passengers to go ashore. The rest of the cargo is going to Cherbourg."

"And the cargo landed here?"

"Rhein wines for the four naval wine merchants in Portsmouth. Nothing else."

"Colville, I suppose, was one of the four."

"Naturally. The goods went into bonded store at once, and this afternoon Elliot examined them, accompanied by several intelligent satellites, some disapproving customs officials, and the four wine merchants in question, who had been invited to be present. Any more coffee in that pot, Franz?"

"A little, and I will make some more if you want it. What happened then?"

"Elliot and his men opened cases and examined the contents for mysterious packages, but all in vain. The four wine merchants exhibited baffled rage in about equal degrees, I don't think the good Colville was any more agitated than the others."

"Doesn't look as though the stuff were there," said Bellair. "If it were, one of those men has really wonderful self-control."

"But it must have been there," said von Krug. "I heard them say so."

Hambledon shrugged his shoulders. "All I know is that they didn't find it."

"The visitor to the *Hulda* couldn't have taken it away with him," said Bellair, "not enough explosive to blow up several battleships."

"There's no such concentrated explosive in existence," said Hambledon, "at least I sincerely hope not."

"It must have been there," repeated von Krug.

"You know," said Hambledon, "I think you'd better come down to Portsmouth with me tomorrow and we'll wander round and see if you can spot your visitor. It's a long shot, I know, but it's worth trying. After all, he is not likely to recognize you."

"Not in the least, I shouldn't think they saw my face at all, looking out from a lighted room into the darkness outside. In any case, I am not afraid."

"Good, we'll do that then."

"I think I'll turn in now," said Franz, yawning. "I am still a little tired, and if we're going to spend tomorrow wandering round Portsmouth looking for an inconspicuous man with a bald head—"

Hambledon laughed. "I am quite sure we shall find one," he said. "The only thing that worries me is that we shall probably find five hundred. Good night, von Krug. Going to turn in too, Jim?"

"In a minute, I'll just finish this cigarette. You know," he added, after von Krug had left the room, "I am not quite completely satisfied about Bettine."

"Oh, aren't you? You do surprise me."

Bellair flushed slightly but continued. "She was at the d'Albertini on New Year's Eve. I know she was inside and anyone inside automatically had an alibi, I'm not accusing her of murder, needless to say. I still believe she didn't know Macgregor was murdered till I told her so. But, supposing they hadn't killed him, don't you think they'd have had somebody inside to report progress? Of course they would. Somebody inside the d'Albertini knew Macgregor was coming there to meet me."

Tommy Hambledon nodded. "But why Bettine? Surely—" he paused.

"You can take it from me," said Bellair incisively, "that that young lady is by no means such a fool as she seems. It's true she is the daughter of a superintendent of police, but—"

"Quite."

"She gave a false name and address, she and the egregious Stafford Wilkins, and then pretended she thought it didn't matter. Yet she knows quite a lot about police procedure, really."

"She could hardly help it."

"Of course not. The police seem satisfied, but they might be mistaken. Then again, she's very friendly with Siddall."

"So I noticed."

"I made all that fuss to see if she'd throw him over to please me. Would she? No."

"I gathered not," murmured Hambledon.

"In short, there may not be anything in it, but I think it's worth investigating."

"I agree with you. If only she'd come to Lynbourne after we did instead of before, I should be sure of it."

"Sent here to keep tabs on us, eh? I'm afraid we can't conclude that, she was here first. Still, perhaps they had a stroke of luck."

"Going to run down tomorrow evening and keep an eye on the lady?"

"I think so," said Jim Bellair.

CHAPTER XVI

"And Still She Wished for Company"

HAMBLEDON and Franz von Krug took Bellair's car and went to Portsmouth in time for lunch. "Snacks in several places, I think," said Tommy. "I hope your digestion is as good as ever. You aren't a teetotaller like Reck, are you? Of course not. That makes things much easier."

"I used to have a fairly hard head, but it hasn't had much exercise lately," said Franz wistfully. "I hope it hasn't atrophied."

"You'll come down by train, Bellair. I expect we shall probably manage to come back together, depends how things pan out. I'll try and leave a message at the d'Albertini about our movements."

Bellair went to Portsmouth by a train half an hour later than Bettine's and treated himself to cold tongue, coffee and roll and butter in a teashop opposite the main entrance of the Leviathan Stores. There were several entrances, but if Bettine were merely going to have her hair dressed and come away again at once this was the entrance she would naturally use, especially if she had any lingering idea that he might be there to meet her. The ebb and flow of customers slowed down and ceased, and on the stroke of six-thirty the commissionaire came out and slid steel lattice gates across the entrance. He locked them, closed the imposing doors inside, and there was a sound of bolts and bars. Bettine was not coming out that way.

Bellair moved nearer the teashop window to watch the employees of the Leviathan streaming out of a passage at the side of the building which he knew led only to the staff entrance. In a few minutes the exodus began; tall men, short girls, fat men, slim girls, small men, large girls, but never the graceful form of Siddall or Bettine's moorland stride. They must have left earlier by another door, it was impossible to imagine them chatting happily in an environment of dust-sheets, charwomen and clanking pails.

Jim paid his bill, walked down to the Clarence pier, and strolled along the front. There was to be a dance at the South Parade Pier that evening which would attract Bettine. On second thoughts, no, not in tweeds. He took a bus to Commercial Road and dropped in at the d'Albertini. No sign of Bettine, with or without escort, and no message from Hambledon. Jim had a glass of sherry and a chat with Albertini, and thought the matter over.

Portsmouth and Southsea were full of places to which Siddall might have taken Bettine; it was quite impossible to make the round of all of them even if he wanted to. There was a faint suggestion of humiliation in chasing the wench round Portsmouth which repelled him, it was all very well for him to tell himself that he was only doing it because it was part of the Job; she would think it was because he was jealous of Siddall and couldn't keep away from her, a revolting idea. He could picture Bettine's sidelong glance and faintly exultant smile, and he began to get angry. Always clamoring to be engaged to him—"it would be so lovely, Jimmikins darling, to feel we belonged to each other"—and yet if any other man held up his finger she must respond. Probably they were in some cinema, holding hands, Bettine was great on holding hands. He thought of Siddall's over-manicured nails and shivered, drank off his sherry and crossed the road to the Hippodrome. Might meet Hambledon and von Krug there, a queer bird, von Krug, and it was obvious that Hambledon trusted him entirely. Bellair wondered who and what the German could be, and what the connection was between him and Hambledon who had introduced him without explanation as "von Krug, an old friend of mine."

But the Hippodrome yielded only a few chance acquaintances and Bellair was not in the mood to be amused, so he walked up to the Empire with some idea of asking Molly if she had any more news about the Newton girl. Why did she commit suicide? She also had known Siddall though it appeared she disliked him; perhaps that was only a pose, perhaps Siddall—

He shook himself impatiently and walked into the Empire, but Eileen in the pay-box was too busy to talk to him and Molly was flitting about finding seats for people. Bellair drifted disconsolately into the lounge at the top of the stairs. It was empty except for the barmaid and one lonely figure on the far side, the Wax Doll. He thought absentmindedly that she always came here on Thursdays on account of Macgregor, but this was Friday. His brain reawoke. Here was a link with Macgregor who died on New Year's Eve because he knew too much. Perhaps she knew something too; he picked up his glass and crossed the room to the table at which she was sitting. With her customary tact she had pretended not to see him till he noticed her, but she looked up brightly when he greeted her.

"May I sit here? And won't you have one with me?"

"Oh, please do, I'm ever so pleased to see you. Thanks ever so much, I'd like a glass of port."

"I haven't seen you about for a long time, not since New Year's Eve, I think," he said deliberately, and was rewarded by a straightforward glance from her intensely blue eyes. He noticed how unnaturally bright they were, but surely cocaine was beyond her means.

"I suppose we just haven't happened to meet," she answered calmly, but he noticed she drank her port straight off instead of sipping it slowly as she usually did. "I heard you had an accident here on Monday," she went on, "was it true? I hope you weren't really hurt."

"Very little, thanks, it's practically well again now. Serves me right for making an ass of myself in public. You'll have another, won't you? You weren't in the theater when it happened, were you?"

"No, I was told about it, and there was a bit in the paper, too. Thanks ever so much for this. No, I only come here Thursdays as a rule, but I couldn't manage last night so I came tonight instead. I wish I hadn't, though."

"Doesn't it seem the same?" he asked in a quiet voice, being careful not to look at her.

"Not a bit the same," she said unhappily, "an' I wish I hadn't missed yesterday. You see, I used to come here every Thursday night with a friend of mine, every week for years we did. He used to buy the seats and we'd meet here and just sit together like old times, and he'd buy me a box of chocolates, too. I wish I'd kept the last box now, but I wasn't to know it was the last, was I?"

"Of course not. Somebody you'd known a long time, then, was it?"

She smiled a little at that. "He was my brother, though nobody knew it, it didn't do, you see. His wife, she didn't like me, and he had a good job in the dockyard—"

Her voice trailed off and Bellair waited, hardly daring to breathe lest he should break her train of thought.

"We were always special friends though he was so much older, he always wanted somebody to talk to when he got into trouble—he was always getting into trouble." She paused and turned those bright eyes on Jim.

"Mr. Bellair, sir, what did he die of? Poison?"

Of course, the police had hushed it up. The explosion had distracted attention from Macgregor's sudden death, and the inquest had been adjourned indefinitely, "for the attendance of important witnesses." If she had missed the original newspaper notice of the inquest she wouldn't know.

"What makes you think that?"

"'Cause I knew it wasn't heart. He had a doctor examine him for life insurance end of last year, not long before, you see, and the doctor said to him, 'Macgregor,' he said, 'you ought to live forever, it's not often I find such a heart as yours in a man your age, it's like a boy's,' he said. So I knew it wasn't heart. What was it, please?"

Bellair did not hesitate. This woman could keep a secret and anyway she had a right to know.

"He was shot," he said gently. "It was quite instan— it was all over at once, he did not suffer at all."

"Shot," she whispered. "Who shot him?"

Bellair shook his head.

"And why did they blow the place up afterwards? Didn't they know he was dead?"

"They must have known that, it was in the papers next day."

"Perhaps they didn't believe it and wanted to make sure. How they must've hated him! Why should anybody hate him so?"

"Perhaps they feared him, instead."

"Feared him? Why?"

"Perhaps he knew something."

"Can't you find out?" she said.

Bellair looked her squarely in the face. "I am trying to," he said. "Keep that to yourself, or perhaps the same people might get after me."

She crossed herself. "I swear I will. You can trust me, I've kept more than enough secrets in my time, I can tell you."

He nodded. "I know I can. The same people who shot him have killed other men, and may kill more. I and some others are trying to find out all about it. Don't you know anything you could tell me?"

She sat in silence, thinking, and Bellair waited patiently, watching her. "I can't think of anything that's any good, really," she said at last. "But maybe things'll mean more to you than what they do to me. He was a foreman fitter in the dockyard, you know that. He was a good workman, too, but he must have his whisky. Lots of men do, but his wife wouldn't have it at any price, beer she didn't mind but whisky was sin to her. Well, what's beer to a Scot? Just something wet, that's all. Still, whisky's expensive and she knew what his pay was. So he used to steal it off the ships he worked on, or do a little job for the wine-steward and get it given him. Not right, you know."

"How did he get it out?"

"On the swill-lorry. The driver was a friend of his but he was killed when the lorry blew up. Jim Barker his name was. I do think they're careless in the Navy, throwing explosives away with the rubbish."

"I don't suppose it'll happen again," said Bellair quietly. So Macgregor had been mixed up in that queer affair, the pieces of the puzzle were beginning to fit together. "Your glass is empty—"

"Oh, thanks ever so, just one more. Well, I don't know as there's much else, not that I can really tell you. Donald was worried about something that last week, ever since Christmas that was. Seemed like he'd something on his mind. I tried to make him tell me about it, like he always did, but this one time he wouldn't. 'It's nothing,' he said, 'or rather, it's nothing I can talk to you about. I'd like to tell someone, though, if I knew who,' he said once. Do you know what I think?"

"Please tell me."

"I think he'd got to know something, don't know what, about German spies maybe, or perhaps it wasn't that at all. I think he got to know about it somehow through getting the whisky, and he was afraid to tell anybody for fear he lost his job for stealing. That's what I think."

"It does look as though it might be something like that, doesn't it?" said Bellair.

"He would tell me now, if he could," said the Wax Doll. She looked past Bellair so interestedly that he glanced round, but there was nothing there. "Perhaps he will be able to tell me soon."

Bellair, feeling a little awkward, began some phrase about hoping she had many happy years to come, but she seemed not to hear him.

"He knows where to find me, you see, on Thursdays, he's always there in the other seat. I wish I hadn't missed yesterday, he wasn't there tonight. Do you think perhaps he won't come any more?"

Jim muttered something reassuring, and told himself firmly that the Wax Doll's last glass of port had been a mistake.

"He's never said a word yet, but it's just nice to be together again. After all, there's something about one's own folk, isn't there? He was always a good brother to me. Maybe one of these evenings he'll say a word or a name, and I'll come and tell you right away."

Bellair tried to imagine himself telling Elliot that Macgregor's ghost had said he was shot by the Archbishop of Canterbury, but he saw the Wax Doll looking over his shoulder again and the feeble jest fell down flat. "You idiot," he said to himself, "she's only watching the door." He had not had enough experience to have acquired the intelligence man's dislike of doors behind him, but there seemed to be a distinct draught blowing in at this one.

"I wish he'd come," she said.

At once there was a long burst of applause in the theater, doors were thrown open, and many voices were heard talking. It was an appreciable instant before Bellair realized it was only the interval. People began to stream into the lounge and Jim rose to his feet.

"I must go," he said, "I promised to meet a man before the interval." It was a lie, but he felt if he sat there listening to that matter-of-fact voice much longer he would be looking about for Macgregor himself. "Don't worry, he'll come," he added. "Perhaps he wanted us to have this chat tonight."

She looked up at him eagerly for a moment. "Oh, thanks ever so much for saying that," she said, and immediately fell to watching the door again.

Bellair retired to the wide passage behind the dress-circle seats and leaned against the wall, watching the people pass by. It seemed a harmless amusement enough, but when he found himself trying to remember on which side Macgregor's hair was parted, he went along to the foyer bar and stood himself some whisky. Presently a hand was laid on his shoulder. He looked round to find Hambledon and von Krug just behind him. He was very pleased to see them, nice wholesome people drinking beer and smelling of cigar smoke.

"What have you been doing all the evening?" asked Hambledon lightly.

"Listening to ghost stories," answered Bellair.

"You look it. Listen, I'd better not be seen talking to you, I want to see Elliot a minute, but there's no sense in dragging von Krug down to the Guildhall and back. I'll leave him with you for half an hour, see you later." He vanished behind a company of carefree sailors who came in. The place was rather overfull and Bellair led the way to a corner by the storeroom door where they could see everyone without being pushed about.

"Is it always as full as this?" asked von Krug.

"Not on Friday nights as a rule, but the aircraft-carrier *Sagittarius* came in today and these are some of the liberty men. Had a pleasant evening?"

"Very, thank you, though I have not yet seen anyone I know."

Bellair nodded and asked no more, as although they were talking German there might easily be half a dozen people within earshot in this press who could understand.

"Perhaps you would like to see some of the show," said Bellair, "I'll get hold of Molly and ask if there's a vacant box."

"It would be very pleasant," said von Krug politely, and at that moment Molly and Eileen Trotter came round the corner. Jim gathered them in and presented Franz, who clicked his heels and bowed.

"These little ladies," said Bellair, "were at Wiesbaden when their father was there with the Army of Occupation."

"We still talk German together sometimes, though I fear it is rather rusty," said Molly.

"*Guten abend*," said Eileen carefully.

"*G'n aben'*," laughed von Krug. "It is easy to see why the British Army of Occupation was popular in their sector."

"But we were only little girls then."

"The bud foreshadows the rose," said Franz gallantly.

Eileen was about to say something when she caught sight of two people edging their way towards the bar and her expression changed so suddenly that Bellair leaned forward to see what had attracted her notice.

"Dear me," he said coolly, "Miss Gascon and our Siddall. Wonder what they're here for, she saw the show last night with me and he was here on Tuesday."

"If it comes to that," said Molly, "you're here again, aren't you?"

"Touché, but I came to see you. Both of you," he added hastily.

"The honor is almost more than we can bear," said the disdainful Eileen.

"Yes, but what did you want to see us for?" asked the practical Molly.

"I was lonely and wanted comforting, and that's truer than you think. What is it, von Krug?"

"The tall man there," said Franz in a low tone, "who came in with the tall lady, I know him."

"The devil you do! Where have you seen him, in England?"

"I have never been in England in my life before, and in France only during the last war, in the Army, you understand. No, I saw him in Berlin."

"Is there a vacant box, Eileen?"

"The one nearest the stage this side."

"Can I have it, please? Von Krug, if you wouldn't mind—it will be more private there."

In the seclusion of the box, well away from the partition dividing it from the next, von Krug said the tall man's name was Siedle.

"Siedle—Siddall. Please go on."

"He was a hairdresser in Berlin with a very smart shop in the Unter den Linden, very expensive, *sehr modisch*, and a flat in the best quarter of Berlin. A friend of mine was his manservant," added Franz with a sardonic smile.

"A hairdresser with a flat and a manservant? Some hairdresser."

"He was not only a hairdresser, he was in the Intelligence, working in with the Gestapo. Ladies talk, you understand, when they are having their hair dressed. What is he doing here?"

"Same thing. Ladies' hairdressing."

"The wives of the Navy?"

"Doubtless," said Bellair dryly.

Franz grunted. "Has Hambledon not seen him? And did not recognize him? No, well, Berlin is a big place, one cannot know everybody. I wonder Siedle did not recognize Hambledon, though."

Bellair, who did not know Hambledon had been in Berlin, blinked slightly, but merely suggested that Siddall probably had not expected to see him.

"There is a lot in that," assented von Krug, "and anyway he would think Hambledon was dead. I did myself."

"Did you really?"

"Considering I attended his funeral! With the Fuehrer making the oration and half Berlin in the streets. Did he not tell you, that when I saw him the other night, first I fainted and then I tried to run away? No, well, he does not talk much." Bellair smiled and Franz laughed outright. "I mean, however much he talks he does not tell you anything, had you not noticed that? Of course you have."

"You were working with us then, were you?"

"No, no. I did not even know that Hambledon was English. No, I had a line of my own and sometimes we helped each other, that's all. He should be back soon, will he know where to find us?"

"Molly Trotter will bring him here. I also have a little news for him about

Macgregor—the man who was murdered on New Year's Eve, did Hambledon tell you?"

Von Krug nodded. "He gave me an outline of the affair, though we have spent most of our time talking over old days."

The lock clicked and Hambledon entered, silhouetted for a moment against the dim light in the passage outside. Bellair made sure the door was really shut, and in as few words as possible repeated to Hambledon what von Krug had told him about Siedle. "I have also a few more details about Macgregor," he added.

"Requiring immediate action? No? Then tell me afterwards. It is now more important than ever that Siddall should not see us together, he might think my visit to his flat even funnier than he did before. You clear off now and if we should meet you don't know me. The car is on the car-park just up the road, you know. I think you had better take it home. Elliot has gone out for an hour to get some supper so there's no object in our rushing straight back to the Guildhall, ten o'clock will do for that. I shall suggest his pulling Siddall in tonight. Von Krug had better come with me to identify him. We may have to stop in Portsmouth tonight, if we don't I will hire a car to take us home. Siddall and your girlfriend are still in the bar, I saw their backs as I came past. I don't think they saw me but there are mirrors in that place, endeavour not to be seen leaving this box. That is all for the present."

"Very good," said Bellair. He slipped on his coat, listened at the door for a moment and went out; Hambledon shut the door quietly after him. Outside there was no one about and Bellair leaned on the barrier watching the show for a few moments, thinking. If Siddall were to be arrested tonight, possibly on leaving the theater, Bettine would have to be detached. Positively a neighborly duty. Jim took his elbows off the barrier and strolled carelessly into the bar.

CHAPTER XVII

Pasteboard Adonis

BETTINE and Siddall were leaning against the bar talking to an elderly habitue of the Empire who also knew Bellair, he saw him come in and nodded to him. Bettine turned her head and gave Bellair a charming, if fleeting, smile before returning her undivided attention to Siddall, who was discussing The Ballet. Eileen and Molly Trotter, the day's work nearly done, were finishing up odds and ends before going home, and the bar attendants were tidying up and getting ready for the last gush of custom before closing-time. A tranquil scene.

Bellair joined the twins and a few minutes later Siddall's acquaintance became tired of his choreographic monologue and strolled across to talk to them instead.

"Evenin', Bellair," he said. "Not a bad show tonight, what?"

"No, quite good," said Bellair.

"Sad about that little gel gassin' herself, what?"

"Don't talk about it, please," said Molly. "I think it's too dreadful."

"Saw her Wednesday night myself. Seemed quite chirpy then. Can't think why she did it, most upsettin'. Fact is, I went behind to see her, known her ever since she was a kid."

"Did you really?" said Bellair.

"You know, I can't think why she didn't tell me about it if she was worried about anythin', I can't really. All these little gels come runnin' to me with their little troubles, you'd be surprised."

"I'm sure I should," said Bellair solemnly.

"If only she'd had the sense to tell her old Uncle Bertie all about it, she might have been alive now. They all call me Uncle Bertie, you know."

"Do they, indeed?" said Bellair.

"Yes. Makes me feel about ninety, but dammit, I like it all the same. Poor little Dulcie! What are you having?"

"Nothing more, thanks, I'm just going home."

"Not really? What about you two?"

"We're just going home too," chorused the twins. "No more, thanks awfully."

"I'm just going to toddle round behind," said the elderly bore. "I want a word with that conjurer fellow, what's he call himself, Signor Maggiore, that's it. One or two things I want to know about that poor little gel."

He wandered away and Molly said she hoped the conjurer would make him vanish into a top-hat and bring out a white rabbit instead.

"Then somebody could shoot the rabbit," said Eileen.

The swing door opened for a moment and closed again, Bellair glanced round to see who had come in but there was no one there so he assumed that someone had merely glanced in in search of a friend, and went on talking. A moment or two later Siddall excused himself and went out, leaving Bettine by herself.

"Anyone would think," said Bellair softly, "that he wasn't coming back."

"Why?" said Eileen.

"Because he finished his drink before going, although it was a full and fresh tumbler of whatever-it-is. Surely he doesn't think Bettine will scoff it while he's away."

"I don't think he's coming back, either," said Molly, and it was Bellair's turn to say "Why?"

"Didn't you see who looked in just then? Doris Baker, his dazzling blonde, you know. She just gave him one of those 'Heel, dog!' looks of hers and went out again, but I'll bet she's waiting for him outside."

"With a swishy stick?"

"Look out," said Eileen in a low tone, for Bettine had grown tired of being rather conspicuously alone and decided to join the party.

"Hello, Jim," she said calmly. "Good evening, Molly. Is this your sister? Oh, how d'you do?"

"Good evening, Miss Gascon," they said, almost together.

"Good evening, Miss Gascon," mimicked Bellair. "Had a jolly evening?"

"Oh, I've had a lovely time. Such fun," she said, patting her hair with a glance in one of the mirrors behind the bar which Hambledon had noticed earlier.

"Splendid," said Bellair, "but wasn't it a bit monotonous seeing the same show again?"

"Really, I didn't notice the show much. We were talking most of the time."

"We must be going home," said Eileen, who found the atmosphere a little trying since Bettine had joined them.

"No, please don't," began Bellair. "I thought—"

"Yes, or mother will be getting fidgety," said Molly.

"Gracious," said Eileen, "look at the time. Where's your coat, Molly? Good night, Miss Gascon."

"Downstairs, where's yours? Good night, Miss Gascon."

"Good night, twins," said Bellair, who knew perfectly well they were going because they disliked Bettine, since it was not really late at all. "I'll see you again soon, I hope."

"Oh, we hope so. Good night, Jim."

"Your cavalier seems to have deserted you," said Bellair.

"So tiresome," complained Bettine. "I can't wait much longer, I've got a train to catch in twenty minutes."

"Of course, you arranged to return by train."

But when they were in the car, he turned left up Commercial Road instead of right towards the station.

"Here," said Bettine, "this isn't the way. I'm going home by train."

"No, you aren't, my lady. You're going home in my car," said Jim, who was determined that the girl should not get mixed up in the arrest of Siddall if he could help it. He still thought it quite possible that she knew more about Siddall's affairs than was good for her, but the man was dangerous and there might be some shooting. He could not have been arrested already, Hambledon was not going to the Guildhall till ten and it was then barely half-past nine.

"I would rather go by train, thank you."

"I dare say you would," said Bellair, driving faster, "but not tonight."

"Why not tonight?"

"I'd rather not tell you, if you don't mind."

"I can't describe to you," said Bettine energetically, "what a bore I find you when you go all mysterious over nothing. You went on like this the other night about my having my hair done today. Well, I went, and nothing happened."

"Delighted to hear it."

"Well, doesn't that show you how silly you are?"

"Not necessarily." Bellair realized perfectly that if Bettine were completely innocent of any part in Siddall's doings, his own warnings and unexplained requests must indeed sound absurd. "Listen to me," he went on. "Can't you believe me when I say that there really is a reason why I ask you to keep away from Siddall? Perhaps some day I'll tell you all about it, I'm only sorry I can't now. There is a reason, and a good one, that's all I can tell you at present."

Bettine thought it over. On the one hand, if dear Jimmy thought he could dictate to her after this fashion, the sooner he was undeceived the better. On the other hand, the police superintendent's daughter had had enough experience of official secrets to recognize their characteristic shushing note whenever she heard it. But what had Jimmy to do with official secrets? Still, Jim was on the spot in Lynbourne and Siddall was far away in Portsmouth; besides, one was only a hairdresser while the other belonged to the same social strata as her employers, even if he did talk to restaurant keepers, taxi-drivers and chocolate girls. Probably he was only getting local color for that play of his. Anyway, if it came to a choice between them there was no question which it should be. It was even a little absurd to quarrel with darling Jim over Siddall, who was Siddall, anyway?

She laid her long fingers caressingly on his coat-sleeve. "Angel, why didn't you put it like that before?" Bellair thought he had, but refrained from saying so. "Of course, Jimmikins, if you perhaps think you know something about him and you aren't quite sure about it, you're perfectly right not to repeat it. Is it something like that, sweetness?"

"Something very much like that, Bettine." After all, taking it by and large, it was.

"Then I'm sorry I was cross with you, Jimmikins darling. Let's make it up, shall we? Look, here's a nice quiet stretch of road and I can't talk to you properly when you're so busy driving. Let's stop under those trees, shall we, and make it up properly."

Bellair did so. After all, there was this about Bettine, whenever they quarreled she was always ready to be the first to make it up again, there must be a lot of good in a girl who would do that. Besides, he had ordered her about rather a lot lately and she was quite entitled to resent it, he had no real right to do so since they were not even engaged. If they were, no doubt he would be able to influence her, rather a fascinating occupation to watch her finer qualities developing and her selfishness and silly little affectations gradually fading away. She could not have had a very easy life, thought Bellair, she must have worked hard to have got on as she had. As for her being mixed up in this Siddall business, that was all nonsense; he felt a stab of remorse at having suggested to Hambledon that he was not satisfied. Most unfair.

He did not, of course, admit having done so, but he did his best to make up to her for it. Bettine explained that she didn't really like Siddall at all and only went out with him because she was so unhappy about Jim. The whole evening had been a horrid bore and it served her right.

"No, it didn't," said Jim.

"I don't ever want to see him again. Let's be together a lot more in future, darling, then everything will be all right."

"Of course it will. I do think that fellow might have entertained you better, though."

"Oh, he did his best," said Bettine generously. "We went for a walk along the front, had dinner in a funny little restaurant in Southsea, and then on to the Empire. I was hoping you'd come."

"You didn't look particularly delighted to see me."

"Oh, but I was. Only I couldn't show it just then, could I? Besides, I wasn't sure you wanted to see me," said Bettine in a timid voice.

"I think you're a little goose."

"But you can't always be wanting to be with me, you've got such a lot of friends."

"When I'm with you," said Bellair magnificently, "I feel as though I had a flower in my buttonhole." He was so busy wondering what on earth had made him say it that he missed Bettine's next remark.

When he eventually arrived home at the bungalow, having deposited a lingering Bettine at Lynbourne House, he was glad to find Reck had gone to bed and Hambledon and von Krug not yet returned. He sat down in Hambledon's big chair before the dying fire and wondered why nobody had ever told him how fatally easy it is to become engaged. One soft, unguarded moment, and you fall into it even as the soap slithers from the soap-dish into the bath, and there's no one to fish you out again.

Doris Baker refused Siddall's offer to drive her home and took a taxi back to her flat. She let herself in with a latchkey, hoping that the maid would be in bed. She did not want Helen's sharp eyes on her tonight, nor to feel the air heavy with unspoken questions. No, the kitchen was all in darkness. Now if only Leonard were out she could sit down quietly and think over what was to be done, though even as she thought of it she felt it would never be possible to sit down quietly again. Leonard could always be relied upon to be out when she wanted him in, it would be like him to be in tonight when she wanted the place to herself, with no one to notice she had been crying. Tears of anger at first but of naked grief afterwards, how amused Leonard would be. He always told her she would have trouble with Rodney one of these days. "Your pasteboard Adonis," he said once. "Better leave him to me, my dear. I know exactly of what he is made, but women always take gilt for gold." But she said she could manage Rodney, till now he had revolted against being managed. "Even a dog," he told her, "is let off the chain sometimes." Who would think his eyes could be so hard?

Doris Baker awoke to the fact that she was still standing in the tiny hall leaning against the wall as though her knees would not support her. She straightened herself and walked into the sitting-room, dark except for the firelight; it was not till she stood by the hearth that she saw her husband was sitting quietly in a deep armchair, watching her in silence.

"Good gracious, how you startled me!" she said. "I didn't know there was anyone here—why don't you have the lights on?"

"I like sitting in the firelight," he said, "it changes the appearance of this rather formal room into something warm and comfortable. I will turn the lights on if you wish."

"No, no, don't bother," she said hastily. "Perhaps you are right, this room has a chilly atmosphere about it, I don't know why. I never noticed it before." She sank down on the hearthrug in her favourite attitude, her hands together in her lap, her graceful head thrown back.

"Have the room redecorated," he said. "Warmer tones would make a lot of difference."

"I don't think it's worth it," she said listlessly. "Such an upset, and the room is perfectly tidy. It is not so long since it was done."

"That's what's the matter with it."

"What?"

"Too perfectly tidy. If the cushions were sometimes crumpled and there were newspapers on the floor, dangerous bits of sewing with needles stuck in them on the chairs and a few neglected cigarette-ends in the ashtrays—"

"And a Noah's Ark and a rocking-horse in that corner out of the draft, I suppose," she said acidly.

"So you've noticed which corner has no draft," he said, but she made no reply and he went on. "In a word, if the room looked like home instead of an hotel sitting-room, it wouldn't matter what color the walls were."

"Oh, for God's sake don't go all Darby and Joan, I am not in a sentimental mood tonight."

"Something has evidently vexed you, what is it?"

"Nothing. It has been a long and tiresome day, that's all."

"The beautiful Siddall giving trouble, eh? I always told you he would. You take too much notice of that young man, you should treat him merely as a business associate, that is all he is."

"No he isn't!" she cried passionately. "You are so cold-blooded you'd never understand."

"Understand what?" he asked in a hard voice. "I thought you were a clever woman, I am to hear no nonsense from you, I hope."

"I think it is you who are talking nonsense," she said, controlling herself. "Romantic visions about dainty fragments of needlework are hardly in your line, Leonard. I thought we were 'merely business associates.' "

"True, we started like that—"

"And we are going on like that."

"Probably we shall. At the same time, you are still my wife, and I shall be glad to hear what it is I am too cold-blooded to understand." She showed no sign of having heard him but sat staring into the fire, with an unaccustomed droop at the corners of a mouth usually so firm, and after a moment his face softened and he went on. "Listen, Doris. We only married because we are both servants of one master and marriage appeared necessary for that service. I remember all that, but I also remember that we used to be better friends than this. When you were in trouble or difficulty you always came to me about it. Won't you do so now?"

"It is too late," she said.

He disregarded this. "You said I was cold-blooded, it is not true. I only pretended to be to please you. I know you never cared for me, Doris, but I have come to love you."

She shook her head. "It is too late."

"I don't think so. I have no intention of forcing your will in any way, but I wish you would think things over some time when you are not tired and agitated as you are tonight. Don't you think it possible that we are throwing away something that might be rather lovely, if we had the will to grasp it?"

She looked at him with curiosity. "What makes you talk to me like this tonight, Leonard?"

"Because you are more human tonight, and very lovely, Doris. You know, usually I am a little afraid of you. That amuses you, but it's true. You are so very sure of yourself, so efficient, so successful, you are rather like a marvellous piece of mechanism, wonderful but soulless. Tonight I notice you have been crying, and I want to comfort you. That's all."

She was in an emotional mood, and tears rose in her eyes. "You are very good to me, Leonard, I am sorry I have neglected you lately. Take no notice of my mood tonight, it will soon be gone. I put all my eggs into one basket and I have lost my treasure. That's all, as you said just now."

"Tell me what has happened."

"It is Rodney, as you guessed. I made a mistake—several mistakes. I thought we could run our marriage entirely on business lines and be happy. I was wrong, a woman wants something more than intelligent companionship and common interests. Then I met Rodney." She laughed unpleasantly. "Another mistake. Never call me clever again, Leonard, I'm just an ordinary fool. I thought he would give me the one thing in life I wanted, the human touch. Now I find him running about after that tall, gawky girl who is usually with Bellair. Have you seen her? Well, do you see anything in her?"

"She looks sympathetic," said Leonard calmly. "I've never spoken to her."

"Looks sympathetic, no doubt that's it. He told me tonight I was too masterful, he said he was tired of being bossed about like a little dog on a string. Why I'm telling you all this I don't know, except that I am unhappy and you spoke kindly. All my fault, of course, I ought to have remembered that men like to be the master. But there was the business to consider, and Rodney was not always very intelligent, he had to be made to do what he was told. I didn't mind, I didn't want him to be intelligent. I just wanted him—" She caught sight of Leonard's face and stopped abruptly.

"So that was it. I also have been a fool, I thought I could trust you. You slut!"

She cowered down on the rug, not daring to answer.

"So now you know what will happen? You have seen it happen before to people who were in my way. Don't get up, stay on your knees, you can stop there and pray for his soul, if you can remember how to pray."

He rose to his feet and she thought confusedly that he seemed suddenly to have grown taller.

"The cheapjack hairdresser to dare to meddle with my woman! Stay exactly where you are, I will speak to you again when I come back."

He went out of the room, she heard him moving about the house and a few minutes later the front door slammed.

Doris sprang to her feet and ran to the telephone.

CHAPTER XVIII

Siddall Seeks Sanctuary

HAMBLEDON and von Krug came to the Guildhall as the clock struck ten and were shown up to Elliot's room at once. "Von Krug here has recognized Siddall," said Hambledon abruptly. "He is an agent of German Intelligence." He went on to repeat what Franz had told him, and was nearing the end of his story when the telephone rang.

Elliot said "Excuse me a moment," and picked up the receiver. "Superintendent Elliot speaking." When he had listened a moment to what was being said to him, his bushy eyebrows went up, but his voice remained perfectly calm as he said "Certainly," and "I understand," and "I will send a car for you at once. Yes, now, it will be with you in about seven minutes. Yes, of course. Good-bye." He put the receiver down and wrote a note on a pad with one hand, pressing his bell with the other. When a constable came in he handed him the note. "Orders for a police car at once. Urgent."

Hambledon waited patiently till he had Elliot's attention again, and said, "I recommend arresting Siddall tonight on any charge you like, I think the—"

"Apparently Siddall agrees with you," said Elliot, "that was him ringing up."

"Asking to be arrested?"

"In those words. Will we please arrest him at once on any charge that occurs to us and lock him up in the strongest cell we've got, the Boss is after him."

"Dear me," said Hambledon.

"And will we send a police car for him at once, at once, at once. In return, he's going to tell us all about the Boss, that'll be nice for us, won't it?"

"I shall be there," said Tommy, with pleasurable anticipation. "With your permission, that is," he added quickly.

"You're welcome," said Elliot handsomely.

Siddall walked impatiently up and down his flat while he waited for the police. How slow they were, how long in coming, if the Boss arrived first they'd only be in time to arrange the inquest. Blast that girl of Bellair's, letting him in for this, blast Doris for getting so idiotically jealous, there was nothing in it. He tried to occupy his mind by packing a few necessaries in a suitcase, but when he found himself putting in a dress shirt, a paperweight and two ashtrays he gave it up for the moment. So Doris had spilt on him to that cold-blooded devil of a husband who looked like a prosperous greengrocer and had the soul of Attila or Bluebeard or some other ruthless tyrant of history, their names escaped him for the moment. Even at school he'd never been any good at history, the tannings he'd had because he never could remember who succeeded Frederick Barbarossa. The maddening thing about it was that he'd never really wanted to make love to Doris at all, it had seemed to him in the first place a bright idea to get on the right side of the Boss's wife, and he had succeeded only too well. Then she had taken charge of him in the masterful way he always resented, and since then he had never been able to call his soul his own. So it wasn't really his fault at all and it was most unfair that he should be punished for it.

He threw the dress shirt and the other undesirables out of his suitcase and packed pajamas, shaving tackle, hairbrush, and clean underwear. He paused with a shirt in his hand to consider what he should tell Elliot, it would be very difficult to tell all he knew about the Boss without incriminating Doris too, but that couldn't be helped. She'd brought it on herself, she would have to take her chance. If only the Boss were under lock and key or, still better, dead, Siddall felt he would breathe freely for the first time for five years. Of course, he would have to serve a sentence too, but they dealt very leniently with a man who'd turned King's Evidence, as it was called in England. That there might be other people, not in England, who would deal anything but leniently with the provider of King's Evidence occurred to him but did not worry him much. The Boss was imminent and dreadful, the other was remote and could be dealt with later.

There came a ring at the front doorbell, the two short rings repeated which he had asked that the police should use. Siddall ran down the stairs to admit them, his heart so inflated by relief that he found it hard to breathe. There were two policemen outside, ordinary men enough to the casual glance but to Siddall they had the air of heavenly visitants. Not Angles in short, but Angels. One moment to shut down his suitcase, and they were off.

Once on the road, however, fresh terrors beset him. The Boss might pass by and see him, leap on the running-board and shoot him; or if he was driving, turn his car in pursuit and shoot him. Or guess by some malevolent telepathy that he was going to the Guildhall, wait for him outside and shoot him in the act of crossing that undesirably wet pavement …

"Are these windows bulletproof?"

"Bless you, no," said the sergeant. "This isn't America."

The driver appeared to have increasing difficulty with the steering, the car pulled obstinately to the right and finally began to bump.

"No good, George," said the sergeant. "You'll have to change the wheel."

The driver pulled the car in to the curb and stopped in spite of Siddall's anguished entreaties. "For God's sake don't stop here. Drive on, I'll pay for a new tire."

"Can't drive on a flat," said the constable driver. "Shan't be a minute."

"It's not safe to stop here," argued the prisoner passionately. "Get a taxi and let's go on."

"You're all right," said the sergeant encouragingly. "Nobody's going to hurt you while we're here."

"I tell you, you don't know who you've got to deal with."

"Besides, it'll take just as long to get a taxi here as it will to change the wheel. George is being as quick's he can; there, he's got her jacked up already."

Siddall, incoherent with terror, babbled something and suddenly slid off the seat to crouch trembling on the floor. The sergeant watched this performance with the air of one whom nothing any longer surprises, but was sufficiently impressed to get out and give George a hand with the wheel.

"Seen some odd prisoners in my time," he remarked in a low tone, "but never one so anxious to be jugged as this one."

"Seems to have something on his mind, certainly," agreed George, running up wheel-nuts. They put the spare on at the back, started up the car and drove on without incident.

"There," said the sergeant, "I told you nothing would happen. Here we are at the Guildhall an' all's well. Come on, hop out."

Leonard ran down the stairs which Doris had ascended so wearily half an hour before, and went into his office on the ground floor to fetch something he wanted. He listened in the hall for a moment before going into the street, but there was no sound from upstairs, Doris was waiting for the door to slam before she telephoned. He took a bus to Palmerston Road and walked from there to Buckland Mews with a parcel under his arm.

He let himself in at Siddall's front door with his latchkey and walked unhurriedly up the stairs. As soon as he entered the flat he became aware that the place was empty, there is no mistaking the blank atmosphere of a place without human occupant. Possibly Siddall had not yet come in, it was not really very late.

Leonard switched on all the lights and strolled round the flat noticing signs of recent occupation, the day's paper thrown on the settee, cigarette-ends in the ashtrays, used sherry-glasses on the table. He put his parcel down and strolled into the bedroom. Here were drawers half-open, a dress shirt on the floor where it fell when Siddall threw it out of his suitcase; hairbrushes were missing from the dressing-table and the sponge was gone from the washstand. The Boss regarded these indications with a hard stare.

"So you've bolted, have you? Well, you shall come back. I do not choose that you should run away."

He returned to the sitting-room and unpacked his parcel which contained merely a bottle of John Haig. He held it to the light and said aloud: "If I should miss him perhaps you'll act for me." He put it in the cocktail cabinet in exchange for Siddall's similar bottle, which he packed up and took away with him. "So you think you escape from me, *lieb* Siedle. I do not think so, somehow."

He went into the garage on his way out and found there a man washing Newton's car. "Newton about?"

"No, sir."

"Mr. Siddall expected back shortly, do you know?"

"Couldn't say, sir, I'm sure."

"What's amusing you?"

"Well, seeing as the police come and took him—"

"When?"

"Only a moment before you come. I wonder you didn't pass—"

"Get out of my way."

"Here! What you doing—"

But the man had only time to jump clear as the car's engine roared up and swung out of the yard heading for the Guildhall. So Siddall would rat, would he? Not if it meant shooting his way into the Guildhall itself and—

He swerved violently to avoid a police car being driven towards the flat. It had occurred to Hambledon that Siddall really meant that the Boss was coming in person to the flat and it would be as well if somebody went and took a careful look at all visitors. Elliot, however, said that the mere visit of a police car would scare him away, everyone in Portsmouth knew the police cars. "We should have left Siddall like the cheese in the mousetrap if we wanted to catch the Boss. Besides, what's the use? Siddall's going to tell us."

"Send a car all the same."

"It's too late, he won't go there now."

"Send a car," repeated Tommy obstinately.

So a car was sent but Elliot was right, they were too late, though not as he meant it. In the meantime Siddall's evil genius laid a nail in the path of the car he was riding in and they were delayed.

"Here we are at the Guildhall," said the sergeant, "an' all's well. Come on, hop out."

Siddall, who was literally stiff with terror, dragged himself out of the car, stood for a moment eyeing the distance across the pavement to the police-station door, and then made a dash for it. A large saloon car came rapidly round the corner, slowed down, and there came flashes from the window with the repeated crack of an automatic. The car instantly accelerated, swept past, turned towards the dockyard and out of sight.

The driver of the police car let in his clutch and went off in pursuit, but was balked at the corner by a large furniture van and trailer, which also blocked his view. He came back five minutes later to report having missed the car completely and no one seemed to have noticed it. "Did he hit anybody?"

"I'll say he did," said the sergeant sourly, for the swinging car door had knocked him down. "He got the prisoner."

"Bad?"

"His troubles are over."

"Did he say anything," said Tommy Hambledon anxiously, "before he died?"

"Only asked for whisky."

"Did you ask if he knew who did it?"

"Yes, sir. He said, 'The Boss', then 'whisky' again, and died straight off."

"Did you get the car's number?" asked Elliot of the constable driver.

"Yes, sir. I know the car, too."

"Whose is it?"

"Belongs to a man named Newton, sir, licensed hackney—"

"General call to all stations," snapped Elliot. "Put on every available man and pull Newton in at once. Also the car. Detective-Inspector Grogan here? Ah, Grogan. Take a couple of men and go through Siddall's flat, bring all his papers and anything suspicious here; then seal the place up. Take a photographer with you, there may be fingerprints, but I don't suppose we shall identify a single one of 'em."

Newton was found without the slightest difficulty, for the police watchers of Buckland Mews reported that he had returned to the garage ten minutes before Grogan arrived. The car also was found without undue delay on the car-park in Grand Parade at the bottom of High Street. Newton was not in the garage itself but in Siddall's flat above it, when the police got in they found him drinking Cointreau out of a small tumbler. It is true he had not been doing this for very long, but Cointreau is a powerful liquid and not intended to be drunk from tumblers, even small ones. Besides which, it subsequently appeared that this was by no means the first drink he had had that evening. The result was that when Grogan eventually entered by breaking in the front door—the trapdoor had had a bolt put on it—Newton, in reply to questions, merely said "Iggle urg," and went to sleep.

"You would," said Grogan acidly, after various restorative methods had failed. "Take him to the Guildhall."

He was put into a cell there for the night till sleep should have worked its healing upon him. The man who had been cleaning Newton's car was also brought in for questioning, and was very ready to answer since he was still indignant. He said it wasn't right, might have knocked him down, driving off like that. Would have, if he hadn't jumped for it. No, he had only worked there a week, so he didn't know the gentleman, so to call him. The gentleman had let himself into the flat with a latchkey, come out again quite quiet, and suddenly flown off like that when told about the police. Not right at all, and goodness knew what he'd done with the car.

"That's all right, we've got that," said Elliot.

The cleaner also wanted to know who would pay him since the police had arrested his employer also.

Elliot said he really couldn't say. "Incidentally, what were you doing washing the car at this time of night?"

"Hire cars," said the man, "have to be washed between runs as an' when possible if it's two in the morning, that being made clear to me when I was engaged."

Newton's car, brought up from the car-park, yielded up only some smeared fingerprints and a bottle of John Haig. Hambledon opened it, smelt it and finally tasted it.

"Yes, that's John Haig all right. Not even poisoned or anything dramatic like that, at least not so far as I can detect, though if I'm writhing in agony in ten minutes' time you'll know—hullo!"

"What's the matter?" said Elliot.

"This is the whisky-bottle from Siddall's flat. It's got a chip off the bottom which I cut myself with the other night and I've just done it again."

"Why should a man go to another man's flat to murder him and then steal his whisky?"

"Perhaps he took it as a consolation prize," suggested Hambledon. "When he found he'd missed his prey. Anything interesting in Newton's pockets?"

Newton's pockets contained a pocketknife, a micrometer and the remains of a packet of Player's, a piece of string, some loose change, three grubby pocket handkerchiefs and a letter from his late daughter. Elliot read it through, whistled, and tossed it across to Hambledon.

"Dear Dad, I am sorry if this upsets you as I am afraid it will but I am so upset myself I don't know what to do except that I can't stand it any longer."

"Curious," interjected Hambledon, "how the feminine mind, when distressed, soars above punctuation." He continued reading. "You know I never liked a lot that went on though I never understood half of it but if it had been alright it wouldn't have been made such secrets of. But the attack on Mr. Belare the other night at the Empire was murder and nothing else. I tell you Dad it was cooked up between Mr. Siddall and Signor Maggior and when it went wrong they rowed like anything. I went to his dressing-room to ask if anything was going to be done about it and they just went on rowing as though I didn't matter well if I don't matter it's all right he can find somebody else and Dad they said it ought to have been you done the shooting only some other man turned up instead I can't believe Dad that you knew it was going to be the real bullet as was fired but if you didn't why was you supposed to come at all though perhaps you repented I'm sure I hope so. Well Dad you know I've often wanted to leave him but you said if I did you wouldn't have any more to do with me and he said if I did he would say such things about me as I'd never get another job and have to go on the streets and I'd rather die than do that so that's what I'm going to do. So good-bye Dad do get out of all this wickedness it can't lead to no good. Your loving daughter Dulcie."

"Well," said Hambledon, drawing a long breath, "no wonder Newton went out and got drunk. I suppose he got that letter today. I see she posted it to him."

"Will somebody tell me," said Elliot, banging the table, "why the devil the poor kid didn't come to the police?"

"What, and land her father in jail?"

"He's there now, isn't he? I'll make that Signor Maggiore wish he'd never been born, bullying that poor pretty little nitwit into suicide. A fine father Newton was, to let it go on."

"Anyone would think you were a father yourself."

"I am, I've got a daughter myself. She's two months old."

CHAPTER XIX

Newton Talks

HAMBLEDON CAME to the Guildhall to be present at Newton's examination and sat in a chair with its back to the window, a little apart from the superintendent's desk. Elliot came hastily in and said "Good morning. That conjurer fellow has hopped it."

"Gone? But you're sure to get him."

"Unless he's started to walk to France. He gave his show at both houses at the Empire last night and went off exactly as usual. It is possible that on his way home he saw the police car with Newton inside. Anyway, he went back to his rooms and said good night to the landlady as usual; she locked up the house and went to bed. In the morning the front door was unlocked and the conjurer had gone."

"Taking his money with him?"

"Presumably. Also possibly a small suitcase."

"You don't generally take even a small suitcase if you're going to drown yourself," said Hambledon. "I expect you'll get him."

"I hope so," said Elliot viciously. "I'd like to, very much. Let's have the prisoner in. We found some useful notes about him under a floorboard in Siddall's flat."

Newton was brought in, an unpleasant sight on a sunny morning, for he was grubby, unshaven, disheveled, and looking extremely ill. He glanced round for a chair, but Elliot looked at him with distaste and said, "Stand there, in front of my desk. You may go, Mullins. Your name?"

"Patrick Newton."

"Nationality?"

"Irish. County Clare," he added defiantly.

"Age?"

"Fifty-two, I think. What am I charged with?"

"At present you are not charged at all. You have been brought here to answer some questions."

"Then I demand to have a solicitor with me."

"In your own interest, Newton, it would be better to be civil, although as I say, you are not charged with anything at present," said Elliot, emphasizing the last two words.

"You've nothing against me."

"Oh, haven't we? Suppose I said that we wanted you to answer some questions regarding the murder of William Geraghty in London in 1923?"

Newton took a step back. "You can't pin that on me. I wasn't anywhere near the place that night."

"I never said you were, did I? No doubt you can disprove it."

"Who says I was there? I'll—"

"Several people. Mr. Siddall, for one."

"Siddall! The lying—I don't believe it. You're telling me this to—for your own purposes. Well, it isn't coming off."

"Listen," said Elliot. He picked up a small sheet of paper from the table and read aloud from it. "Patrick Ahearn Newton, born 1886 in Ireland. Enlisted Munster Regiment 1911. Taken prisoner May 19th, 1915. Joined Casement's Irish Brigade end of '15. Returned to London February 1920. Concerned in murder of William Geraghty August 1923, fled to Germany. 1923-34, no trace. 1934 employed by German Intelligence, sent 1935 to Portsmouth and assisted to start business as a garage proprietor. Well, Mr. Newton, now will you talk?"

"Where did you get all that pack of lies from?" asked Newton in a voice which tried to be contemptuous.

"From underneath a floorboard in Siddall's flat."

"Oh. Well, you can put it back where you found it and forget about it."

"I said you could be charged with being concerned in the murder of William Geraghty, but there are other more recent charges which will also be brought. You will be asked to explain what share you took in the murder of Donald Macgregor on New Year's Eve last."

"Don't know anything about it."

"And in the attempt on the life of James Bellair outside your garage in the second week of February."

"I heard about that, Siddall told me. I was out that night." Newton wiped his forehead.

"No doubt you can prove an alibi," said Elliot sarcastically. "You were wise enough to be absent when a further attack was made on Mr. Bellair during a performance at the Empire the following week, although it appears that you were expected to do the shooting."

"That's a lie! Who says that?"

"Siddall was overheard saying so to the conjurer. You should avoid associates, Newton, who are stupid enough to talk secrets with the door ajar."

"Don't believe a word of it," said Newton, still defiant but showing increasing distress. "I won't listen to this pack of lies you've cooked up, I want a solicitor here to—"

"Was your daughter a liar, too?"

Newton opened his mouth but no sound came from it.

"Here is her letter, it is—"

"Have you got that?" gasped Newton. "I thought I'd—"

"It was in your pocket, you cold-blooded scoundrel," snarled Elliot. "If only that poor child had come to the police she'd have got more help and pity than she ever did from you. She's dead and it's your fault, you realize that?"

Newton looked down and made no reply.

"It is not, unfortunately, a crime for which the law can indict you, Newton, but you will answer for it at the Judgment. We have enough against you without that, and the most serious of all is your complicity in the sabotage which has occurred on several of H.M. ships during the past year or more."

"That's the blackest lie of all—"

"Your comments are monotonous, we know better than that. Siddall—"

"Siddall knows no more about it than I do!" shouted Newton, losing control of his temper at last. "If he says I—"

"So you do know something about Siddall."

Newton turned sullen again and did not answer nor look at Elliot.

"Siddall is dead," said the superintendent abruptly. This brought Newton's eyes up to his and a look of genuine surprise crossed his face. "He was coming here under police protection to give us some information about these explosions and who was responsible for them, but he was shot as he was in the act of entering the Guildhall. You would have seen the marks on the pavement last night, Newton, if you hadn't been so drunk when you came in."

"Who shot him?"

"A man—presumably a man—whom Siddall called the Boss. Siddall telephoned to me saying that the Boss was after him and he wanted police protection here; if we would kindly arrest him he would tell us all he knew. So we arrested him, but the Boss got him all the same. Siddall was shot from your car, Newton."

"My car! But it was in the garage—"

"It was being washed just outside, actually. Who is the Boss, Newton?"

"I don't know," answered Newton, almost absentmindedly. "I wonder what Siddall had done to annoy him."

"Who is the Boss, Newton?"

"I tell you, I don't know. If I did I probably wouldn't tell you, but I don't know."

"Ever seen him?"

"Not to my knowledge," said Newton, in the same abstracted tone, and then appeared suddenly to wake up. "I'm not answering any questions, and while you make up your minds which of those ridiculous jumped-up crimes you're going to frame me with, I'm going home." He walked towards the door.

"One moment, Newton. You shall certainly go home, but not just now. This afternoon you shall go home, after the first evening papers are on sale— if you still wish to, Newton."

"What's the *Evening News* got to do with it?"

"A paragraph will appear in the *Evening News* to the effect that Siddall was in the act of coming here to give us information about—smuggling, shall we say. You were brought here under suspicion of being concerned in it, but in view of the great help your information has proved to be, you were released at 4 p.m."

Newton stood perfectly still holding the door-handle for a moment, and then slowly let go. He turned undecidedly towards Elliot who observed with interest that the man had turned perfectly white. The superintendent began to feel a certain sympathy for the undisguised panic of Siddall, pursued by a man capable of cowing even this truculent Irishman. Hambledon sat quiet and said nothing at all.

Eventually Newton made up his mind. He came back to Elliot's desk, leaned his hands on it, and said abruptly, "You win, blast you. You know I daren't do that, nobody would."

"So you don't want to go home after all."

"If you showed me the door this minute I'd hurl a brick through your window to be taken in again!"

"You might not find a loose brick handy, Newton, this isn't Ireland. Well, will you talk now?"

"On one condition."

"What is it?"

"That you arrest me for something, the devil I care what, and keep me under lock and key till the Boss is dead and buried, and for God's sake make sure you've got the right man."

"You can be arrested for the murder of Siddall if that will suit you. You will be sent to Winchester, you won't be too uncomfortable there."

"I wouldn't care if it was the Tower of London, ghosts and all," said Newton frankly. "Can I sit down now?"

Elliot nodded. "You can have a cigarette too, if you like. Now then. Who is the Boss?"

"I don't know. Siddall knew but he never told me."

"He came to Siddall's flat, I suppose?"

"Yes, but lots of people did, I don't know which he was."

Elliot was inclined to believe him, a man in the Boss's position would be known to as few people as possible, for his own safety. The superintendent let that subject go, and started on another matter.

"The murder of Donald Macgregor, what do you know about that?"

"Nothing firsthand, Siddall told me about it. He had the wind up over that, he lived with the wind up," added Newton, with contemptuous pity. "I always thought he'd crack up one day."

"Did he do it himself?"

"He said no, it was that blonde he went about with, Doris Baker, he said. She shot the Scotty through the car window and Siddall drove off. All I knew about it was I was ordered to have the cab at a certain point in Commercial Road to pick up Siddall and Doris, and I was to keep the engine running, ready to start. I didn't know what they were up to, nobody told me."

Hambledon spoke for the first time. "Why was Macgregor shot?"

"Boss's orders," said Newton briefly, and glanced at him with curiosity.

"Yes, but haven't you any idea why?"

"I don't know, nor did Siddall, but he thought Macgregor had somehow stumbled on something about those explosions you tried to pin on me. I don't know why he poked his nose into it, if he'd minded his own business he'd have been alive today. Siddall thought the Boss had an idea he knew too much and had him watched; Smith was one of those on that job, you know, the man who was killed in the car when it crashed."

"Who was Smith?" asked Hambledon.

"One of the Boss's lot. He worked for that naval wine merchant, Colville, I think myself he used to get dockyard information about ships and that. I knew him a bit, not well."

Hambledon nodded, and Elliot said, "Why was he killed?"

"According to Siddall that was an accident. Smith had been following Macgregor about all the evening from one pub to another, he was drinking hard and dropping hints, you know, boasting, 'If you knew what I know'— ken, he said—'ye'd ken something fearfu', mon,' all that sort of tosh. He let out he was going to see someone important at the d'Albertini; when Smith heard that he went off and told Siddall. They pinched a car standing near by, Smith hopped in behind, they did the job and drove off. Then Siddall said what with the excitement and having to crash the car and all, he clean forgot about Smith in the back. He could ha' jumped out, of course, I suppose he just wasn't quick enough. I didn't see it, I drove off. Hell of a job it was, too, after the cop smashed the windscreen, I was driving out of the side windows as you might say."

"And long live the man who invented Triplex."

"Ah," said Newton, and lit another of the cigarettes Elliot had returned to him. "Thirsty work, talking." The superintendent poured out a glass of water at which the prisoner made a wry face, and the examination was resumed.

Newton could not tell them so much about Siddall as von Krug had told them already, only that he was a German named Siedle with a job in Intelligence, "I met him in '34," and that the hairdresser only came to Portsmouth three years ago, which they knew already. "Wasn't nearly so good as he had been, got the wind up." He knew practically nothing about Doris either, didn't know where she lived. "Fiery little bit of fluff, I've heard her handing it out to Siddall good and proper."

With regard to the attack on Bellair at Buckland Mews, "I didn't know who he was, but I was told to slog him so I slogged him." Of course he had no intention of going the length of murder, "I should ha' just taken him somewhere quiet and dumped him." Of the second attack at the Empire, "I was delayed, it was quite accidental. Fact is, I'd been talking to my girl and what she told me worried me no end though you don't believe it. I told her not to be silly, she was imagining things, and then went outside to think things over. Then I met a man I knew and couldn't get rid of him. 'Course, I shouldn't ha' killed the young feller, only winged him like the other man did," and so on.

When it became evident that the now garrulous Newton had no more to tell them, Elliot and Hambledon looked at each other. Tommy nodded, hitched his chair forward, cleared his throat and began in his mildest tones.

"You have given us an immense amount of helpful information—I thought you would—now tell us just this one thing more. Why have you got such a grudge against Doris Baker?"

"Grudge? I haven't," said the surprised Newton. "Why the devil should I? I never have anything to do with her—she never speaks except to pass the time o'—"

"Come off it. What has she done to you that you should accuse her of murder?"

"Accuse her? I didn't accuse her, it was Siddall who—"

"Siddall be damned—he probably is. You were there, you drove her."

"I did, yes. I don't see what you're driving at."

"What I want to know is this. Why are you telling us it was the blonde Doris who shot Macgregor, drove off in the Beverley, and was picked up by you?"

"Because it was," said Newton, but his tone of confidence wavered a little.

"You don't sound quite so sure now, somehow."

"Because I—it was Doris, I heard her voice," said Newton with returning certainty. "I've driven her often enough, I ought to know."

"Why did you hesitate just now?"

"Now I come to think of it, I didn't actually see her that night, that's why. You see, the Beverley passed me, they hopped out and ran up to me from behind. They got in, Siddall said 'All right', and I drove off quick, I didn't look round. Then, when they got out, she—"

"Siddall said it was Doris Baker, did he?"

"Yes. Besides, I heard her voice, I—"

"Yet the woman in the car with Siddall that night had black hair. Quite black."

"But—"

"Which of Siddall's lady friends has smooth black hair?"

"I don't know, I—"

"Which of your Boss's gang of assassins has smooth black hair?"

"Don't know of one."

No amount of questioning shifted Newton from this point of view, and as he eventually turned sullen again he was removed.

"Well," said Hambledon, "what d'you know about that?"

"I believe he thinks it was Doris Baker. Some woman with a voice like hers, a sister possibly?"

"Doubtless time will show. Any results from Siddall's flat?"

"Only the notes about Newton, in German of course, I had to get them translated. Probably supplied to enable Siddall to put the screw on. Oh yes, one thing more. There were two used sherry-glasses there, one had Siddall's fingerprints on it, those on the other tallied with the set you supplied the other day."

"Oh, did they," said Hambledon. "Now that was a shot in the dark if there ever was one, and lo! it hath boomeranged."

He returned to Lynbourne and found Bellair looking through the jewelry section of the Army and Navy Stores Catalogue.

"Engagement ring or a consolation prize?" asked Hambledon unkindly, and went on without waiting for an answer. "Does Miss Gascon work during the afternoons?"

"I don't think she teaches the children, but she's supposed to be there. She takes them out for walks and all that."

"I see. What's the telephone number? Five-three." Hambledon dialled the number and Bellair heard him say "That Mrs. Bingham? Hambledon speaking, from East Bungalow. Good afternoon. Quite fit, thank you. And you? Splendid. Look here, I want to ask you a favor. Bellair and I want half an hour's conversation with Miss Gascon this afternoon if it's not too inconvenient. Oh, that's extremely good of you, will about two-thirty be all right? No, don't tell her, if you don't mind, we should like it to be a surprise. If you'd just arrange for her to be somewhere about the place—thank you very much indeed, I am most grateful. Thanks awfully, I'd love to, some time. Next week, perhaps? I have got rather a lot on this week. Thanks very much, I shall look forward to it. Good-bye."

"What's all this?" asked Bellair.

"D'you remember the account Miss Gascon gave you last night of her evening with Siddall? You told me about it over breakfast this morning. Yes—well, we're going to hear the real story this afternoon."

Bellair stared and turned slowly red, but asked no questions. After a moment's thought, he closed the jewelry section of the Army and Navy Stores and put it back on the sideboard.

Bettine's dark eyebrows rose in surprise to find Hambledon and Bellair waiting for her in the schoolroom at Lynbourne House, but she was given no time to ask questions. Tommy Hambledon shook her warmly by the hand and said "I am afraid the news of Siddall's murder last night must have been a shock to you."

"Oh, it was," she said, and held Jimmy's hand tightly in both of hers as though seeking comfort and protection, the very picture of clinging, trusting womanhood. "The poor man! Who could have wanted to shoot him?"

"We are trying to find out," said Hambledon earnestly, "and with that end in view I am going to ask you to give us a careful account of everything you can remember during the time you were with him. Where you went, whom he spoke to, whether he changed his mind suddenly at all—'No, don't let's go in there, let's go so-and-so,' that sort of thing."

"Oh dear, I'm afraid I'm terribly stupid at that sort of thing. Couldn't you get it from somebody else?"

"I'm very sorry indeed to have to worry you about it at all, Miss Gascon, but as bad luck would have it, he did spend more of that evening with you than anyone. If anything happened which you didn't understand, it might mean something to us."

"I quite see that and I'll do my best." Bettine frowned with thought and gave Hambledon a slightly expanded version of the account she had given Bellair the night before. Siddall had greeted several people in passing as they walked along the seafront but had not stopped to speak to anybody. She named the restaurant where they had dined and thought Siddall had been there before because the head waiter seemed to know him. They had a taxi to the Empire and talked to some people in the bar, Jimmikins must have seen them. That was all she could remember. No, he didn't seem at all nervous or anything like that, quite happy all the time. She was terribly sorry to be so unhelpful.

"That is really all?"

"That's all. Oh, if I think of anything else I'll just ring you up and—"

"That being so," said Hambledon in his blandest tones, "will you explain how it comes about that your fingerprints were found on a glass in Siddall's flat?"

CHAPTER XX

So Ends Romance

"I CAN'T IMAGINE," said Bettine, coloring to the hair.

"Oh, come now."

"I think you're simply horrid, trying to suggest horrible things about me."

Bellair disengaged himself from Bettine's clinging fingers, walked across to the fireplace and lit a cigarette. He was surprised to find himself feeling cold and rather sick.

"What were you doing in Siddall's flat?" persisted Hambledon.

Bettine glanced at Jimmy and saw no help there. She stamped her foot and flared up.

"I won't answer your beastly horrible questions! I'll complain to Mrs. Bingham about your coming here on purpose to insult me—"

"If you would prefer to answer these questions to the police, you are perfectly at liberty to do so," said Hambledon coldly. "You will then probably have to repeat your evidence from the witness-box in a murder trial. I only came here to give you a chance of explaining yourself in private out of courtesy to Jim's fiancée, personally I don't care what you do. Good afternoon." He picked up his hat. "Coming, Jim?"

"I am," said Bellair instantly, and walked towards the door.

Bettine hesitated, bit her finger, and said, "Wait a minute!"

Hambledon turned on the threshold and said that certainly they would wait a moment but he hoped if she were going to change her mind she would do it quickly. He and Jim were busy men, especially just now, and if she had anything to tell them—

"But that's just it!" cried Bettine. "There wasn't anything in it, I can easily explain all that. I only didn't say anything because I knew Jimmy would be silly and jealous about it."

"Never mind what anybody thinks. Tell me what happened," said Hambledon peremptorily.

"Well, it's such a silly thing to make a fuss about. Only, Rod—Mr. Siddall said he wouldn't be comfortable spending the evening in the same suit he'd worn all day and would I mind coming to his flat while he changed. Of course I said no, so we went there after our walk and he gave me a glass of sherry in his sitting-room while he changed, that's all. I sat in front of the fire and looked at *Picture Post.* That's all."

"How long were you there?"

"Only about twenty minutes, not long. You see, Jimmy, don't you, how silly it is to be so jealous; if I could have trusted you not to make a fuss I'd have told you all this last night and we shouldn't have had all this scene," said Bettine reproachfully.

"I wonder whether he found any letters waiting for him," said Bellair to Hambledon.

"Did he open any letters while you were there?" asked Tommy.

"No."

"Receive any phone calls?"

"No—yes, I believe he did. I'm not sure."

"Will nothing get it into your head that this enquiry is important?" snapped Hambledon. "I don't think we'll waste any more time here, if you agree," he added to Bellair. "Let the police finish the job."

"Somebody did ring up," said Bettine sulkily.

"Who answered the phone?"

"He talked for a few minutes, it wasn't a—"

"The telephone is the sitting-room, where was Siddall when it rang?"

"In his bedroom."

"Who lifted the receiver, you or he?"

"I just lifted the receiver, I didn't say anything—I was afraid whoever it was would ring off if it wasn't answered at all."

"Man or woman the other end?"

"Woman."

"Give her name?"

"I didn't catch it, I—"

"What name did she give?"

"None at all."

"What did she say?"

"She said 'Is that Mr. Siddall, please?' "

"Then what happened?"

"Rodney dashed out in a dressing-gown and took the call himself."

"What did he say?"

"He said he was sorry he couldn't manage tonight, he'd see her tomorrow, he was very sorry, a previous engagement, all that sort of thing. Then he rang off."

"Answer this question very carefully, please," said Hambledon. "Did you make any sound at all to betray your presence, apart from lifting the receiver?"

"I sneezed," said Bettine. "I couldn't help that, could I?"

"You could if you knew how. He didn't call her by any name, of course?"

"No."

"Anything else happen before you went out together? You did go out together?"

"Of course we did. No, he came and had a glass of sherry himself, that's all."

Hambledon looked at Bellair and said, "Any more points occur to you? No? Very well. Miss Gascon, you will probably have to repeat your evidence upon oath."

"I thought you said if I told you all about it I shouldn't have to tell anyone else," said Bettine indignantly.

"If you had told the truth in the first place, yes. As it is, I think it would be better to have it repeated on oath, you might remember something else," said Hambledon unpleasantly. "Good afternoon, Miss Gascon."

"Good afternoon," repeated Bellair. "Excuse me, I have to go now. I will see you tomorrow if I may?"

"You know, I think that was probably all that did happen," said Hambledon as they went down the drive. "The rest was just girlish irresponsibility."

Bellair snorted, but made no other comment. "Did you think Siddall was shot by a woman?" he asked.

"I think it's possible. If it's true the black-haired woman shot Macgregor from a car, she might have performed again on Siddall if she were sufficiently annoyed with him."

"He said the Boss shot him, didn't he?"

"He may have been mistaken. Or the Boss may be a woman, have you thought of that?"

The following day being Sunday, Hambledon and Bellair spent it quietly at home with Reck and von Krug. Not that its being Sunday would have made it a day of rest for them if there had been anything particular which wanted doing, but the case of Siddall was in the hands of the police for enquiry and there was not very much they could do in the matter till their enquiries had borne some fruit. They sat in the wide front porch in the spring sunshine talking idly of this and that while Bellair tried to make up his mind to walk up to Lynbourne House to see Bettine. She must be very much annoyed, she had not rung him up either the previous night or that morning. Jim listened with half an ear to Reck talking about making a seedbed and sowing cabbages, turnips, carrots and leeks. "We haven't enough room to grow potatoes," he said, "but that rough grass at the side will never be a decent lawn. D'you mind if I dig it up?"

"Not in the least," said Hambledon. "Can you grow radishes—those big ones we used to have in Germany, sliced and sprinkled with salt?"

"If I could get the seed, I would, but I don't know if you can get it in this country and I hardly like to—"

"Quite," said Tommy. "I feel a certain delicacy about writing to Germany myself. Let the dead past bury its dead, including me. We might get somebody to write for us, though."

"Or possibly I could get some through," said von Krug. "Our gardener at home used to grow them, round balls like young turnips, he would send the seed if he were told where to send it. At home, they used to grow along under the peach-trees on the garden wall. When we were boys we used to eat them together, alternate bites, you understand. A remarkable combination." He looked away at the green line of the downs and fell silent.

"Aunt Ludmilla could write, perhaps," suggested Hambledon. "I see no risk in that."

"To a seed-merchant in Berlin?" said Reck.

"Better let me get them," said von Krug. "There are no radishes anywhere like those we grew at home."

"Someday," said Hambledon, "when this tyranny is past, we will go back to your garden, von Krug, and I'll try that ingenious mixture you recommend. After all, I've often thought before that I should die in Germany."

Von Krug's ugly face lit up. "It would be curious, my old friend, if I should succeed where Goebbels so signally failed."

"I'd love to plant nemophila on Goebbels' grave," said Reck wistfully.

"Why nemophila, whatever it is?"

"Cats love it," explained Reck, "they like to sit in it. In pairs, singing. I may be wrong, but I don't think Herr Goebbels likes cats."

Jim Bellair came to the conclusion that after tea would be quite soon enough to see Bettine. She seemed very small and far away beside these three middle-aged men sitting in the sun discussing radishes. He felt like a schoolboy having tea with the masters and had a sudden schoolboy wish that they would tell him a story about their adventures; a fruitless wish, for men like Hambledon, Reck and von Krug do not indulge in reminiscence as a rule.

The gardener's boy from Lynbourne House rode up to the gate, dropped his bicycle in the hedge and came up the path with a note for Bellair in Bettine's curiously unformed writing. Jim gave him twopence and dropped the note in his pocket, that would do later.

"Any news yet of who shot the industrious Herr Siedle?" asked von Krug.

"He was shot by the I.R.A. in mistake for a prominent politician," said Hambledon sleepily. "He was shot by a small boy with an airgun in mistake for a tomcat."

"He was shot by the police themselves by means of an automatic device concealed in the car, which comes into operation when the prisoner steps out," suggested Bellair. "Saves the trouble of a trial."

"He shot himself and then threw the automatic up on to the dome of the Guildhall," said Reck. "It will not be discovered till they go up there to affix peace-celebrating decorations after the next war."

"When will the war start, von Krug?" asked Hambledon.

"Unless it starts this month it will be next September or next March. It is always March or September with Hitler, he should have been a tax-collector."

"He should have—" began Reck, but the telephone bell rang and Bellair, from habit, rose to answer it. He came back and said, "Elliot on the phone, he wants you, Hambledon."

"Tell him it's Sunday and I've gone to church," said Hambledon, but he got up from his chair and went into the house. When he came back some time later he said, "There now, just fancy that."

"What's happened?"

"Siddall has exploded, just like Macgregor. Elliot is hopping mad because one of his best men went up too. He says that Siddall was neatly boxed up and returned to his flat to await the usual ceremonies, but Elliot apparently had an idea that something like this might happen. In fact, I suggested it myself in jest, but he seems to have taken it in earnest. 'Look out,' I said, 'that he doesn't blow up like poor Macgregor.' 'If he does,' said Elliot, 'we shall know it's the work of the same man, shan't we?' Anyway, he put a cordon of police round the house watching it intently from every angle, had the place searched so thoroughly that it took six men four hours to tidy it again, put a man on the inside to see, presumably, that Father Christmas didn't come down the chimney because I can't see who else could have got in, and allowed no visitors except wreaths at the door. They examined the wreaths, too, they thought of that." Hambledon paused. "All this excitement is making me thirsty," he added. "I think whisky is indicated." He went into the house and returned with a decanter and a siphon.

"Whisky," murmured Bellair thoughtfully.

"I am glad you agree with me because now you can go and fetch the glasses."

Bellair went, plunged so deep in thought that he came back with sherry-glasses.

"What's the matter with you?" asked Hambledon, staring. "Have you had an idea, or what?"

"Eh?"

"Look what you've brought."

"Oh, I'm sorry, I'll go and change them."

When he returned Hambledon said, "What are you thinking about?"

"This case. There's too much whisky in it to be natural, I think."

"Go on, please."

"Macgregor was blown up, wasn't he? He was smuggling whisky out of the dockyard. Now Siddall's place has gone up too, after the police had gone through it with Grogan's well-known thoroughness. The only mysterious thing about Siddall's flat is that you found his whisky in Newton's car. Suppose it wasn't just taken away, suppose it was exchanged. Did the police find a bottle of whisky in the flat?"

"I don't know but I'll find out in a minute, I'll ring up Elliot. Go on."

"Then the *Hulda von Gronau's* cargo was delivered to the Navy wine suppliers in Portsmouth. I know they don't buy their whisky in Germany, but the connection is pretty close. I suggest we look up those four naval wine merchants and see if we can find anything funny."

Hambledon looked at his whisky, tasted it carefully, drank it off and went to the telephone. When he came back he said, "You were right, there was a bottle of whisky in Siddall's cocktail cabinet when the police went through the place. Elliot is turning up the records of the four Portsmouth firms who supply the Navy. They have to supply the licensing magistrates with pretty good credentials before they are allowed to trade, and I imagine the Navy gives them a look-over too. They have dockyard passes and walk about just where they like, you know."

Bellair nodded, and Reck asked if the man, who was cleaning Newton's car when the Boss so abruptly borrowed it, were shown round these four firms, would he not perhaps recognize somebody as the borrower.

"He's gone all shy since he knew it was murder," said Hambledon. "Elliot told me so. He don't remember nuffin' and don't know nobody. What about you, von Krug?"

The German looked doubtful. "I also could not be sure, the man who came aboard the *Hulda von Gronau* was so very ordinary-looking. If there were only one commonplace man among all these wine merchants, that would be he."

"I don't know that it would help us much if you did," said Bellair. "What we want is the man who is responsible for all this Navy sabotage, the Boss in short. We aren't primarily investigating murder. We know that either Siddall or his girlfriend shot Macgregor, but Siddall wasn't the Boss. If the car-cleaner identifies the man who took Newton's car, we shall know who killed Siddall but we shan't be certain then who the Boss is. Siddall said the Boss was after him but somebody else might have got in first, or he might have been lying. If von Krug identifies one of the Portsmouth wine merchants as the visitor to the *Hulda von Gronau* who talked about explosions, we still don't know who the Boss is, the commonplace man may have been merely another subordinate like Siddall."

"You do make it sound difficult," said Hambledon, "but you're perfectly right. I assume that the fingerprints and note I took from Siddall's flat belonged to the Boss, but I can't prove it."

"I don't see how we're ever going to," said Bellair disconsolately, "unless somebody who knows will talk. Doris Baker, for example, where's Doris?"

"Nobody knows, and the police can't find her."

There followed a short silence which Reck broke by saying in consolatory tones that at least there had been no further explosions on board any ships since the *Araucaria* went down.

"That's mainly because the Admiralty have been keeping their pet lambs away from Portsmouth lately," answered Hambledon. "I don't attribute that to the refining influence of my dignified presence. And anyway, that only happened two months ago, that was early January and it's only Sunday March the fifth today. Explosions didn't occur very often before, you know."

"I hope Elliot finds one of the wine merchants has a mysterious past," said Bellair. "Otherwise what do you suggest we should do?"

"That reminds me," said Hambledon, evading the question. "Elliot says he is coming out here this evening to get a breath of fresh air, and talk to us. I don't know why the Portsmouth air isn't fresh enough for him, but he's coming out by train to Mark at five o'clock and will one of us meet him."

"I'll go," said Bellair, "but why come by train?"

"Because his car's laid up and he hates driving a strange car. He can't get a driver this evening, apparently."

Bellair drove the Triumph Dolomite into the station yard at Mark and noticed the Lynbourne House Daimler pulled up just in front of him. A lady got out, presumably a visitor, followed to his surprise by Bettine Gascon, and there was a good deal of luggage.

"Oh my hat, I've forgotten to read her note," thought Jim, with a frightful stab of conscience. "I suppose she's been sent for to go home for some reason, wonder if pa's ill or only one of the goldfish. How very awkward."

His first instinct was to get out of the way and stay there till Elliot's train came in—the same, presumably, by which Bettine was traveling, but she recognized the Triumph and came to him at once with a look of delight. He greeted her with guarded cordiality, what had she said in that wretched note?

"How are you?" he said. "Sorry I couldn't come up before, been frightfully busy all day." She looked at him as though that was not exactly what she had expected him to say and the radiance of her welcome faded perceptibly.

"Sorry you've got to go away," added Bellair, convinced by the sight of a suitcase bearing her initials that he was on safe ground this time.

"Are you really?" asked Bettine with one of her lingering glances.

"Course I am," said Bellair cheerfully. "Don't be silly."

Bettine's face fell, evidently the cheerfulness was out of place. Perhaps father had had an accident—if only he'd read the note! Sympathy appeared to be called for.

"Of course," he went on in a subdued tone, "I'm terribly sorry for the cause of your going."

"But I think I'd better, don't you?"

"Oh yes, rather. Definitely. I don't see how, under the circumstances, you could do otherwise."

"So you do agree with what I said, don't you? You did get the note, didn't you?"

"Yes, thank you very much for it. Of course I agree entirely," he said, in tones of the deepest conviction, but once again he received the impression that that was not the answer which was desired. What could the wench have said with which he was expected to disagree? "Let me carry your suitcase across," he added, picking it up. "Got anything to read in the train? You go and get your ticket and I'll meet you by the bookstall."

She looked at him doubtfully but went, while he collected an armful of literature with a bright feminine interest of the sort in which Bettine delighted. "Look," he said when she came up the platform, "are these all right?"

"Thank you so much," she said in a flat voice.

"And cheer up, I expect things won't seem so bad when you get home."

"No," she said uncertainly, "though of course there's always father."

(So it was father, now we're getting somewhere.) "Of course, of course."

"He always makes such fusses."

"Men always do, don't they?" said Bellair encouragingly. "Go right up in the air over the least little thing. Naturally, it's horrid for you, all this sort of thing always is, but I always find that when you really come to look these things squarely in the face, they aren't half so serious as one anticipated."

Bettine gasped audibly and the horrified Bellair thought it was the prelude to tears. Could the poor old skate have suddenly died? Happily the train came in at that moment and caused a diversion. Intending passengers and their escorts pushed about and separated Bettine from him for a moment. Just opposite to him a carriage door opened and Elliot stepped out.

"I say, Bellair," he said, raising his voice above the insistent hiss of escaping steam, "this is frightfully good of you. I'm sorry to be such a nuisance, really I am, but—"

Jim met Bettine's eye through a gap in the crowd and her expression made him lose the rest of Elliot's apologies altogether. It was emphatically not a loving look, either, nor did it linger except as a rapier momentarily lingers before it is withdrawn from the quivering body of the victim. She immediately dived into the compartment which happened to be the nearest, and Bellair, excusing himself, dashed after her with the suitcase. Evidently there were to be no protracted farewells on this occasion, no doubt she had thought he had come to Mark on purpose to see her off and was annoyed when she found he hadn't. Very awkward, Elliot hailing him like that.

"Good-bye," said Bellair, handing up the case to a helpful Marine who was already in the compartment, "let me know how you get on, won't you?

I'm quite sure, when you get home, you'll find matters aren't half so serious as you think. I expect you'll be having a good laugh over it in a couple of days' time, when you remember how upset you were."

But Bettine only said, "Thank you so much," and engaged in animated conversation with the Marine, so Bellair retired to drive the superintendent to Lynbourne, congratulating himself that, apart from the unfortunate Elliot episode, he had got out of an awkward situation rather neatly.

CHAPTER XXI

The Tall Man

"I CAN'T STAY very long," said Elliot, "I must drop in at the Guildhall on my way home to see if anything has come in. Doris Baker, for example."

Hambledon pushed him into a chair before the fire and said, "You're staying to supper anyway. Blow Doris for the present, we want to talk about wine-merchants, a much juicier subject."

"I can tell you about three of them. You see, I started in Portsmouth as a young constable walking a beat, thirty years ago now, so the present heads of the firms and me were boys together as you might say. Mifflin and Bogarty. There's no Mifflin in the firm now nor has been these fifty years, they're an old-established firm who've been here for generations. The Bogartys were Irish originally but they've quieted down now, though I remember young Bogarty getting into a bit of a bother at Petersfield when he was a lad. Nothing serious at all, just a sort of college prank, he was at one of those colleges at Oxford then; we had to tell him Petersfield wasn't Oxford and we couldn't have those goings-on down here. He's been perfectly all right ever since and I know him well." Elliot paused for questions.

"What's he like?"

"Tall, thin, stoops a bit, wears spectacles."

"Next please," said Tommy Hambledon.

"Weston and Angell. Another old firm, was Weston and Son for generations but the present Weston has no children and young Angell is his nephew. Weston—always used to be called 'Aggie' of course—is as steady as they make 'em. Hardboiled old Tory—well most of the liquor trade are that," said the Lowland Whig. "Lost a leg in the last war, walks heavily with a stick. Young Angell's only been here about eighteen months, he learned his job in the firm's other branch at Plymouth. Good cricketer. Redhaired. About twenty-eight." He paused again, but Hambledon only repeated "Next, please."

"Darrell Brothers. Two old chaps, twins they are, must be nearly eighty and so much alike nobody ever knows t'other from which even now. Young Darrell does most of the work, Mr. William Darrell's son, Wilfred Darrell, never married. But the two old fellows do keep the boy in order—boy I said, he must be forty—not allowed to do a thing on his own, I understand. Oh, they're all right."

"Next please."

"Colville. The firm was started about ten years ago by John Harroway, it's still John Harroway Limited. He ran it for about five years and was just making a decent business out of it when he died, leaving a young widow with one child, a girl if I remember right. She—the widow—didn't sell the business, she advertised for a manager and Colville got the job. Of course he may have bought her out by now, I don't know, though one could easily find out. Companies are registered as you know. Colville came here from Edinburgh with first-class references. I don't know any more about him except that I'll swear he's no Scot and I don't even believe he was long in Edinburgh, he's no trace of an accent. Very reserved man, doesn't talk much at all. Married, his wife's a thin dark woman, got no personality I should say, for though she's nice-looking enough when you do notice her I never can remember the woman for some reason. You know how it is with some folk."

"We know what Colville's like," said Hambledon. "Shortish, stout, rather pallid, going bald—" He stopped and hit his knee with his fist.

"What's the matter?"

"I ought to have recognized his back—in Siddall's flat that night, I mean. Can you get his fingerprints?"

"I expect we can manage somehow."

"I should be interested to learn if they coincide with those on the glass I scoffed for you."

"But that wouldn't prove he was the Boss," said Bellair.

Elliot stared, and Hambledon went through Bellair's arguments for the superintendent's benefit. "It all arose because Jim thought there was too much whisky in this case."

"Could there be?" said Elliot wistfully.

"I beg your pardon, I do indeed," said Tommy, making a dive for the sideboard. "I can't think what came over me, I must be getting feebleminded or teetotal."

"So much talking does make me thirsty," admitted Elliot. "I'm not so used to it these days, I sit back in my chair now and induce other people to talk to me. But I think Bellair's right, at least I hope so. It's worth trying, anyway."

"Could you arrange for von Krug to have a look at him too?" asked Hambledon.

"Of course," said Elliot.

"Preferably from a first-floor window," said von Krug when translation had been made. "I saw him from above before."

"I'll bear it in mind," said the superintendent. "Will the top of a corporation dust-cart do as well?"

"Even that wouldn't prove he was the Boss," said Bellair.

"Too true, Cassandra," said Hambledon.

"But if we had him locked up on a minor charge," said the superintendent, "we might find the rest of the evidence among his effects."

"If he is the Boss we probably should," answered Hambledon, "but if he isn't, the real Boss will take alarm and leave, and we shall never catch him."

"I think somebody ought to go to Edinburgh," said Bellair. "One might come across something."

Hambledon made a long arm for Bradshaw and spent a few minutes in research.

"There's an express leaves King's Cross for Edinburgh at 10:35 p.m., another leaving Euston at 11:05," he said. "Why shouldn't we go tonight? If we can't catch the earlier we'll go by the later, it's barely seven now and only an hour and a half to town."

"There's a verra good reason why ye'll no' travel the nicht," said Elliot in good broad Scots.

"Why?"

"Because it's the Sabbath. There's no night trains to Scotland tonight."

"I cannot but think," said Hambledon, "that a short compulsory stay in the British Isles would do Hitler such a lot of good. I mean, what is Man, anyway? When may we travel to Edinburgh?"

"By the ten o'clock from King's Cross tomorrow morning," said Elliot, "that's the Flying Scotsman if that'll suit you. You'll get there at five-twenty, four hundred miles in seven hours twenty minutes."

"You'll get up early tomorrow, Jim, my lad. Though what you suppose we shall find when we get there I really don't know. Still, perhaps something will present itself."

"In the meantime," said Elliot, "an example of Colville's fingerprints shall be unostentatiously procured and compared with those you brought from the flat, though what good that's going to do us I don't see at the moment. It's not a crime to possess a latchkey to a friend's flat with his permission, or even to drink his drinks. Still, it shall be done, it may come in handy."

"Any news about the gun?" asked Reck. "I mean the Mauser we found in Siddall's Greek Lexicon. Was that the gun which killed Macgregor?"

"Have a heart," said Elliot. "They've only had two days to look at it, you didn't bring it in till the small hours of Thursday morning. I sent it off at once together with bullet extracted from Macgregor but you can't expect the Home Office to move as fast as that. Besides, there's no hurry, Siddall's very dead." He retired into morose thought.

"Cheer up," said Tommy Hambledon. " ''Tis all decreed, The rise and fall of nations, war's red tide.' "

"I am familiar with the doctrine of predestination," said Elliot sourly, "but even that doesn't explain how the trick was worked. Grogan is fair demented. He walks about muttering, 'I searched the place. I searched it myself, and when I search a place—' I tell you, I'm sorry for him."

"I'm perfectly certain," said Hambledon, "that when we find that out we shall know how the *Araucaria* blew up."

"So am I, but that doesn't mean we shall have enough proof to secure a conviction. The whole trend of British justice is towards—"

Elliot was interrupted by a strangled howl from Bellair. They all looked at him, he was reading a letter.

"What's the matter?" asked Hambledon. "Bad news?"

"N-not exactly," stuttered Bellair, scarlet in the face. "No, it's not that—but Lord! how I did put my foot in it!"

"May we hear?"

"I saw Bettine at Mark station when I went to meet Elliot and suddenly remembered I hadn't opened a note she sent me. Of course I couldn't admit that, so I fenced and agreed with everything she said. I got the idea she was going away because her father'd had an accident—I don't know where that brainwave came from—and told her it would be quite all right when she got home, nothing was ever so serious as it seemed, probably she'd be laughing about it in a day or two—all that sort of thing."

"Well?"

"Well, it wasn't father at all, that's all," said Bellair. He rose from his chair, stalked into his bedroom and shut the door after him.

The letter ran:

"MY DARLING JIMMIKINS,

"You know I am terribly fond of you and I simply hate hurting you, but I hope you will be sensible and take what I'm going to say in the right way. I have been thinking about things a lot lately and you know I'm awfully sorry but I don't think we should ever be happy together. We might be happy for a fortnight or so, but I'm sure it wouldn't last and we should make each other ever so unhappy.

"You see Jimmikins you're so terribly possessive and jealous, I mustn't look at another man or do the most ordinary things like going to dances or anything like that. I do hate it so because it makes me feel so guilty when I'm not, I feel all the time as though you're looking at me though I can't see you, and it's so horrid. Besides, I don't want to be tied, I want to be free. I know I'm changeable but I can't help that. The real trouble is you don't trust me."

Bellair's mind reproduced a few stray sentences from that awkward dialogue at Mark station. "Of course I agree with you entirely. Oh, definitely." He mopped his brow and went on reading.

"Besides, nearly every time I go out with you something awful happens. First there was that poor man on New Year's Eve, I wasn't with you then but you were there. Then those horrible men nearly killed you and threw you in the car and frightened me to death. Then Mr. Hambledon was so horrid to me yesterday about Mr. Siddall, I couldn't know he was going to be shot, could I? I think it was most unfair. Besides, there was the time you got shot at the Empire. I'm always wondering now what awful thing is going to happen next, how can a girl be happy when somebody is always getting murdered?"

"She's perfectly right there," said Bellair justly.

"This is making me most dreadfully unhappy, I cried for hours last night, but I've decided that it's better for both of us really to break it off. So I'm giving Mrs. Bingham notice and going home this evening, it is nearly the end of term anyway. I can't stop here and see you every day, I couldn't bear it, besides it would be so awkward.

"So I'm catching the five o'clock at Mark tonight. I am terribly sorry to leave here, it's a wonderful place and the children are sweet, but I really can't do myself justice with all this hanging over my head and I've got my career to consider. I hope we shall meet again some day soon, it will be lovely to see you and of course we shall always be friends.

"Wishing you every happiness, always

"Yours,
"BETTINE.

"P.S.—If you like to come up when you get this we could talk things over but you won't make me change my mind."

Jim read the letter carefully twice and returned to the sitting-room; the others looked at him with interest.

"I've been jilted," he announced.

"Congratulations, my dear chap," said Hambledon warmly.

"Cynic," rebuked Elliot.

"I'm not a cynic, I'm a realist. Honestly, Jim, were you ever really conscious of how you came to be engaged?"

"No. A sort of rosy mist supervened; when it cleared I found I was discussing engagement rings."

"Minx," said Reck. "I said so the first time I saw her."

"Where's she gone?" asked Elliot.

"Home to Wellstone."

"Then her pa will have to take a statement from her *re* Rodney William Siddall, deceased," said Hambledon gleefully. "The goldfish will turn silver in the twinkling of an eye."

"Not silver," said Jim. "Bright blue."

"You seem to be bearing up very well, I must say," said Elliot, but Bellair merely grinned at him and made no answer.

"I suppose she really has gone home?" said Reck. "She's such a hussy, one can't be sure."

"One can't be sure with any woman, Reck, that's why they're such an interesting hobby," said Hambledon.

"I prefer photography," said Reck acidly. "The camera cannot lie."

Hambledon and Bellair arrived in Edinburgh on a clear March evening, ascertained from a directory the private address of the senior partner of Messrs. Wilkie and Simpson, wine-merchants, and took a taxi to Coates Crescent where the door was opened to them by a parlormaid of severe demeanor.

"Is Mr. Wilkie at home?" asked Hambledon.

"Is't Mr. Wilkie senior or Mr. John Wilkie?"

"Mr. Wilkie senior," said Hambledon, with the idea of finding someone who had known Colville. The parlormaid looked at them with plain distrust and asked them to come in. She took their cards on a silver salver which lay on the hall table, as an afterthought picked up a lady's handbag which happened to be there too, and left them standing in the hall while she went upstairs. A few minutes later a white-haired man came down, holding their cards in his hand. "Mr. Hambledon?"

"My name is Hambledon, this is Mr. Bellair. Mr. Wilkie, I am extremely sorry—"

"You wish to see my father, I understand?"

"Actually, I wanted to see someone who could give me particulars of a previous employee of yours, a man named Colville."

"Ah, in that case we will not trouble my father, I think. I hope sincerely that you do not bring us bad news of Lewis Colville, we have often been anxious about him and he has proved such a singularly bad correspondent, my father is really hurt that after all his kindness—come into this room, gentlemen, we shall be more comfortable. I will switch on the fire, these March evenings are chilly. Please sit down. What is it that you want to know?"

"Anything that you can tell us. Perhaps you will begin by saying how he came to you and where from—how long have you known him?"

"Ever since he was a child about four years old, and that's some twenty-five years ago."

A silence settled on the room so profound that the very furniture seemed to be listening, and the faint clicks from the electric fire as it warmed up were plainly audible. Mr. Wilkie glanced up in surprise, apparently he too had noticed it, but the faces of his hearers were completely impassive and he went on with his story.

"In a sense he is a connection of ours. My aunt, Mrs. James Wilkie—an aunt by marriage, you understand—had a sister who married a Mr. Colville, an Englishman. They lived in London and had this one son. When he was, as I say, about four years old, they were both killed in a cab accident and my good aunt, having no children of her own, immediately sent for him to come to Edinburgh and brought him up as though he were her own. I believe Colville was a man almost without relatives, I never heard of any. I am taking you at your word, Mr. Hambledon, are you sure you really wish to hear all this?"

"It is exactly the sort of thing I want and you are interesting me beyond measure," said Hambledon truthfully. "That makes Mr. Colville about thirty years old now, doesn't it?"

"Twenty-nine or thirty, yes. To continue, he went to Loretto with his cousins—we regarded him as a cousin though actually he was no relation—and after he left school we took him into the business. He was clever and adaptable and prepared to take an interest in it, besides, he used to say that Providence had designed him for a wine-merchant, it was so easy for him to lift bottles down from high shelves. His enormous height, I mean."

He paused, and the abysmal silence fell again.

"I seem to have surprised you," he said, no longer pretending not to notice it. "You cannot have overlooked my cousin Colville's unusual height, that is, if you have ever met him."

"I am afraid," said Bellair gravely, "that neither of us has ever seen your cousin Colville."

The wine-merchant looked at them for a moment and was plainly about to ask a question. He changed his mind, however, and said, "I think you have something to tell me, but you want to hear my story first. I have not much more to say and I think a drink of some kind will be welcome, will you have a glass of sherry? I can recommend this—I frequently do, in fact," he added with a faint smile. "Now I will go on. He had been with us for about six years—no, seven—when circumstances arose which made a change desirable. No, nothing to do with our business relations. In point of fact he formed a strong attachment to a lady who was a newcomer to Edinburgh, nothing much was known about her. We did not like her—in the family, I mean—but the boy was his own master and she was very beautiful. She allowed him to take her about and give her presents, all quite openly, for deceit was no part of Lewis' character; in short, she encouraged him to make a public exhibition of himself," said Wilkie acidly, "and then suddenly produced a husband from somewhere abroad to whom she was ostentatiously devoted. Lewis came to my father and myself and said he would rather go away somewhere, at least for a time. He was bitterly hurt and in addition he felt that the whole of Edinburgh was laughing at him. He was mistaken there but he would not believe it. So he answered this advertisement from Portsmouth, we gave him the highest references, which were completely justified, and he left. That is five years ago and we have never seen him since."

"Have you ever heard from him?" asked Hambledon.

"We wrote repeatedly to his business address—he never gave us his private one—and at last got a typewritten letter in reply, excusing himself for not writing before as he had had an accident to his right hand—as though he could not have dictated an answer long before! But the whole tone of the letter was so cold and uninterested that we were rather hurt about it and did not write again for some time. I think we had one more letter from him and then the correspondence lapsed. My father took up the line that a man who could allow himself to be so unpleasantly altered by an unfortunate affair with a worthless woman must have some fatal weakness of character, and if you knew my father," added Wilkie with a trace of amusement, "you would realize that weakness is the unforgivable thing. A bad man, he says, is better than a weak man, for the bad man may repent, whereas the weakling—but you will not be interested in that. Is there anything else I can tell you?"

Hambledon looked at Bellair, who said, "Have you a photograph of him?"

"I think so. Excuse me a moment," said Wilkie, and left the room.

"Well, we've certainly found something in Edinburgh," said Hambledon, "though I must admit I hardly expected that, did you?"

"Not that, no," said Jim. "But when Elliot said Colville wasn't a Scot and hadn't been long in Edinburgh, I thought we'd find something, if only his previous address, before he came here, I mean. What do we do now, telephone Portsmouth to arrest him for impersonation?"

"No, I don't think we telephone on the subject of Colville. Telephones are occasionally less private than one thinks they are, a fact that at your age you will do well to remember."

Bellair flushed slightly and changed the subject by saying, "I wonder what happened to this Colville?"

"Murdered, poor chap, I expect."

"Do we tell this uncle?"

"Leave it to me," said Hambledon, as Wilkie came back to the room with a fat book in his hand.

"We are an old-fashioned family, gentlemen, we keep our photographs in albums."

"Much better than having them scattered all over the house," said Bellair.

"He had this portrait taken shortly before he went away," said Wilkie, turning over thick pages, "here it is."

It was a rather uninspired likeness of a pleasant-looking young man with a turned-up nose, a wide mouth, a long neck and a thick thatch of fair hair. Hambledon looked at it, passed it to Bellair, and asked, "What was his height?"

"Just over six foot five. He had rheumatic fever as a lad and had to lie up for the best part of a year, as a result he grew enormously."

"May we borrow this photograph? I will see that it is returned to you."

Wilkie nodded. "May I know now, gentlemen, something of the purpose of these enquiries? I do not wish to be indiscreet, but the lad was dear to us—"

"I will ask you to keep all this business entirely to yourself for the present," said Hambledon, "I should like your definite promise on that point. Thank you. I have no definite news of your cousin Mr. Colville, but I will try to obtain some. I can tell you that he is not with John Harroway Limited of Portsmouth and never has been. I am afraid he is not such a bad correspondent as you thought him," added Hambledon in a quiet voice, "you will understand me when I say I am afraid."

CHAPTER XXII

The Boss

THEY came out into Coates Crescent to find the lamps lit in the streets, lit but not yet giving light, for the daylight was still falling from the clear northern sky and the tall gray buildings gained in mass what they lost in detail. The shops were closed but some of them kept their windows illuminated for display purposes, bright colored rectangles in the gathering shadows. The pavements in Shandwick Place were full of hurrying people, trams slid past them and stopped at the corner to drop their passengers among the cars and buses, and at the six roads where Princes Street begins, traffic swirled in all directions round a redhaired policeman.

"Back to London, now, I suppose," said Bellair.

"Have you no soul?" said Tommy. "This is Edinburgh."

"I know. Are you going on a sightseeing tour now?"

"I've a very good mind to take you on one, we've got four hours before the train goes. But no, I'm ashamed to admit it but I want some dinner. We will compromise by doing as Dr. Johnson recommended."

"What was that?"

" 'Sir,' he said, 'let us take a walk down Princes Street.' "

"Oh, did he?" said Bellair doubtfully.

"Well, he would have done if it had been here in his time."

"Where's Wilkie's office?"

"In George Street I believe, that's behind here. Why?"

"Only wondered if young Colville used to look at that every day on his way to the office," said Bellair, regarding the great mass opposite to them, irregularly thrust against the fading sky. "It's rather nice, what is it?"

"The Castle, you oaf. Portsmouth would seem a little flat after that, don't you think?"

"He never saw Portsmouth," said Bellair.

"And I fear he never saw that again, either, and that is one of the things which short, fat Colville is going to swing for."

The night express to the south, and King's Cross at the uncomfortable hour of seven-fifteen on a cold gray morning. The great station was full of loud echoes, for most of the passengers at that hour were milk-churns.

"This station reminds me of me," said Tommy plaintively.

"Discolored with age and grime?"

"Discol—blast your impudence. No, it's so empty that it makes hollow noises."

"Breakfast?" suggested Bellair.

"Bath and shave first, I think. We can get breakfast on the train if we haven't time before. It doesn't leave Waterloo till ten to nine, I should think we could manage both."

In the end they had to run for the train and leap into one of the rear compartments, most of which were fairly well filled. "Let's go along the corridor," said Hambledon, "we'll find an empty carriage somewhere, I expect."

"Emptiness no longer repels you," said Bellair, and led the way forward. At the entrance to the restaurant car, however, he recoiled so abruptly as to cannon into Hambledon and tread heavily on his right foot.

"What the devil's the matter? Seen a ghost?"

"No. Get back, or let me get back, she knows me too well. Doris Baker."

"Next thing to it," said Hambledon, retiring into the previous corridor. "I thought she was dead, myself. You are quite sure it is Doris? Yes, now what happens? I wonder if she's going to Portsmouth, because that would mean a lot of odd things, wouldn't it? That she didn't know the police wanted to talk to her, for example, or that she wanted to talk to the police, which would be odder still. That she's just heard about Siddall's murder and is coming back to see about it, or that she hasn't heard of it at all and is coming back to see Siddall. That Siddall alive was a danger to her and she's coming back because now he's dead it's safe. That she killed Siddall herself and has been away to cook up an alibi. Or that she—"

"Stop, for pity's sake. If she's not going to Portsmouth, where will she go d'you think?"

"Where's my railway timetable? It's got a map somewhere. This train only stops at Guildford, Haslemere, and Portsmouth. You can go in almost any direction by changing at Guildford, but you only change at Haslemere to get into a stopping train. So I think if she doesn't alight at Guildford she'll go on to Portsmouth. I love that word 'alight', it suggests brightly-colored birds flitting gracefully from carriage to platform, the pretty little dears. I love to see 'em, don't you? Here's the right page at last. If she doesn't hop out at Guildford, Elliot must be instructed to meet her at Portsmouth. Guildford nine-twenty-six, Portsmouth ten-twenty. No time to wire. So I'm afraid you'll have to alight at Guildford, my lad, and if she doesn't you will telephone to Elliot to be at Portsmouth Station at ten-twenty with a suitable barouche. If you're quick and lucky you'll be able to catch the nine-thirty-one, which stops at all stations to Portsmouth and arrives twenty-four minutes after I shall. If you don't get your connection quickly you will have my sympathy at

Guildford till one minute past ten, arriving Portsmouth eleven-fourteen. Well, I don't suppose all the excitement will be quite over even then."

"Suppose she does get out at Guildford?"

"Then I shall do the same, for beauty draws me with a single hair if it's blonde enough. This one does, anyway. The train's slowing now, this is Guildford. *Au 'voir*, Jim. When you've gone I shall go and sit in the restaurant car myself, the seats are soft and wide and the lady doesn't know me."

When the train stopped at Portsmouth Doris Baker called a porter and went with him to the luggage van for her suitcase, but before it was handed out a quiet man in plainclothes came up to her, took off his hat politely, and said, "Miss Doris Baker, I believe?"

"That is my name," she said coldly, but her eyes looked quickly from right to left.

"The superintendent would be very grateful if you would come to the Guildhall for a few minutes, madam, just to answer a few questions."

"Questions—what about?"

"The superintendent will tell you himself, madam."

She looked over the man's shoulder, for she was a tall woman, and saw behind him one or two other unostentatious men of a type she recognized, for Elliot was taking no chances.

"Oh, very well," she said lightly, "but it's a frightful bore and I'm sure I can't tell the police anything they don't know, how could I? May I get my poor little suitcase out first?"

"Bring the lady's suitcase, Richards."

Elliot was sitting behind his big desk with a police stenographer at his elbow and Hambledon in a chair by the window when Doris Baker was brought in. They rose to their feet and Elliot said, "Give the lady a chair, Mullins. Miss Baker, I should be very grateful if you could help me in a small matter. Formalities first of all and let's get them over. Your name?"

"Doris Baker."

"Married or single?"

"Single."

"Age?"

"Twenty-four."

Hambledon raised one eyebrow but made no other movement.

"Where were you born?"

"In Kent somewhere, I forget where at the moment, does it matter?"

"Present address?"

She gave an address in Portsmouth.

"Nationality?"

"British, of course. Why do you want to know all this about poor little me?"

"Purely a formality, Miss Baker. Now, you went up to town on Friday night last, was it?"

"No, Saturday morning early. Why—"

"Where did you go to, madam?"

"I stayed with friends in town," she said defiantly. "I think you are—"

"One moment, please. You came back this morning, why?"

"Because I wanted to. Why not? I live here."

"Why did you come back today, madam?"

"I tell you, I—"

"Had you no special reason for coming back, madam?"

"If you must pry into my private affairs, I came back to see a friend."

"What is your friend's name?"

"That's no business of yours."

"What is your friend's name?"

She twisted her gloves round her left hand and answered, "Mr. Siddall, if you must be—"

"You came back to see Mr. Siddall?"

"Yes I did, there's no crime in that, is there? And when I tell him about the way you—"

"I don't think you will tell him anything of the sort, madam."

"Why not? I shall tell him exactly what I like. Why shouldn't I——" Her voice trailed off. "What are you looking at me like that for?"

"Because Mr. Siddall is dead."

"*Dead*. Dead? I don't believe it."

"He was shot dead on Friday night as he was entering this building, madam."

She stared at him till the color drained out of her face under her makeup and her eyes became as glassy and unintelligent as a doll's. Elliot, who thought she was going to faint, got up hastily, but his movement aroused her and she sprang to her feet, transformed and flaming with fury.

"You shot him, you yellow dogs, you curs, *schweine, Teufel*," she stormed.

"Madam," broke in the horrified Elliot, while Hambledon said, "Just fancy that," to nobody in particular.

"I suppose you will allege he was attempting to escape—"

"You forget you are not at home now, Fräulein," said Hambledon in German. "This is England, not Germany, and people are not executed here without a trial."

She looked at him and he noticed her hands were beginning to shake. "Of course—I forgot," she said in the same language. "Who shot him?" She repeated the question in English to Elliot since Hambledon did not answer. "Who shot him?"

"The Boss," said the superintendent ponderously.

At that she sat down suddenly and remained so still that she hardly seemed to breathe. "Of course," she said at last, "I knew he was after him because I told him I cared for him, but I never thought he'd do this. He never took any interest in me or minded what I did, so long as I worked for him all right—"

"Worked for Siddall?" put in Elliot, confused by all these pronouns.

"Siddall? No, Colville," she said impatiently.

"Colville. But why should Colville shoot Siddall because—"

"Oh, you are a fool," she cried in an exasperated tone. "Because Colville is the Boss and I am Mrs. Colville."

She dragged roughly at her hair; to the men's amazement the wonderful blonde coiffure came off in a piece.

Beneath the wig was a sleek dark head cropped like a boy's, and her face, made up with a pink-and-white complexion, looked so unnatural as to be quite horrible. Elliot leaned forward and stared at the masklike face which stared back with a mocking expression.

"You think yourself so clever, you English police," she said. "Different hair, a different makeup, high-heeled shoes, a little swagger in my walk, and you are all fooled so easily. You think Mrs. Colville the little dark mouse, don't you, so quiet and dull, so uninteresting that when you look at her you see nothing, fools."

"I suppose that's where Siddall came in," said Hambledon contemptuously, "for dolling you up, I mean." She looked piteously at him and he went on, "But you went a bit too far, I suppose, so Colville got rid of him, phut! Like that. One of those strong silent men, evidently."

"He killed Rodney for me, I did not know," she said. "So now I will kill Leonard and as for me it does not matter. Tell me can I see him? Rodney, I mean."

"No," said Elliot.

"Buried already? When did he die?"

"On Friday night. No, he's not buried, he never will be. You see, your dear husband, not content with shooting him, blew him up as well, coffin and all, as he did Macgregor, as he did the *Araucaria*, as he did the—"

"More whisky, I suppose," she said, and shivered violently.

"Whisky?"

"That was how it was done, you know. A new explosive that looked like whisky, the detonator was in the cap," she explained in a hard voice. "If I tell you all about it you will catch him and shoot him, won't you? I want him shot, he shot Rodney."

"Won't hanging do?" asked Hambledon in a matter-of-fact voice.

"Better," she said eagerly, "much better, he'll hate it more. Can I see it done?"

"No," said the scandalized Elliot, "certainly not. But we'll attend to that all right, after due trial, of course. He put this explosive whisky of his aboard ships with the rest of the wine stores, I suppose?"

She nodded. "Spirits sent on board ships have caps on the bottles, you know, not corks. The detonator—oh, I told you that. Did you notice if there was one like that in Rodney's flat?"

"I'll ask the inspector who searched it," said Elliot. "The whisky bottles had been changed, we do know that."

"How did you know?"

Hambledon told her about the chipped bottle found in the car after Siddall's murder. "I knew it was the same because I cut my wrist on it in Siddall's flat and again in the same way at the Guildhall."

"In Siddall's flat?" she repeated. "When were you there?"

"Don't you remember me?" he asked, and turned towards the light.

"I know now. You were the funny little drunk who climbed up a water-pipe because I was so beautiful," she said. "I remember how we laughed about it. It seems queer, now, to remember laughing."

"Are there many more in Colville's gang?" asked Elliot. "Besides Siddall and Newton, I mean."

"No, not really. There are men working for him, but they don't know anything about it. Like Smith, you know, the man who was killed on New Year's Eve in the car crash, he thought Macgregor was nosing out trade secrets or something, that's why he had to be watched. It was rather awful for us, we completely forgot about Smith in the back of the car."

Elliot nodded, this agreed with what Newton had said.

"No, you don't tell anybody what you're doing on a job like that," she said. "It wouldn't be safe."

"About Macgregor," said Elliot. "What had he done to be bumped off, and who did it? Siddall?"

"No, I did. Rodney never killed anybody, he was much too—too *gemütlich*. I suppose you'll hang me for that, but I don't care. Nothing matters, now. Macgregor used to steal whisky from the dockyard, and on one occasion he got a whole case of explosive—that was the time the main gate blew up. That made him think, because there'd been explosions before, and he stole again till he got another sample. Then he was going to tell somebody, but he talked too much so we stopped him." She leaned back with closed eyes. "If you want to know any more, will you ask me some other day? I am a little tired now. Rodney—"

Elliot looked at Hambledon, who said, "The original Colville from Edinburgh, his name was Lewis. What became of him?"

She shook her head. "I don't know, that was before I came over to join Leonard. He said he'd got rid of him, I never asked how. He may have killed him too, I don't know. It was lucky their names beginning with the same letter, otherwise I should have had to call Leonard Lewis. As it was we should have said it was a pet name if anyone had ever asked, but nobody ever did. Pet name!" she repeated, and laughed unpleasantly.

"Tell me one thing more," said Hambledon. "I cannot understand why you didn't know about what happened to Siddall, it was a newspaper sensation, didn't you see any papers while you were in town?"

She looked at him in evident embarrassment. "No, I didn't go out much—I didn't bother with the papers—I—the fact is," she added in a burst of frankness, "I have never got used to the stupid letters you use here, the type do you call it? So different from ours, it fidgets me to read it."

Elliot asked a few more questions, her real name and Colville's; where she had stayed in town—at a small hotel which she and Siddall frequented, because she expected him to come to her there. She only left it to return to Portsmouth when there was no sign of or word from him.

"This statement of yours will be typed out as quickly as possible," he said, "then you will be asked to read it through and sign it, if you agree that it is a fair account of what you said. If there is any place where you think a mistake has been made, you will please say so."

"How extraordinary," she said.

"Extraordinary?"

"It seems so funny to me," said the servant of the Third Reich, "to be so tender of the feelings of prisoners."

"It isn't their feelings we bother about, madam," said Elliot. "It's their rights."

"Rights? Have prisoners rights?"

"What can you expect," said the superintendent after the door had closed behind her, "from people as badly brought up as that?"

Bellair entered the room simultaneously with the escorting constable, and burst out with, "Well? What did she say?"

"Colville is the Boss," said Hambledon. "He is in his office, unwittingly surrounded by hordes of police. Elliot put them on as soon as your call came through from Guildford."

"So now we will go and pluck that lily," said Elliot, taking a revolver from a drawer and dropping it in his pocket.

"You were right about the whisky," said Hambledon. "The explosive was bottled and the detonators were in the caps."

"I thought there was too much whisky to be quite normal in this affair," said Jim.

"Not whisky," said Elliot. "Firewater, if you like."

"Wasn't it nice of Colville," said Tommy appreciatively, "to murder Siddall? Because now he can be arrested for that, charged with that, and hanged on account of that. No awkward disclosures of subversive activities, no treading on the corns of an unduly sensitive Great Power, and we can only hang him once anyway. Besides, who wanted Siddall? Except, of course, Doris. I think this affair has arranged itself extremely neatly."

"By the way," said Elliot, as they ran down the stairs to the waiting car, "I received a report from Superintendent Gascon of Wellstone of his interrogation of his daughter, and a copy of her statement."

Bellair looked enquiringly at Hambledon, who said, "Yes, I thought we'd better make sure she did go home. What's your opinion, Elliot?"

"I think the girl is only silly, no worse. She has got a bit out of her depth this time, though, I hope it'll be a lesson to her."

" 'Small fry,' " hummed Tommy, " 'should keep in shallow water.' I suppose she's all right, but I shall always have my doubts about that young woman."

"Oh, I think she's harmless in that way," said Elliot. "Stop by St. George's Church, Wilson, we'll walk along The Hard. For one thing, I don't see men like Colville putting any trust in a flibbertigibbet like that. No, I think she's innocent of complicity in that affair."

"Though not, generally speaking, far above rubies," suggested Hambledon.

"Far below, in my opinion. This is where we get out and walk."

"All the same," said Hambledon, sliding out of his seat, "I would have given something to be present at that interview."

"The only comment Gascon made to me," said Elliot, "was that he thought there was something to be said for nunneries."

Bellair took no part in the conversation.

Anyone walking along Portsmouth Hard towards the main gate has the sea on his left and houses, shops and offices on his right. Narrow streets break the line of buildings at intervals, narrow because this is Old Portsmouth, and if Nelson had walked there in 1939 he would not have lost his way. At the corner of one side turning there was a neat office on the ground floor with residential quarters over it. The office had wire blinds across its windows, with "John Harroway Ltd." in tarnished gilt letters. There was the usual number of people about, officers, noncommissioned officers and ratings of the Royal Navy, Marines, a few soldiers, still fewer women, some boys on the sea side of the road shouting to each other, gulls swooping overhead, and a smell of seaweed and wet mud, for the tide was out. There was also an unusual number of respectably dressed men of imposing physique who seemed to have nothing in particular to do this fine morning, as well as a good many uniformed police.

"Why, the place is stiff with cops," said Bellair, observing all this. "Colville must have noticed it, surely."

"There are no uniformed police within sight of his windows, not if my instructions have been carried out," said Elliot. "They generally are."

"Personally I shouldn't hesitate to call out the Brigade of Guards to this fellow if I thought it necessary," said Hambledon. "He's a lot worse than those Sidney Street hooligans years ago."

"I wouldn't flatter him," said Elliot bluntly. "Here is the place. His private entrance is in the side street." He said a word in passing to two men who were looking into a tobacconist's window and they fell in behind. The office door was set at an angle right across the corner of the street; as they turned into it Bellair glanced up the turning and saw Colville's inconspicuous private door beyond the shop and two policemen standing close outside it.

There was a small anteroom filled with packing-cases stencilled "H.M. Ships. Duty free." The place smelt, as all wine-merchants' establishments smell, of a warm, comfortable mixture of wines, spirits, beer, cigars, cellars, and old age. Between this anteroom and Colville's office there was a swing door, Elliot pushed it open and the three men walked in. The two plain-clothes men remained outside.

Colville was sitting at a large desk on the left, facing the window, he rose to his feet and said calmly, "Good morning, gentlemen. Ah, good morning, Mr. Bellair. What can I do for you?"

Bellair walked across to the inner door, communicating with the house, without reply.

"Leonhard Vinzenz Schumbacher," said Elliot formally, "alias Lewis Colville, I arrest you for the murder of Rodney William Siddall and I warn you that anything you say may be taken down and used in evidence."

Hambledon was standing by the entrance door as Colville fired from his pocket and immediately dashed at him. Hambledon, hit in the right shoulder, staggered forward, Colville pushed him against Elliot and dodged out through the doorway. Here he met the two plainclothes men who had heard the shot and were in the act of entering; Colville, who for all his appearance of fat was astonishingly hard and heavy, put his head down and burst out between them winding one and sending the other staggering. The winded one caught his fingers in the collar of the German's coat, but it split to the waist and he shot across the path and into the roadway. There followed a shout and a screech of brakes simultaneously, then a crash and a woman screamed. Colville had run slap into a Portsmouth taxi coming fast from the dockyard with a fare who was trying to catch a train.

Instantly the taxi was surrounded by police who appeared like magic from every corner and doorway. The taxi-driver climbed hastily out of his seat.

"I call you all to witness," he said, loudly and unsteadily, "as I couldn't do nothink. Run straight out inter me cab—Gawd 'elp us, you're all busies. An' cops, dozens of—Gentlemen, I couldn't 'elp it, straight I couldn't. What are you all 'ere for, who 'ave I run over for the love of Mike? Royalty?"

   * * * * * * *

Hambledon sank into the armchair before the lounge fire in East Bunga-low, Lynbourne, and stretched his legs gratefully towards the fire. He winced slightly as he leaned back, since the damage to his shoulder was less than a week old, and Franz noticed the fleeting grimace.

"Is it your shoulder that is hurting you? Have a cushion under your el-bow."

"No, thanks, it's quite all right, I only bumped it. It's very slight, really."

"I think you got out of that very lightly," said Reck, settling down to his favourite spot on the fender. "He might have damaged you much more se-verely than that. He couldn't have been trying."

"I think the whole thing went off extremely well," said Hambledon. "We are even spared the trouble of a trial, thanks to the taxi-driver."

"Will he get into any trouble with the police for killing the man?" asked von Krug.

"No, no, far from it. The inquest brought it in as accidental death and said he was not in the least to blame. You can't expect a car to leap sideways like a startled gazelle whenever impulsive citizens charge at 'em broadside on. Colville killed himself, and very suitable, too. It's the only decent thing he's done."

"What happens to that other garage fellow, Newton?" asked Reck. "It'll be a bit awkward trying him, won't it? Various obscure points will be brought to light, won't they?"

"Newton's being tried for a murder committed in London in '23, Elliot tells me, he'll probably do a stretch for his share in it and we'll let the rest go."

"A stretch?" said Franz von Krug, puzzled because Hambledon had trans-lated English slang into German. "Do you mean—" He sketched a rope round his neck with a gesture.

"Not stretch his neck, no! He'll serve a term of imprisonment, that's all. Elliot is rather pained about it, he thinks Newton deserves to swing. So he does and his conjurer friend too, for the way they drove that poor silly girl to death."

"And for the attacks on Bellair?" suggested von Krug.

"Oh, Bellair was fair game, besides, he did ask for it. He'll know better another time," said Hambledon comfortably. "He's in no danger tonight, I think."

"Unless he gets himself engaged again," said Reck.

"What, to the twins? They have not confided in me, but I've a feeling that each of them will protect him from the other," said Hambledon.

"The so-charming young ladies I met at the Empire," said von Krug. "I think you are right. I thought, by the way, you were also going tonight, was that why you stayed at home?"

"Partly," said Hambledon. "Besides, when I take little ladies out to dinner I prefer a duet. The twins are quite charming and they deserve a dinner because they really did help, but—well, I subscribed towards it and thought that was enough. My shoulder, you know."

"Your shoulder my foot," said Reck. "You didn't want to go, that's all. Talking about the Empire, what happened to the conjurer in the end?"

"He is being detained for enquiries and will soon be deported as an undesirable alien. Signor Maggiore will be Signor Piccolore—Piccolevi—my Italian is not what it might be."

"I think I shall go to bed," said Reck, yawning. "Otherwise I shall oversleep in the morning and the Awful Woman will be angry again." He rose to his feet, stretched himself, and strolled into his bedroom. "Going to sit up for Bellair? He's forgotten to take the key."

"Heavens, no, I shall turn in shortly. What about you, Franz, old friend? Will you mind sleeping in a house where the front door is not even locked?"

"It is strange, but I shall not mind at all. One of the nicest things about England, I find, is to lie awake at night listening to noises I don't recognize and yet not be alarmed."

"When the war comes, Franz, there will be plenty of noises at night, I'm afraid. Goering has been preparing them for long enough."

"Then your Air Force shall go and make bigger noises in the Wilhelmstrasse, and in the end the loudest bangs will win. They do not know your England, these herd-leaders, they are too—how shall I put it?—too insular. They are not sufficiently by-intelligent-travel-instructed, you understand?"

"I hope you're right. Well, I shall go to bed, I think."

"I will come and help you off with your coat," said Franz. "It is awkward for you, with that shoulder."

"I can manage the coat," said Hambledon, "It's the shirt that's the difficulty."

Lights went out in the bungalow one by one, and the neglected fire in the lounge sank to red ashes in the dark. A loose trail of ivy, shaken by the March wind, slid, scratching across Hambledon's window. "I'll cut that in the morning," he murmured sleepily. "I thought I was going to like England—and I do." He fell asleep.

THE END

About the Rue Morgue Press

"Rue Morgue Press is the old-mystery lover's best friend,
reprinting high quality books from the 1930s and '40s."
—*Ellery Queen's Mystery Magazine*

Since 1997, the Rue Morgue Press has reprinted scores of traditional mysteries, the kind of books that were the hallmark of the Golden Age of detective fiction. Authors reprinted or to be reprinted by the Rue Morgue include Catherine Aird, Delano Ames, H. C. Bailey, Morris Bishop, Nicholas Blake, Dorothy Bowers, Pamela Branch, Joanna Cannan, John Dickson Carr, Glyn Carr, Torrey Chanslor, Clyde B. Clason, Joan Coggin, Manning Coles, Lucy Cores, Frances Crane, Norbert Davis, Elizabeth Dean, Carter Dickson, Michael Gilbert, Constance & Gwenyth Little, Marlys Millhiser, Gladys Mitchell, James Norman, Stuart Palmer, Craig Rice, Kelley Roos, Charlotte Murray Russell, Maureen Sarsfield, Margaret Scherf, Juanita Sheridan and Colin Watson..

To suggest titles or to receive a catalog of Rue Morgue Press books write 87 Lone Tree Lane, Lyons, Colorado 80540, telephone 800-699-6214, or check out our website, www.ruemorguepress.com, which lists complete descriptions of all of our titles, along with lengthy biographies of our writer